RED SKY IN THE MORNING

Claude I. Owens, Sr.

Red Sky in the Morning
Copyright © 2000 Claude I. Owens, Sr.
All rights reserved. No part of this book may be reproduced or transmitted in any form or by any means without the written consent of the publisher.

This novel is the work of fiction. Any resemblances to the names or characterizations of any person(s), living or dead, or to any events depicted are purely coincidental.

Published by MysteryeBookstore.com, Inc.
Thomasville, Georgia USA
www.MysteryeBookstore.com
ISBN: 0-97110-118-3
LCCN: 2001118311
Book design by Summer Mullins.
Printed in the United States of America.
Published August 2001

Cover Image: Copyright 1998, Corel Corp., Clipart, Evening Skies #79086

*This is dedicated to my wife, Linda.
She was my inspiration for writing this book.*

The story actually begins in the mid 1950's in the town of Conway, South Carolina, where Wendy Wenslow was reared; however, it unfolds in Thomas County, Georgia in 1997, when a forgotten, sinister figure from Wendy's past projects himself into the present, leaving pain and death in his wake.

1
"THE FIRE"

Two Thomas County Sheriff's Department cars tore out of the parking lot of the Thomasville Justice Center and screamed out of town on Smith Avenue. They didn't slow until they turned onto Summerhill Road about a mile east of town. Sheriff Matthew Young pressed his accelerator to the floor as soon as he reached the first half-mile straight stretch of highway on Summerhill. He got a quick glance of the rear of Captain Bill Stanley's car as it started into a sharp curve a good half-mile ahead.

"Bill!" Jack screamed as the captain's car skidded sideways in the middle of the sharp curve, almost colliding with an oncoming car. The driver of the car, a woman, had a cellular phone in one hand and was fighting with the steering wheel to keep her car on the road with the other. Neither Captain Stanley nor Jack Jackson had noticed her.

"You got a death wish or something?" Jack strained to ask as he held onto the armrest of the passenger door, trying to keep from sliding across the seat.

Captain Stanley laughed, and answered, "We all gotta die sometime."

The speed of the captain's car easily reached 100 miles per hour on the next straight stretch of road. Within minutes they swung onto the lane that led to Wendy and Jack's house.

Jack saw the huge column of white-hot fire rocketing toward the sky across the tops of the slash pine saplings where his house should have been. The sight of the spiraling tower of smoke made him feel both anger and fear—anger that his little piece of the world was being destroyed, and fear, real fear, that Wendy, his wife, might be trapped inside the burning house.

He thought he had known fear before, but the kind of fear he felt now was different. It was the kind of fear that began deep down in the pit of his stomach, the kind that reminded him of how small he was and how little control he had over the events in his life.

There was a bend in the red clay lane leading to the house and only the roof of the house could be seen until the captain's car skidded around it, bringing the house into full view. It was a straight shot to the house from the bend. Suddenly, Jack's heart began to beat so fast in his throat that it was difficult for him to breathe.

There was a gravel walk, flanked by landscaping timbers and a row of boxwoods that led from the front steps out into the front yard for about seventy-five feet. At the end of the walk stood two pine saplings where the lane suddenly turned ninety degrees to the left and continued for about forty feet or so before making another sharp turn to the right, straight into the carport.

When Captain Stanley's car hit the middle of the turn at the end of the walk, he knew he going too fast. He crammed his foot down hard on the brake, causing the car to skid to the right, severing one the sapling as clean as a chain saw. The car continued the sideways skid into the front yard, mowing down the first three boxwoods boarding the walk and coming to a stop within fifty feet of the front steps.

Jack had begun to open the door before the car skidded. The sideways inertia rolled him out of the door and into the front yard. He rolled several times and sprang to his feet midway between the car and the front steps and stood frozen in his tracks for a moment.

The fire was hot, damned hot. It was hotter than any fire he had ever felt yet he didn't seem to really feel the intense heat.

The sheriff had stopped his car short of where the captain's car had skidded. The fire was too hot for anyone to be near, so he had backed down the lane away from the house.

"Captain Stanley!" the sheriff yelled, getting out of his car. "Move your car back! Y'all get away from the house! You're too close! Get back!" Neither the captain nor Jack could hear him.

Captain Stanley stood inside his open car door, shielded his face from the heat with his hat, and screamed, "JACK! COME BACK! COME BACK!"

But the roar of the flames or Jack's frame of mind kept from hearing the warning. The tower of whitish-looking flames mesmerized him.

Wendy's car, which hadn't been at the house when Jack went into town that morning, was now parked beside the west porch. As Jack turned to look in that direction, its gas tank exploded with a thunderous sound, making the hilltop tremble underfoot.

It reminded Jack of napalm, from his Vietnam days. The liquid fire, a different color than the fire from the burning house, spewed outward. The carport, the covered walk, and the hedges on that side of the house were engulfed in flames, disintegrating in a matter of seconds.

Pieces of burning metal from the car rained on the hilltop like steel hail. Large pieces fell near Jack's workshop about a hundred feet east of the house. The workshop didn't catch fire, but the force of the blast shattered the two front windows, blew them inward and ripped complete sheets of tin from the roof. Everything else on the west side of the house ignited instantly. The small pines planted about the yard dissolved into a vapor of nothingness.

"WENDY!" Jack yelled in a long scream, turning to Captain Stanley as if begging for him to do something.

"JACK!" the captain yelled, motioning with his arms. "PLEASE COME AWAY FROM THE HOUSE!"

But still Jack wouldn't or couldn't hear. Instead, he began to move toward the front porch with hesitant steps, trance-like as the nylon flag of the United States that hung on the flagstaff ignited and literally melted in seconds.

The captain stood watching with his arms reaching out for someone he was powerless to help and saw Jack's hair as it suddenly singed from his head.

The lone sapling remaining at the end of the gravel walk burst into flames like someone striking a giant match, while the leaves of the boxwoods bordering the walk ignited like hundreds of tiny sparklers. Their leaves evaporated from the small branches, curling like spent matches.

The captain knew that he had to do something. He couldn't just stand there and let his friend walk to his death. He pulled his shirt up to cover his head with one hand, and, holding his hat toward the flames, he ran around the front of his car, trying to shield his body from the searing heat. The blaze fed on the free oxygen in the air like a school of hungry piranhas, their red tongues flicking outward to feed on the captain's flesh. His lungs were starved for the oxygen stolen by the fire and his mouth gasped for a breath that wasn't there.

Jack's face looked like it would catch fire at any moment. The skin was a mass of blisters that hung from his cheeks like gigantic tears.

"WENDY! WENDY!" he screamed over and over, continuing to inch toward the house.

He tripped on the blackened skeletal limbs of a boxwood, stumbled, and fell on the gravel walk with his outstretched hands landing a few feet from the front steps. But still he didn't stop. He began to crawl on hands and knees in the gravel still screaming his wife's name, but the roar of the fire was his only answer.

"She might be in there! Oh God, please don't let her be in there. Please help me, please God!" he begged as his toes dug in the gravel, trying to push his body forward.

Suddenly, the ammunition in the drawer of Jack's gun cabinet detonated, blowing the two huge bay windows in the living room outward as a tremendous explosion rocked the house. Jack had purchased a full case of 12-gauge shotgun shells only a week before in preparation for the upcoming hunting season.

Captain Stanley was standing within a few feet of where Jack had fallen, and his body took the full force of the blast. The thick plate glass of the windows was propelled outward in long jagged arrows as if shot from a bow of fire. A large shard of the glass like a crystal-tipped spear knifed through the captain's upper right leg and severed it at mid thigh. Blood spurted from the flesh and was evaporated by the intense heat before it could fall to the ground.

The captain never knew the leg was gone. His face was expressionless, holding only a blank stare as moments passed before he started to slowly fall to the ground, landing with his right hand inches from Jack's feet. His fingers crept forward in the gravel until they caught Jack by an ankle. The toes of Jack's feet still dug in the gravel, trying to push him forward, but Captain Stanley held him firm. Jack lay face down, crying, but his tears were gone almost before they could form.

The explosion of the ammunition and the windows caused Sheriff Young and Deputy Jamerson Young to crouch behind their car. That reaction probably kept them from serious injury or even death, because an instant later, another explosion roared, an explosion much greater than the first. The force blew the towering column of white flames and what remained of the house out and over the parked cars.

It came from the rear of the house—from the small propane tank on a gas barbecue grill that sat on the north porch. A small amount of C4 plastic explosive with a remotely operated ignition device had been attached to the side of the tank. A number dialed from a cellular telephone activated the detonator. The force of the exploding propane tank was directed toward the house. It was meant to obliterate the evidence and leave only residue to be found.

Jack and the captain lay on the ground with their clothing smoldering. Captain Stanley rolled over onto his back and lay in a pool of blackened, cooked blood. The melted polyester shirt covered his head like a cocoon, and his right leg was missing below the knee. His right hand held to Jack's ankle and the left hand clutched at a bare chest burned so badly that the rib bones were visible.

Jack still lay face down and digging with his hands. "God please, please!" he begged.

Sheriff Young ran toward the house and knelt, crying, beside the captain. He had been helpless to assist him and blamed himself for what had happened. However, there was nothing he could have done. He cried as he tied his belt around the stump of the captain's leg and tried to tear away part of the melted shirt from his face as the tanker truck from the Thomasville Fire Department and an EMS vehicle arrived at the scene.

Jack and the captain were still alive, but barely. Captain Stanley kept pulling on Jack's leg and trying to speak but only white foam came out of the corners of his mouth. His left hand clawed at his burned chest, causing bright red blood to ooze from the charred skin. The emergency personnel worked feverishly, but it was hopeless. It had been from the time he ran around the front of his car.

Suddenly, the captain's body flexed, became rigid for an instant, and then began to convulse as he gasped for a breath of air from the oxygen mask. His eyes rolled back into his head and slowly returned to a blank stare as the hand on his chest relaxed. His right hand still held fast to Jack's ankle. The emergency personnel pounded on his chest and tried CPR, but Captain Stanley was dead.

Jack's body lay on the ground with a hand outstretched toward the doorsteps, his fingers making twitching movements. Cries for "Wendy" could still be heard, but ever so faint.

"Please, God," he prayed.

The words rumbled inside his chest like distant thunder. One of the emergency technicians attending him looked at the sheriff and just shook his head.

An ugly spiraling column of black smoke had replaced the radiant, red sky of that autumn morning, almost as if signaling that a sailor's proverb had not been heeded—"Red sky in the morning, sailor take warning."

***

The hell of that Saturday morning had begun when Jack Jackson entered the city limits of Thomasville on Friday afternoon.

"Every day! Ev-ver-ry day!" Jack growled with a very tired sounding voice, and continued, "What are the odds that I'd catch this train every afternoon? What are the odds? Well, it won't catch me next week. Thank the good Lord I'm on vacation." His brother and his wife's two brothers had planned a hunting trip on one of the plantations near town.

Jack was employed by a boiler manufacturing company located in nearby Coolidge, Georgia, a little town about 15 miles northeast of Thomasville. The company had been in the process of installing a new boiler at a sawmill in Bristol, Florida for the past three weeks. Jack wore multiple hats where he worked. He was the Service Manager and Field Erection Division Coordinator and had recently been assigned the additional duties of investigating the possibilities for the company to establish a joint venture building their product in China. A trip was planned in the near future to China, but in the meantime, he had taken the opportunity in his capacity as Field Erection Coordinator to observe the erection crew first-hand in Florida. Since Bristol was only a short drive from his home just outside Thomasville, he made the daily round trip.

As it happened, Jack had been stopped at the tracks that crossed West Jackson Street every afternoon on the trip home. He knew when he headed into town that Friday afternoon that the train would probably block his path again, but it seemed to be a contest between his personal schedule and that of the railroad. He could have taken Pine Tree Boulevard and avoided the tracks altogether, but not Jack. He had lost the battle each and every day and was determined to win once, just once. Not only was he a creature of habit, he was also a little hardheaded, to put it mildly.

In a way, Jack had become accustomed to the daily delay and sort of looked forward to it. It gave him time to mentally run through the events of the day and jot down things that he had questions about—there was a lot about the boiler business he didn't know. But he hadn't been hired for what he knew about the boiler business. He was hired because of his background and his ability to organize things and make things happen, correctly.

He glanced at the lotto tickets on the seat beside him that he had just purchased at convenience store entering town.

"Fifteen million! Fifteen big ones! That would be just enough to get by, I reckon. But, Lord, I don't want to be greedy. I'd settle for just enough to pay my bills," he said aloud, laughing a little; then he stuck his head half out of the car window, looked up toward the sky, and said in a mock earnest sort of way, "Lord, this ain't no laughing matter. I really, really would love to get my hands on all that money! Just give me a sign, Lord! Please, just give me a sign!"

Just then, a horn blared from behind and Jack jumped like he had been shot. His face turned as white as a sheet, and, before he could compose himself, the horn blared again. He jerked his head back into the car so fast he forgot to duck, causing his graying head to graze the edge of the molding at the top of the window.

"Shit!" he yelled, rubbing a red, nearly hairless spot on the side of his head just above the ear. He looked at a small spot of blood on the tip of his index finger and then at the top of the window.

"Damn!" he exclaimed, very loudly, at seeing the little tuffs of his salt and pepper hair that were sticking out from the edge of the molding. It looked almost like an old bottlebrush. "What are you trying to do? Scalp yourself?"

He drew his fist back, intending to hit the molding, but the horn sounded again from behind, stopping his fist in mid air. He looked into his rearview mirror in time to see the front of a pickup truck bump into his rear bumper. He could see the reflection of at least four people in the cab of the pickup, all high-school-aged kids. The back of the pickup truck was full of kids, too. He had seen a few other vehicles packed the very same way on his way into town that afternoon.

Jack snapped back to reality as the pickup fishtailed around him with its rear wheels smoking.

"Drive it or park it, you old gray-haired fart!" a very large young lady with stringy green-looking hair yelled from the back of the truck as she shot Jack the bird. Behind the pickup bounced a dirty, mangled, stuffed toy bulldog on the end of a short chain.

Jack started to yell something back but refrained. Smiling instead, he just shook his head, and mumbled to himself, "They could tattoo Goodyear in big yellow letters on the cheeks of her fat ass, strap a camera to her belly and fly her over the stadium tonight."

He was still smiling at what he had said when he put his car into gear, crossed the track and continued through the downtown area.

Once he was on East Jackson near the football stadium, high school students seemed to be everywhere. They were almost like little ants. The traffic was backed up for blocks. Water balloons filled the air like a hail of rubber breasts. Some of the kids, who weren't inside cars or pickup trucks, walked or ran between the rows of stopped vehicles, throwing the water balloons at each other. Those without water balloons were tying red or gold ribbons on radio antennas, door handles, bumpers, drivers' arms or anything else they could find.

Mingled with the kids were a few adults, acting almost as goofy as the kids were. In fact, everything around Thomasville seemed to get a little goofy during the Labor Day weekend because it was the night of the annual Rose Bowl game, southern style.

Thomasville was the Deep South's City of Roses. It was the night of the annual slugfest between the two local teams, the Thomasville High School Bulldogs and the Central High School Yellow Jackets—the city high school and the county high school.

The Bulldog's colors were red and black, and the Yellow Jacket's were blue and gold. Most people who lived in or around Thomasville went to one of the two schools. The battle lines were drawn for every game between the two archrivals.

He thought of the fun everyone were seeming to have and smiled most of the way home, until he began the turn onto the red clay lane that led to his home off Summerhill Road.

"Ev-ver-ry time!" he grumbled in a not-so-serious tone as he jammed the gearshift into park. "Why won't Wendy stop for the paper? Just one time!"

The rule was simple: "The first one home stops for the newspaper." It was a rule that he had made and that Wendy had never obeyed. He always complained, but she never stopped for the newspaper, not once.

Wendy used the newspaper as a gauge of Jack's daily disposition. If he walked through the back door bitching, she knew he was fine and all was well. It was when he was quiet and withdrawn that she knew something was wrong.

"I swear! If I left the paper in the box until it got so full the weight tore the thing from the post and they piled three feet high and blocked the road, you'd park out there and walk to the house before you'd pick up the paper. But, sure as shit, before I can read it, you're clipping them coupons. By the time I finally get to read it, it looks like the rats got a hold of it!"

Jack started talking as he walked up the back porch steps and finished after he came through the kitchen door, carrying the newspaper in one hand and rubbing the already sore spot on the side of his head.

Wendy always bought groceries on her way home from work on Friday. Grocery bags were scattered around the kitchen floor, and Jack stomped a zigzag path through them, stopping at the counter between the kitchen and dining areas and waited for Wendy to look his way.

"Allow me to show you, my dear, the ease with which this task can be performed. It's really not terribly difficult, but if I go too fast for you, tell me, and I'll slow down, okay?" Jack continued, trying to keep a straight face while he mimicked a British accent.

He laid the newspaper on the edge of the counter beside the mail Wendy had picked up from their post office box that day, turned and stomped over the bags, retracing his route back to the kitchen door; then stopped, turned, and added, "It's done thusly, my deary."

Jack made the revving sound like a car engine and held his hands in front of him just above his protruding waistline like he was holding a steering wheel. Wendy watched him drive by in his imaginary car and had to put a hand to her mouth to keep from laughing out loud. His physique wasn't exactly fashion plate material, never had been. Though she sometimes referred to him as "Mister Buttless" or having a severe case of "no ass at all," she loved him just the was he was, butt or no butt.

Jack stopped at the counter, made a squealing sound like braking tires and lifted the newspaper. Wendy watched his antics out of the corner of her eye as he turned to face her with the newspaper held high. She quickly looked downward to avoid his eyes, straining to keep from laughing.

"See?" replied Jack, trying to hold back a grin. Wendy wanted to laugh so badly until her cheeks were beginning to cramp.

Finally, she cleared her throat, pointed at Jack's feet and began to laugh. She attempted to speak but her laughter stopped her three times before she managed to say, "Didn't know a fat truck with no rear end could spin its wheels, deary."

Jack looked at his belly and began to laugh as well. All the pressures of the week were released from inside both of them as they met in the middle of the kitchen, embraced, and kissed.

However, Wendy's laughter couldn't be stifled even with a kiss. With her lips pressing against Jack's, she began to laugh again as she pushed herself away, grabbed her stomach, crossed her legs, and bent her knees.

"Jack," she finally managed to say while putting her hands between her legs. "You almost made me pee in my pants!" Jack fell across the counter laughing. It felt good and he needed it. They both did.

"I love you," Jack whispered into her ear, and Wendy's only answer was, "Me, too."

Not long after Jack left the kitchen, the coffeepot completed the brew cycle. Wendy filled Jack's favorite mug, and with cream and sugar blended the way he always drank it, took it to the bedroom. Both enjoyed a fresh hot cup of coffee after a long hard day. Sometimes she poured for him and sometimes he poured for her; there was no dominant party in their marriage.

Jack was in the bathroom when she came into the bedroom. Out of habit and respect for his wife's affectations, Jack always closed the bathroom door when he showered regardless of the fact that the two were generally alone in the house. When they were first married, her idiosyncrasies included sex only at night, with the lights off and always under the covers. It was years before Jack saw her completely nude and then it was when he accidentally walked into the bedroom when she was dressing.

Wendy heard the shower flowing as she tapped on the door, and called, "Jack!" She wanted with all of her heart to tell him that she loved him, words she had never spoken to him, words she hadn't spoken since she was a little girl.

"Jack!" she called again, and hearing no reply, she eased the door open just far enough to reach her arm inside the bathroom so she could set the mug of coffee on the vanity; then, she quickly undressed, put on her robe and went into the kitchen to finish putting the groceries away. After Jack finished showering, he slipped on an old pair of ragged pajama bottoms that were cut off at the knees, moved a stack of pillows from his favorite chair that was in the corner of a very large master bedroom and collapsed into the chair.

"I AM THE KING AND THIS IS MY CASTLE!" he shouted at the top of his lungs, holding the remote control for the television in his hand. It was his favorite saying, and he said it at the end of nearly every day when he could settle back in his chair and relax. Wendy heard him and smiled, for she felt like his queen.

His old chair had very little left of the original covering. Wendy had tried for years to get rid of it but he couldn't or wouldn't part with it. She had told him once, "I've seen better-looking chairs thrown away at the county landfill." Nevertheless, she allowed him to win the battle, if only for the time being and hid the eyesore under an afghan and the extra bed pillows.

***

Wendy and Jack were married in 1964. Jack was in the US Navy and remained enlisted until his retirement, just before they moved to Thomasville about four years ago. They both wanted children at first, but for some unknown reason, they weren't able to have any. Neither had ever been examined to see if it was a medical problem, and although both kept promising, neither did. As time passed, the idea of children seemed to have less importance, with them finding contentment within themselves and each other.

Wendy was born Wilhelmina Grace Wenslow in the little town of Conway, South Carolina, in June 1946, the third of four children. Her father was of Dutch ancestry and named her after a Dutch queen. However, most thought her name came from her grandmother, a Cherokee Indian. Wendy's mother's maiden name was Grace Tanner and her father was Francis Wenslow.

Jack sometimes called Wendy his squaw. She didn't seem to mind. She knew he didn't mean the nickname to tease or to hurt. She had heard hurting words as a child and knew how those words felt inside. Those remembered words and deeds filled her mind at times and still hurt, things that happened when she was a little girl. She tried to hide the memories inside, locked away, but they always returned as they did that night, prompted when Jack had told her that he loved her.

***

The bedroom was dimly lit by moonlight in a house that was more like a shack when nine-year-old Wendy was shocked into full alertness. She was lying on her back and knew that her panties had been pulled down around her knees. Her stepfather's hand was touching her between her legs in the place that her grandmother told her "Little boys mustn't ever see."

Her entire body trembled with fear—her mouth opened in a soundless cry. Lester quickly put a hand tightly across her mouth. She tried to pull herself free from his grasp, but she couldn't. Her eyes opened widely in disbelief, screaming the words her mouth couldn't.

"Shut up!" he jeered, the words hissing through his teeth. She could smell the scent of whiskey on his breath. "I'm just checking to make sure you're all right. Your Momma sent me in here."

Her frightened eyes looked down questioningly to where his hand was touching her.

"That's where she told me to check," he said, looking into her eyes.

His eyes, in the darkness, looked like two balls of fire to Wendy. She could see only a faint outline of his face in the gloomy darkness, but she could see his eyes and smell his whiskey breath. His evil stare seemed to burn her clothing from her, yet a chill seemed to grip her small frail body.

Lester must have seen the fear and the questioning way she looked at him. Her eyes told him what her mouth couldn't. They said, "I don't believe a word you're saying!"

Instantly, a change seemed to come over her stepfather. The hand that had rubbed gently suddenly became hard and rough as he pushed his finger into her tiny vagina.

Wendy's back arched up from the bed as her entire body winched with pain, causing a slight smile to break across Lester's face.

His voice changed when he whispered, "When I let your mouth go, you better not scream or say a word. I better not hear so much as a peep out of you. If I do, I'll march right straight back to your Momma's bedroom and beat the hell out of her some more. Then, I'll beat Emily the way I whipped your little ass. You'll love me. I'll make all of y'all love me. I can do anything I want to you, or to her, and nobody can stop me. I'll make your Momma put you two out by the side of the road like two bitch dogs. DO! YOU! HEAR! ME!"

With every word his finger dug deeper inside her; then, he added a phrase that burned into her mind much more than the fingertip inside of her.

"Say it! Say it!" he hissed, removing his hand from her mouth. "Say you love me! Say it!"

His finger hurt like nothing she had ever felt. She wanted to scream but couldn't. Instead of saying those three little words, she wanted to scream out for help.

She knew that she didn't love her stepfather. She hated him more than any other person or any other thing on earth. But, reasoning that the pain would stop if she said the words, she opened her mouth but no sound came out. Her lips could only mouth them.

Lester nodded his head, and said, "Now, that wudn't so hard, was it?"

Her answer was only a blank stare.

"This ain't over yet!" he snarled. "I'll be back! If you say a word about this, the next time it will be worse."

When he finally withdrew his finger and left the room, Wendy could still smell Lester's whiskey breath and still couldn't cry out.

***

Jack was born William Leon Jackson on a farm near Hemingway, South Carolina, in July 1945. He was the fourth of eight children. He was called Bill at first, but he had an uncle who lived nearby who was named Bill. Consequently, as time passed, everyone began to call him Jack.

The children born in South Carolina, in the little farming community of Pleasant Hill, were not simply children of Sam Jackson. They were treated almost like his chattel, like property. They were farm workers, laborers, someone to work the crops and who wouldn't have to be paid hard cash, pieces of property to be loaned out to work in another farmer's fields much like mules or tractors were loaned. Jack believed that if his father had not had a large farm, there probably wouldn't have been the need for a large family. Large farms needed large families to do the work.

The Jackson children, who worked the sandy, dusty, hot fields of that South Carolina farm, took the blame for whatever happened to the crops, dry year, a wet year, low tobacco prices or whatever. It was "they" who did "it" and "they" who took the punishment. They formed a bond with each other and no single individual took sole blame. In doing that, all took the punishment, the condemnation, the ridicule and even the abuse when something went wrong. Even when separated, each seemed to act as one, as if connected by an invisible umbilical cord. Yet when they were together, they were individuals, one being very much different from the other.

Jack and his brother Carl were the closest in age and the nearest to being alike. There was less than a year separating their ages, and the two brothers looked and acted almost like twins. When Jack caught his brother in the tenth grade, some of the new teachers for the school year thought they were indeed twins.

Just as Wendy formed a shell to try and block out some of her past memories, Jack and Carl also had their defenses. They hid behind a facade of humor. Rather than face the reality that others found sad, uncomfortable, or stressful, they managed to find something within the situation to laugh about. When others cried, they told jokes. Their humor at times appeared cold and misplaced and caused some to scorn. Now, Jack found it difficult to cry.

***

All of those things were a million miles away from Jack's thoughts that Friday evening as he went into the kitchen to get another cup of coffee. Seeing a frozen potpie on the counter next to the microwave and knowing that he wouldn't be getting his customary Friday night steak for supper, he said as he lifted the potpie and dropped it hard on the counter, "This don't look like no rib-eye to me." Behind his southern dialect lay a well-educated mind.

Wendy was standing on a two-foot-high stool, putting groceries on the top shelf of a kitchen cabinet.

"Use your imagination," she replied, sniffing and wiping the tears from her eyes caused by her mind's trip to the past.

"Yeah, right," Jack answered, laughing as he stepped behind Wendy and attempted to run his hand under her robe. "If I had an imagination that vivid, I'd dream up some sweet, young thing."

"Stop!" she snapped, quickly grabbing his hand. Knowing that her tone of voice was too sharp, she gently pushed him away, stepped down to the floor, and added in a softer voice, "Go get yourself a sweet young thing!"

"No way," Jack said as he placed his hands at Wendy's waist. "You're as young as I want. I don't want to train another." He could see that she had been crying. He had seen it many times before and knew she'd been thinking of the past. Attacks of melancholy were normal for her.

He pulled her quickly toward him, kissed her forehead and began to tickle her.

"Stop, now!" she said, twisting from his hold and out of his reach. "I've got to hurry and get ready to go."

"Go?" Jack asked. "Go where?"

"I've got to help with security at the game tonight," she answered, lifting the stool and moving it to a corner.

"Why?" asked Jack. "You're not a deputy! I thought they hired Susan Clark. You don't have any business out there! Why don't they use her?"

"The sheriff says she's not ready yet. Susan doesn't know departmental procedures so I have to go. There has to be a woman on duty at the game," Wendy answered. "Besides, all I have to do is stand in one spot, collect my overtime and come back home. I don't have to do anything unless one of the deputies has to arrest a girl or a woman."

"I still don't like it!" Jack snapped. "If it's all that simple, why can't Susan do it? Didn't you learn a lesson from that fat bitch at the jail? I believe I'll come along with you. It should be a hell of a game tonight, anyway."

"Suit yourself," Wendy answered, but remember what happened the last time you went to a game and sat on those cold damp steel bleachers for two hours? Remember, Jack? Remember your hemorrhoids?" Her voice had a motherly tone.

"I hate to admit it, but when you're right, you're right," Jack replied, refilling his coffee mug. "Yes mother, I remember." He had suffered long and had very painfully memories of the game the year before. It had taken two weeks and a box of suppositories for him to get over it.

"Oh!" Wendy said. "Almost forgot, be sure you wake me up early tomorrow morning, okay? I've got to go into work for a little while. I'm moving into my new office, finally."

She had been promoted the previous week to Assistant Jail Administrator for the Thomas County Jail. However, she wasn't a sworn deputy. She had a uniform and a badge but didn't wear the uniform except for special occasions, such as funerals or when on security assignment. She once worked as a guard, or matron, in the jail but had hurt her back trying to put a 300-pound woman into a cell.

She had worked some cases with the investigators when a woman was needed, or on a stakeout when there was a chance of a woman being arrested. Mostly she worked cases with the investigators when child molestation or rape was involved. She enjoyed taking part in putting those who were responsible behind bars. It was a personal vendetta for her. She loved her job and it was next in her life behind Jack, though he thought otherwise at times.

Wendy soon showered quickly and, dressed in her uniform, said a goodnight to Jack with a peck on his cheek and left for the game. Jack fed the dog and settled down to watch an Atlanta Braves baseball game on television and listen to the local football game on the radio. He planned to do both at the same time, but he never saw the last out of the Braves game or heard the final whistle of the football game. He was fast asleep an hour after Wendy left the house.

2
"AUTUMN DAWN"

It was rare for Jack to sleep later than 6:00 or 6:30 a.m. Years of early reveille in the navy had made him a habitual early riser. He was surprised to see that the time on the bedside clock was after 8:00 a.m. when he opened his eyes Saturday morning. He had slept soundly the entire night.

Without turning over, he reached his hand behind his back to wake Wendy but felt only an empty spot. She wasn't beside him in their bed, but her absence wasn't a big surprise. When she had to go into work very early in the morning on the weekend, she often left the house without disturbing him. Regardless of the fact she had been up half of the night at the game, he knew she would have gotten to work on time that Saturday morning.

Jack went into the kitchen and made a pot of coffee even before he visited the bathroom. He was a coffee-holic. When he returned to the kitchen, he filled his favorite mug with fresh hot coffee, and, with his right index finger curled around the handle, he headed out of the kitchen door to the east porch to enjoy the coffee and the morning. It was his favorite part of the day when he had the time to enjoy it.

The new home fulfilled Wendy and Jack's dreams. It was the only house they had ever owned. They had drawn the plans themselves and did most of the construction. Everything was just the way they wanted, and to them, it was beautiful. It was home, their home. They purchased ten acres of land that had once been part of an antebellum plantation named Summerhill.

The land looked like a scene from a postcard or travel guide, and it had taken every penny they had saved over the years just to buy it. Then the timber was clear-cut and sold to raise enough money to build the house. They didn't like the idea of clear-cutting the beautiful virgin timber, but they had little choice. It was either clear-cut or they couldn't have had a home at all.

The home site was atop a large hill on the back quarter of their land. It was the most prominent hill in the area. It had been the site of the original plantation house that had burned long ago. Huge magnolia trees still lined an old lane that ran to the new home. The magnolias stood as stately and beautiful as when they once marked the entrance to the grand old house.

Pine seedlings were planted on the hill as soon as the logging was completed. The seedlings' four years of growth were now beginning to cover the ugliness done by the logging and the hill's grandeur was beginning to return.

Only the top of their home could now be seen from the road. They wanted their little corner of the world to be private, and if the trees continued to grow at the rate they were growing, in a few years, they would have their wish. Nothing marked the entrance to their magnolia-lined, red clay lane except a red plastic newspaper box and the number 4172 on a small sign to the right of the drive. Their mail was deposited in the post office box in town.

A wide porch encircled the house. Jack named them north, south, east and west. Once a sailor, he loved to sit on the east porch and watch the sunrise over the tops of the pine seedlings, and on the west porch to watch it set. In the evenings after a hard day at work, he sat on the north porch to watch the northern sky and to gaze at Polaris, the North Star. It had always been a reference point for mariners and seemed to be a focal point for him. By spending hours looking at the star, he seemed to gather his composure in preparation for another day.

Wendy and Jack rarely used the front or south porch. It was mainly used as a place for Wendy to hang her flowers and a place for Jack to fly his flag. He was an extremely proud veteran and wanted the flag to be the first thing their visitors saw.

Next to the flag was a small plaque with an alligator head painted in bright green. There were two white dice in the alligator's mouth with the number "6" on one and a zero on the other. Beneath the alligator head were the words, "Gator 60," and beneath that in smaller letters, "YFU-60." It had been Jack's boat when he was in Vietnam. His call sign was "Gator 60."

The front door of the house was seldom used. The kitchen door was the main entrance to their home.

Jack had missed the sunrise when he rounded the northeast corner and strolled onto the east porch. An old Bloodhound lay asleep in the porch swing. Jack called the hound "Earnhardt" after his favorite NASCAR driver, who was known on the Winston Cup circuit as "The Intimidator." Since the old dog's size usually intimidated most, the name of Earnhardt seemed to fit.

Jack enjoyed NASCAR Winston Cup car racing. A huge picture of Dale Earnhardt hung on the wall above the workbench in his workshop. The telephone on the nightstand beside his bed was a replica of the driver's black number "3" Goodwrench Chevrolet.

They didn't know the true age of the old hound, but from the way he looked, his age was estimated to be at least twelve years. His long red ears nearly touched the ground when he decided to walk, but most of the time, he slept. His coat was the color of Georgia red clay except for some intermingled black hairs down the center of the back. There was enough extra skin hanging on his body to cover three more dogs. Wendy said his body was a size 5-short and his skin a size 10-long. She pretended not to like the old hound because of the constant stream of slobber from his mouth, but she did.

It seemed every weekend morning when Jack went to the swing on the east porch, Earnhardt was always there, waiting for his master. However, he really wasn't Jack's dog. He showed up about the time they finished building the house and decided to stick around. Now, he was as much a part of their lives as a child would have been.

Earnhardt's long body completely covered the seat of the swing. Jack lifted his head slowly, and a thick bead of slobber stretched like clear silicone from the seat of the swing. Jack took a seat on one end of the swing, and lowered the dog's head gently into his lap, slobber and all. The hound didn't move a muscle nor did he loose the rhythm of his snoring.

During the weekdays, Jack tended to stay clear of the slobber to keep it from getting on the clothing he wore to work, but, on weekends, he didn't really care.

He held Earnhardt's head in his lap while sipping the coffee, quietly looking toward the eastern sky. Neither seemed to have a care in the world.

The sky was almost blood red that morning. Horizontal bands of clouds looked like strips of red and orange ribbons across the sky just above the tops of the trees as a harvest dawn signaled autumn's approach.

"Absolutely beautiful, ain't it, boy?" said Jack as he scratched Earnhardt's back. The dog didn't move. Jack raised one of the dog's long ears, and said loudly, "Wake up! Reveille! Reveille! Everything's almost as red as your eyes!" The hound still didn't move a muscle.

Jack placed the coffee mug on the porch railing, lifted Earnhardt's head between his hands, pointed his nose toward the eastern horizon, and said, "I said look!"

Earnhardt opened his eyes only slightly, took a deep breath and went back to sleep. Jack placed his head back down in his lap, and rubbed his wet hands in the roll of extra skin on the dog's neck to wipe away some of the slobber.

"I knew you'd like it. Now don't go getting excited and get yourself all worked up. Ain't you glad I woke you up? When I was in the Navy, do you know what they use to say about a sky all red like that?" Jack asked.

He paused a moment, as if waiting for Earnhardt to reply, while he lifted the mug and took a sip of coffee and swung the swing gently back and forth, enjoying the quietness and beauty of the morning.

Finally, he said, "Red sky in the morning, sailors take warning."

The muscles in Earnhardt's stomach suddenly tightened and relaxed as he expelled some bodily gases.

"Christ! Earnhardt!" yelled Jack, faking a cough. "Them Alpo farts are hell!"

He quickly got out of the swing and Earnhardt's head hit the wooden seat with a THUNK.

"That aroma is nuclear, damned-near! Think I'll go take a shower before it eats into my skin. I can't take this shit!" he said, faking another cough and fanning his hand in front of his face as he rounded the northwest corner of the porch headed for the kitchen door.

After a quick shower, Jack refilled his coffee mug and he and Earnhardt walked to the road to get the Saturday morning newspaper from the box. It was actually Jack who walked all the way to the road. Earnhardt stopped about halfway and waited for Jack to walk back then followed behind him to the house.

As Jack approached the house, he noticed the flag was foiled on the flagstaff. He straightened it and walked around to the west porch to find Earnhardt lying beside Jack's favorite twisted vine rocker, waiting.

It was almost as if he knew what Jack was going to do before he did it. Jack swore to Wendy that Earnhardt was human sometimes, or at least more human than a lot of the people he knew. But, Jack being the dedicated creature of habit that he was, even Earnhardt at times could anticipate what he would do next.

It was a beautiful morning even on the west porch. A cool, gentle breeze blew out of the north and across the porch and made the brass wind chime, hanging at the northwest corner of the porch, sing its song. The world seemed at total peace.

As Jack sipped his coffee, he scanned through the pages of the paper, rocked and dozed. And, just as Wendy's mind sometimes slipped to the past, Jack's did, too.

The memories revived by the old sailor's parable began to flash through his mind like individual frames of a film of his naval days, days when he and Carl were stationed on the same ship in Charleston, South Carolina. Those memories were very dear to him. He may have retired years before, but his heart and his mind were still at times far away on some distant sea.

"God, how I miss them days," he had said more than a few times.

***

Jack's oldest sister finished school and was the first to leave the farm, followed two years later by his oldest brother, which left Carl the oldest at home. Then Carl dropped out of school and enlisted in the navy, leaving Jack the oldest at home. Another long hot summer passed, and Jack began his senior year in the fall.

Before Thanksgiving, Jack's father had a very serious heart attack that came close to taking his life. After that, he lost interest in the farm. Before Christmas arrived, the farm was sold and the Jackson family moved to Myrtle Beach during the holiday break from school.

Jack enlisted in the US Naval Reserve, to his brother's displeasure, after moving to the beach. When he graduated from high school, he followed Carl into military service—the US Navy, of course. After basic training, he requested and was transferred to the same ship his brother served aboard, the USS Howard W. Gilmore (AS-16), home ported in Charleston.

***

"To hell with this!" Jack said as he got up from the rocker. "You sentimental old fart."

Rather than continue the journey of yesteryears, he decided he would take a ride into town to run some errands and stop by to visit with Wendy in her new office. He always drove his pickup truck to town on the weekend and Earnhardt always rode in the back.

The carport was on the west side of the house, separated by a covered open walk, or, at least, that's the way the walk started out before Jack planted the ivy. Now it looked like a green tunnel. Except for some scrawny shrubs around the yard, the walk was about the only green thing in the yard.

He didn't take the covered walk to the carport. Instead, he jumped over the porch railing and walked across the corner of the lawn. Their so-called "lawn" looked almost like some thought the surface of Mars would probably look. A sprig of green showed here and there, but mostly, it was hard red clay.

When Jack reached his pickup, he found Earnhardt perched on the aluminum toolbox in the back where he always rode. He always sat with his head pointed straight ahead into the wind like a stone figure, with his long red ears flapping and streams of slobber stretching backwards. Even during love-bug season in South Georgia, Earnhardt wouldn't alter his riding position. Sometimes his face was a mass of splattered bugs. The 60 mile per hour winds parted his lips and the bugs would smash on his teeth like on the windshield.

The love-bugs, as they are called in Florida and southern Georgia, are flying bugs about a half-inch long that join for mating in flight. The male cannot disconnect himself from the coupling. He must fly along with the female until he finally dies. The exhaust emission of gasoline-powered vehicles seems to attract the insects to thoroughfares. There, they become pests as they swarm in thick clouds. Windshields can become completely obscured in less than a half-mile.

Some of the so-called "good old boys" around the county who drove pickup trucks had big dogs riding in the back—sort of a custom, a status symbol. Most had to train them to ride without jumping from the truck, but not Earnhardt. What he knew, and he knew a lot, he already knew when he came to live with Wendy and Jack.

Barking, for instance. Some dogs have to be taught not to bark unnecessarily, but not Earnhardt. He never barked at anything—growl, yes—heist his leg and mark his territory, yes—but bark, no. Wendy thought he couldn't bark, but Jack said he was just too damned lazy.

The Justice Center was along Smith Avenue, or US-84. Jack drove past it that Saturday morning on his way to the downtown area but didn't see Wendy's old Buick in the front parking lot. He figured it must have been in the lot beside the building. When he returned from downtown a little later, he parked his pickup in the front lot, left it guarded by Earnhardt, and went into the main entrance.

A lot of prisoners were in the hallways, moving office furniture and boxes.

"Wendy?" Jack called as he began to open the door to her new office, but he didn't get a reply. He was only able to open the door about a foot as he called Wendy's name again. He craned his head through the small opening but didn't see her. The office was full of furniture, boxes, and many other items, but no Wendy. If she had been there, she would have had to stand on the desk for him to have seen her the way the room was cluttered.

He left the office and looked around for someone he recognized and finally caught a glimpse of Captain William "Bill" Stanley, Wendy's boss, the Jail Administrator. He was headed into one of the offices down the hallway. Jack called to him, but the captain didn't seem to hear. Jack and the captain became friends shortly after Jack came to Thomasville. The two men had something in common; they were both retired military.

Captain Stanley was talking to a group of people inside the office he had entered, so Jack didn't interrupt. He remained in the hallway and waited until the captain turned toward him. Jack saluted the captain, and the captain returned the salute; then he held up one finger toward Jack. Jack pointed toward the front door, and the captain nodded a reply.

Jack exited the front door, walked across the parking lot and waited beside his pickup. Earnhardt nuzzled close, and Jack gave him a good scratch behind the ear while he waited for Captain Stanley to join him.

A few minutes passed and the captain came out of the main entrance. He glanced around the parking lot, saw Jack and began walking toward him.

"Good lord, Jack," Captain Stanley said as he approached. "Don't you believe in washing them love bugs off your truck?" he added as he shook Jack's hand.

"Yeah, but I figured I'd wait till it needed it," Jack replied. You could hardly see the grill of the truck for the love bugs. "I'll be glad when they go back to Florida or wherever they came from."

The captain scraped along the front bumper with the toe of his shoe, and answered, "Me too! There are more this year than I've ever seen. Our patrol cars are taking a beating. A couple of them have the paint chipped from the front of the hoods."

"Speaking of love bugs," the captain said, rubbing Earnhardt's ear. "Where's your love bug this morning?"

Jack looked puzzled, answering, "Love? What love bug?"

"I wasn't talking to this dog. I'm talking about Wendy!" the captain said, paused, looked for a place to wipe the dog's slobber from his hand, wiped it on his lower right trouser leg, and continued, "She's supposed to be here working with the rest of us prisoners. It's her office we're moving."

"You're joking, I hope, Bill," Jack answered.

"Nope," the captain replied with a deep southern drawl. "She ain't here. She's home playing sick, right? Sent you here to give her excuse?"

"Now, does that sound like Wendy to you? I don't think she's ever missed a day of work except when she hurt her back," Jack replied; then continued with some anxiousness creeping into his voice, "She's not at home, and I'm serious, Bill! I thought she was here!"

The captain couldn't mistake the change in the sound of his friend's voice. He knew something was wrong. He slowly turned without a word and walked toward the building with Jack walking beside. No further communication between the two was necessary. Besides, the captain knew Wendy better than he knew Jack. His gut feeling told him something was wrong.

By then, Jack knew something was wrong, as well. His heart pounded in his chest and his face felt hot as he followed the captain to the sheriff's office.

There was a large red-lettered sign on the door that read, "SHERIFF MATTHEW YOUNG," and, in smaller letters, "KNOCK—THEN—ENTER." It had been on the sheriff's door since the first day he assumed the office, but the captain always ignored it. The sheriff got very frustrated each time the captain walked in without knocking and started talking.

"Sheriff," Captain Stanley said as he opened the door. "Jack Jackson here's got a problem."

"I might as well use that sign for a door mat. Ain't nobody round here can read no how. How many times..." a voice said from behind a large oak desk. He was getting some papers from a bottom drawer.

"Jack says Wendy's not at home. She's supposed to be here but she's not here either. Something's dead up the branch, Sheriff," Captain Stanley said, talking like the sheriff wasn't.

The sheriff finished what he was saying, only hearing part of what the captain had said, and asked, "What's dead up what branch?" as he rose and lay a stack of papers on his desk.

"Wendy, Sheriff," Captain Stanley answered. "Our Wendy's missing!"

Jack interjected, "My Wendy, Sheriff. She's missing!"

"Missing?" the sheriff replied. "I know some men who'd pay real good money to make that statement. What do you mean...missing?" His voice had a patented deep southern drawl. He was like Jack in that he knew proper English but chose instead to speak most of the time in the local vernacular.

The tone of his voice, when he had said missing, made Jack feel somewhat awkward. He felt as if he had reported his newspaper stolen or a sock lost in his dryer.

He dug his hands into his pockets, and replied, "I know how it sounds, but all I know is that I thought she was here working, and she's not. She left the house last night to work security at the game and wasn't at the house this morning when I got up. I thought she got up early and came here. I don't know where she is. All I know is she's not at home and Bill say's she's not here."

"Well," the sheriff said with the tone of his voice changing to reflect the concern he had heard in Jack's voice. "I believe we might need a little more to go on. She could be missing, Mr. Jackson, but, you know, not MISSING."

A young deputy, as skinny as a rail, ran full speed into the sheriff's office screaming, "Matthew! Matthew!" at the top of his lungs.

"JAMERSON!" the sheriff screamed. "What in sam hell's wrong with you? Ain't I told you 'bout calling me Matthew? What you yell'n 'bout?" He started around to the front of his desk, adding, "One a these days, I'm gonna run your ass off! If you wusn't my baby brother..."

The deputy came to a stop so fast he nearly fell face-first into the sheriff. He looked as if he was scared to death. His skinny body looked like rigor mortis had set in.

Matthew Young usually had a cool head and wasn't bothered about a lot of things. He had savvy, a lot savvy. He didn't look much like a sheriff, especially a sheriff in the south. If a movie was ever made in Thomas County about its sheriff, he wouldn't have gotten the part. He wasn't fat, or old or hidden behind sunglasses with mirrored lenses nor did he have a big half-smoked cigar hanging in his mouth like a stereotypical southern sheriff. He was only thirty-five years old, five-foot-eight, and weighed at the most 150 pounds.

He had come to Thomasville with his wife and brother by way of Montana, the US Naval Academy and the US Marine Corps. In fact, he had been Captain Stanley's company commander before the captain retired from the marines.

He had proven himself to be cool under fire as a marine and as a sheriff. In his presence, things seemed to always run smoothly. That is, until the red dawn of that particular Saturday morning.

When Jamerson finally managed to speak, he said, "A wa...woman called in and sa...said there's ah, ah house on fire out on Summerhill Road!"

The word "Summerhill" snapped Jack's head toward the deputy.

The sheriff answered, "So, Jamerson, call the fire department!" Then, he turned to go back behind his desk, and added, "Don't come running into my office, yell'n! You hear?"

Jamerson almost took a step toward the door but stopped, pointed a shaking finger at Jack, and said, "Matt, I...I mean, Sheriff, it's his house! It's Mr. Jackson's house!"

Jack felt his face flush, felt lightheaded and had to catch the back of a chair to steady himself.

"Good God!" Sheriff Young said while reaching for his hat that hung on the wall near the door. "Let's all go and see if we can find out what in sam hell's going on 'round here!"

Laying his hand on Jack's shoulder, he added, "Ride with the Captain, okay, Mr. Jackson? It'll be faster. Jamie, you're with me."

The four men entered the hallway from the sheriff's office already at a half-trot and headed out of the building.

"Somebody call the fire department!" Sheriff Young yelled to no one in particular.

"Already been done!" a voice answered from somewhere.

They were nearly at a full run when they left the front entrance of the Justice Center. Jack yelled at a prisoner; clad in a black and white striped uniform, watering flowers near his pickup, "Look after Earnhardt!" The prisoner looked at Jack with a puzzled look, and Jack added while pointing at Earnhardt, "My dog there in the pickup!"

The prisoner answered with a thumb raised in the air.

3
"THE CHURCH"
(DECEMBER, 1954)

It was a bitterly cold morning that December as Wendy held onto her little sister's hand and walked into their Sunday school classroom. Their older brother, Tom, had walked them to the church about a mile from where they lived on Powell Street in Conway. Wendy was five; going on six, and Emily was barely three.

The two girls were dressed only as well as their mother could afford to dress them, but what they wore was clean. Having so-called "nice" clothes was something reserved for others when Wendy was a little girl. She couldn't remember ever having had a new dress, a dress no other person had ever worn. Her dresses had always been hand-me-downs or ones made by her mother from an old dress of hers. Their brothers, Tom and Bill, once even wore the shoes the sisters wore that morning.

What she wore didn't seem to bother Wendy, for it was simply the way things were, the only way she had ever known, the way she thought things was supposed to be. She knew she didn't have the things other little girls had, but those were things of her dreams, like the pictures in a catalog, things she was wishing for on Christmas a week away, things Grace and Francis Wenslow couldn't give her.

Wendy's father was a carpenter by trade and had been bedridden for as long as she could remember. Tuberculosis had slowly drained the life from him. Her mother earned the little money brought into the home by taking in washing, but she didn't have a washing machine. She boiled the clothing in a large iron kettle in the back yard. Her mother's hands were always cracked and bleeding, results of strong lye soap and a scrub board. She also made dresses for other women on an old peddle-type Singer sewing machine.

Wendy's mind that morning was a thousand miles away from the words of her Sunday school lesson as she gazed out of the window at the big white house across the street next to a funeral home. To her it was like looking into a storybook. There were always bicycles and toys scattered about the yard. A pink curtain hung at an upstairs window above the front porch, and she imagined the house being where she lived, and her room, the one with pink curtain.

Emily sat beside her and leaned her sleepy head on her shoulder as soon as they sat in the little classroom close to the woodburning stove. Emily wore a coat that Wendy had worn the year before, so Wendy didn't have one to wear that morning.

Her mother had bundled her up in an old sweater and told her, "It doesn't make any difference what you wear to church as long as it is clean. Jesus doesn't care how little girls look on the outside. He looks inside their hearts to see how they look there. We'll get you a coat before long. The Lord will look after us... Shoot! I'll bet there's a lot of folk who don't have it as good as you. You just be thankful for what you have and don't worry about how you may look to others."

The Sunday school teacher had completed the lesson but wouldn't let them leave the classroom until the bell rang. Wendy sat with her eyes staring at the door because Tom had told her that morning, "The bell will be rung by an angel. If you're looking really hard at the door and you're really quiet, you'll see her when she sticks her arm in the room."

However, Emily moved, and, while Wendy kept her from falling from the bench, the bell rang. She looked back at the door only in time to see it closing. Consequently, she was a little mad as she more-or-less dragged Emily from the classroom.

Tom, who was eleven, was waiting for them in the hallway. "Momma wants you all to come home, NOW!" he told them, and, without another word, he went out the side door of the church.

Wendy took Emily by the hand and hurriedly followed with Emily in tow, around the front of the church and into the street. By that time, Tom was a good twenty yards ahead of them, for one of his steps equaled two of his sisters'.

Wendy gripped her sister's hand tighter and pulled her along as she ran to catch her big brother; then she hooked a finger into one of his belt loops and held on for dear life in a half-trot while Emily's little short legs were in a full run.

"Why are we in such a hurry?" asked Wendy.

Tom replied, "Cause!"

A few steps further, Wendy asked, "Cause why, Tom, cause why?"

Tom stopped dead in his tracks, causing Emily to fall forward face down into the dirt of the street. Wendy almost fell but managed to hold onto the belt loop like she was riding a subway.

Emily had so much clothing on to keep her warm that she nearly bounced when she hit the dirt. She wasn't hurt, but she screamed like she was in severe pain. Tom helped her up, brushed her off and picked her up into his arms for a moment until she stopped crying; then, carrying her in his arms and with Wendy holding to his belt loop, he continued the walk home.

Wendy could hardly keep her eyes off of her brother's face as she tried to skip along, but Tom made her stop. He was usually nice to her, except when he didn't want her around. Nice or not, he wasn't above throwing a rock or two at her to drive her back to the house or away from where he didn't want her. But, all in all, he was okay as brothers went.

Usually Tom and Bill went to church, too, and when their mother could, she went with them. But on that particular December morning, Bill, who was nine, stayed home with his mother and father, and Tom walked his sisters to church only to return to walk them home again after Sunday school. It all seemed strange to Wendy, as were other things around the house that morning.

Her mother seemed very quiet and subdued to Wendy, almost secretive, as she bundled the girls up in their clothing and hurried them away to church. Wendy saw the same look in Tom's face on the walk home.

Grace met them as they entered the house, but, before Wendy could ask her mother what was wrong, the four children were hurried into their father's bedroom.

He lay in an old iron posted bed, the same bed where he had lain for what seemed like forever to Wendy. His face was long and drawn with only the long black eyelashes of his closed eyelids breaking the yellowish glaze of his face.

Wendy thought that her father had beautiful eyes. She had heard some say that they were too pretty for a man. They once had been crystal clear and a bright emerald green. But that morning, time and pain had taken their toll. The eyes that once had known all of the answers and could make things all better simply by a look, could not focus enough to see his children as they stood around the bed. Instead, he stared blankly at the ceiling.

His mouth tried to open but his lips were cracked, dry and stuck together. Grace dampened a white towel and squeezed a few drops of water onto his lips and then placed the towel very softly on his forehead.

Wendy reached her trembling hand beneath the sheet at the foot of the bed and clasped her father's big toe. It felt like a cube of ice to her. Her tears began to flow as she stared at her father's face through the small metal bars. She had looked at him that way every day for as long as she could remember but she had never cried before. Now, she cried but didn't know why.

"Grace?" he said hoarsely in a barely audible voice, moving nothing but his mouth, gazing upward with unblinking eyes.

Grace wiped his face with the damp towel and answered softly, "Hush now, everyone's here." Her voice was that of someone who hurt inside but couldn't show it.

A few days before, Wendy had been mean to Emily and made her cry. Grace had a long talk with Wendy, explaining what love was and that she should always love her little sister enough not to make her cry. Wendy hadn't understood then what her mother was trying to tell her, but, as she watched her mother that Sunday, she believed she understood.

She watched as tears streamed down her mother's face as she looked upward at the ceiling, praying silently. Wendy followed her gaze, and when she looked at her father's face again, her mother's hand was covering his eyes. Her father was dead.

***

Wendy's way of dealing with the reality around her that day was to simply shut down her mind from things that were unpleasant. Her memories of her father's funeral and many details surrounding it were a blank for many years. She remembered her mother received a monthly check from her father's social security. She continued to wash and sew, and the family managed to survive, though barely.

The four children helped as much as they could. Under Tom's watchful eyes, they walked the streets searching for soft-drink bottles to sell for a half cent each. Tom and Bill also earned a little money from raking yards and from odd jobs they managed to find around the neighborhood. It was a very slim existence for the family. However, just when they thought things couldn't get any worse for the little family on Powell Street, things did.

Wendy's grandparents—her mother's parents, the Tanners and their son moved in with them less than six months after the death of her father. At that point, things really got tough for them. The big "plan" was for everyone to pool their earnings so all could live better, but that's not how it all worked out for the next year. Now, eight had to survive off of what had barely been enough for five. To add to an already intolerable situation, Mrs. Tanner had recently had a stroke and was paralyzed, unable to walk. However, she didn't have a wheelchair.

Mr. Tanner and his twenty-two year old son stayed drunk most of the time. Neither had a job nor were they even looking for work. They stayed around the house, for the most part, making excuses as to why that particular day wasn't a good day to try and find a job. However, Grace tried to remain respectful to her father and not criticize him.

Mrs. Tanner spent most of the day in a rocking chair. Wendy wondered why there wasn't money to buy a wheelchair if her grandfather had enough to buy wine, corn whiskey and cigarettes. Even though she probably wasn't quite old enough to know what real anger was, she learned fast or was made to learn.

Tom and Bill were gone most of the time earning what money they could. Mr. Tanner and his son were either off somewhere drunk or at home, drunk.

Mrs. Tanner had to be dragged about the house in the rocking chair, and with almost everyone gone or drunk, it was usually Wendy who did the dragging. Even when the two men were around and relatively sober, they seemed not to hear when the old woman would beg to be taken to the back porch so she could use the chamber pot.

Everyone in the house except for Mrs. Tanner called the chamber pot a "pot". She chose to call it a "slop-jar."

The Tanner men seemed not to care what happened to Mrs. Tanner. Sometimes they even laughed while she begged. They didn't seem to care about anything unless it somehow led to their next drink. Grace helped when she could, but most of the time she was in the back yard at a hot fire and wash pot. Consequently, the chore of looking after the old woman fell upon Tom, Bill or Wendy, but mostly Wendy.

It was not easy for a little girl to drag a rocking chair around with a large woman sitting in it. Her grandmother helped some by pushing with the foot that wasn't completely paralyzed, and Wendy devised a method to leverage the weight and move the rocker.

She and Emily would stand on the right rocker while their grandmother pushed backwards with her good leg. When the rocker turned sideways, Emily would then move to the other side and stand on the other rocker while Wendy pulled the chair around the other way from behind. The process was repeated over and over until they reached the back porch or Mrs. Tanner was where she wanted to go. Grace begged her mother to use the pot wherever she was inside the house, but the old woman wouldn't.

The process was painfully slow but it worked though sometimes it wasn't fast enough to get Grandmother Tanner to the back porch and the slop jar in time. Consequently, sometimes there was a mess to clean up.

Wendy's bare toes often got in the way of the pointed rockers and sometimes a toenail would be pushed backwards or completely torn away. It hurt, and when Wendy cried, her grandmother always took her in her arms, rocked her gently and cried while she told her, "I'm sorry, baby, that Grandmomma can't walk!"

Granddaddy Tanner told his son one day when they were drunk, watching the girls struggle to move the rocker, "It looks like two piss ants moving a horse turd!"

It hurt Wendy to hear her grandfather say things like that, for she loved her grandmother. She loved to climb into her lap and be told stories. Her Cherokee name was Sunflower and she had been given the name because her skin was a golden brown, almost the color of honey. Her face had weathered some over the years but her cheeks still felt soft as she held Wendy in her lap and hugged her.

She had a natural kind of beauty not needing the trappings of makeup. When her hair wasn't braided, it nearly touched the floor behind the rocking chair. It had once been as black as coal and as bright as the gleam in her eyes. Now, it was nearly as white as snow. She was sixty and still very proud.

Tom or Bill helped with their grandmother when they were around, but Mr. Tanner or his son seldom helped. Grace hoped her father and brother would find work soon and help with the household expenses, but things didn't get any better. They continued to drink as much, if not more. When they managed to work a little, which wasn't very often; they only worked long enough to buy a quart jar of corn whiskey or a cheap bottle of wine. The only things they ever brought home were the empty jars and bottles.

The two men made everyone's life miserable and they fussed and fought with each other constantly, sometimes with words and threats, sometimes with fists.

The Horry County Sheriff seemed to be at their house weekly to drag one or the other away to jail. Wendy hoped they would stay gone but they always came back after they sobered up.

Only Grace's strength held the family together in those days. Even with all that happened, Wendy couldn't see that it aggravated her mother very much. Grace tried to keep herself and her children segregated from the others. She didn't have time to worry about her extended family. Her days were filled trying to earn money to keep a roof over their heads and food on the table.

She tried never to let her children, especially Wendy and Emily, out of her sight for long except when they were at school. Sometimes after school and on the weekends, Tom and Bill had to be gone from the house to work, but as soon as they were back home, they too were positioned inside of their mother's protective circle. She tried to always be between her children and the others and try to keep the peace. She usually succeeded, except for one time.

It happened one Sunday when the four Wenslow children came home from church. Their grandfather and uncle had returned home from a night of drinking, and everyone inside, including their mother, argued about something. The children stayed on the front porch listening, mainly because their mother had instructed them in the past to stay out of the way when there was an argument.

The arguing went on for a half-hour or more while the children waited. Wendy and Emily wanted to play in the yard but knew better than to get their church clothes dirty.

Wendy couldn't understand why they were fussing so Tom tried to explain. "Momma's probably fed up with their drinking and freeloading. I hope she throws both of them out on the street," he told her.

Tom and Bill waited until they heard their mother scream and that was all it took to ignite the miniature Wenslow buzz saw. The boys ran through the front door with their sisters on their heels.

Grace was standing with her back to the fireplace and their uncle stood facing her with his back to the attackers. This proved to be a big mistake on his part, for Tom jumped in a full run and caught him around the throat from behind. Bill seized him somewhere around the waist and Wendy and Emily tackled a leg each. All of the children hit him at about the same time.

Grace must have seen her children coming because she stepped to one side just in time for her brother's forehead to hit the fireplace mantle full force. He was knocked out cold and fell backward to the floor, landing nearly atop of the foursome, but not before leaving a large portion of his eyebrow embedded in the wooden mantle. The old clock that hadn't worked in years began to chime.

The children didn't know that their uncle was unconscious, and it probably wouldn't have mattered if they had. They had him just where they wanted him, on the floor and more their size. Grace didn't make them stop right away. She allowed them to have equal turns of biting, scratching, hitting and kicking.

It wasn't funny by a long shot, but what happened seemed to loosen some of the tension in the house that day. After it was all over, nearly everyone laughed over a Sunday dinner of the best fried chicken anyone had ever eaten, except of course Wendy's grandfather and uncle. They didn't find it funny at all and left soon after the meal and stayed gone for three days.

For a change, there was peace and quiet around the house, and when Grace's father returned, he was sober. He soon found a job and went to work. Grace's brother chose to join the US Army rather than return.

Grace held her children close that evening before bed and told them, "I'm sorry that things are the way they are, but I can't turn my family out because of your grandmother. Someone has to take care of her. I'm all that she has. Things will get better. Things will change."

However, as time went by, it was Grace who changed. She became frequently depressed and lonely. Wendy could hear her cry at night and it seemed she never had a smile on her face any more or sang the way she used to sing.

She asked her grandmother one day, "What's wrong with Momma?"

"Your Momma needs someone else to love besides you youngens. She needs a man," her grandmother answered.

Wendy didn't understand why her mother wanted or needed another man around the house. The only men she had ever known were her grandfather, uncle, and her father. Her father was sick and had to be tended to by her mother and the others had been drunks.

When Wendy told all of this to her grandmother, her grandmother laughed and replied, "I know what you mean, child. Never met one of 'em worth a shit either, but your Momma needs a different kind of man. She needs one who'll take care of y'all."

Wendy sat for a minute thinking of what her grandmother had said, and finally answered, "You mean one that's worth a shit, Grandmomma?"

Mrs. Tanner tried not to laugh but couldn't help it. Her little granddaughter was right and without an argument she replied, "Yes dear, one that's worth a shit."

Not long after Wendy's talk with her grandmother, her mother went out one evening alone. It was the first time she had been away from them since their father's death. It almost put Wendy and the others into a state of shock. Wendy was afraid her mother would come home drunk the way her grandfather and uncle had done before so she stayed awake until her mother came home that evening. She wanted to see if she would somehow be changed in one night.

When Wendy finally heard the front door open, she ran to her mother and nearly jumped into her arms. She wanted to see if she smelled like her grandfather and uncle when they came but, all was well. Her mother smelled like Momma.

Something did happen that evening that would change things for the rest of Wendy's life. Her mother met a man that she liked and began to see a lot of in the coming weeks. His name was Lester Flanders.

He seemed to be a nice man, and Wendy couldn't help but notice that her mother seemed to be happier. There was a smile on her face again where there had only been tears and that was reason enough in the beginning for Wendy to try to like him.

Tom and Bill were totally against the courtship. Tom told his mother, "We don't need him around here. Me and Bill can look after things." However, their mother had different plans.

One afternoon in March of 1956, Grace went for a ride with Lester, and when they returned about dark, Grace gathered her children around her. She sat in a rocker and held Emily in her lap while brushing her hair. Wendy sat in her grandmother's lap, and Lester, Tom and Bill sat on the couch. Wendy knew something was wrong. If not wrong, then something was somehow different about their mother.

Finally, Grace told her children, "Me and Lester got married this afternoon."

Tom got fighting mad, and asked, "What's gonna happen to us?"

Tears filled Grace's eyes as she replied, "Oh baby, we are a family and we'll always be a family."

"No Momma, not anymore! To be a family, there's a Daddy, and that man won't ever be my Daddy!" Tom snapped as he rose from the couch and ran out of the front door followed by Bill.

Nothing else was said on the subject that day. Emily and Wendy were soon playing as they had been earlier, and Grace went into the kitchen to start supper.

The thought of having another father kind of excited Emily and Wendy. They had very few memories of their real father.

However, little did either of them realize that the events of that day would shape their lives.

4
"THE CHANGE BEGINS"

After Grace and Lester were married, things began to change quickly for Wendy and her family. They moved from Conway and into the country. Wendy's grandparents remained in the house on Powell Street, and so did Bill and Tom. Grace's motives for marrying Lester were the unity and survival of her family, but it had the opposite effect on her sons. They felt somehow alienated and refused to live under the same roof with Lester. They couldn't get along with him, nor could he tolerate them. It was an impasse that neither side attempted to overcome.

It was difficult for Wendy to make the adjustment of not having her brothers around, but it was more so for her mother. She was sickened at the very thought that her sons were living some place other than with her. Besides, she knew that her father didn't have a very good track record, with his history of drinking and all. He had changed some, but she still worried he might revert to his old ways. However, she had to give credit where credit was due. He had worked almost every day since he found a job and had stopped drinking entirely. He had even bought a wheelchair for her mother.

Their new home was ten miles away from town. It was near Lester's parents, the Flanders. During the first few weeks, Wendy cried nearly every time she thought of Tom and Bill. She missed them terribly.

She begged her mother, "Please make them move in with us!"

But before her mother could answer, Lester made his feelings known on the subject by jeering, "They'll stay in Conway. I won't have dem hellions in my house!" Grace cried and begged more but to no avail. It wouldn't be the last time she would cry and beg Lester.

The house was very large and Wendy and Emily enjoyed discovering all of its nooks and crannies. As time passed, Grace seemed happier and sang as she cleaned. She scrubbed and bleached the wood floors until they were almost white. Her home always seemed to be spotless, for she couldn't abide filth.

A month went by and things began to settle down. Wendy saw her brothers from time to time at school or when they went to church in Conway. On rare occasions, Lester would take them to town just to visit.

He had a car, such as it was, an old beat-up Ford coupe. It looked like it belonged in a junkyard. The lone hubcap on a front wheel looked like a little pie pan to Wendy and it sparkled like a great big moon-shaped diamond. She and Emily liked to look at their reflections. When they moved their heads from side to side, their faces changed shapes from long and skinny to short and fat.

In May, Wendy's continual changing life seemed to move toward the worse. Lester began to drink a lot and lost his job as a brick mason, putting everyone near him through pure hell. A different personality began to emerge. He acted as if he was mad at the entire world, directing most of his anger toward Grace and Wendy.

One Saturday, about midday, after another week had passed of Lester's drunkenness, he told Grace about a friend of his in Baltimore that could supposedly get him a job on a big construction project there. Grace was against the idea from the start and began to cry. Lester had already had several drinks that morning from a quart jar of corn whiskey that he had hidden away from the night before. He wasn't drunk but well on his way.

Grace's crying soon progressed to begging and more crying and more begging until Lester slapped her several times, got into his car and left. He returned late that night, drunk. Everyone had gone to bed, but Grace was still awake and still carrying on the way she had been all day. She had cried until her face was swollen.

Wendy was also still awake. She heard Lester's old car when it came into the yard, and the noise he made coming into the house, falling over things. She could hear him cursing before he entered her mother's bedroom and even louder after she heard the bedroom door slammed shut.

Wendy's bedroom was only separated from her mother's by a thin wall covered with cardboard. Consequently, she could hear everything that was said or done in the other room.

It wasn't the moving to Baltimore that Grace resisted so and had cried about all day; it was the fact that Lester was forcing her further and further away from her sons. That's what she thought her greatest concern was until she confronted him with that fact.

"I don't want to leave my boys behind!" Grace begged.

Wendy heard Lester answer with slurred words, "It won't be for that long!"

"At least now," Grace answered. "I can see them every once in a while when we go to church, but in Baltimore, I..."

Lester broke in, and yelled, "I AIN'T TALKING 'BOUT DEM WORTHLESS HELLION SONS A YOURS! I'm talking 'bout dem two girls, Wendy and Emily."

"My girls!" Grace screamed. "No! I won't leave my girls! I won't!"

"Now Grace," Lester said, trying to keep his voice down, but his drunken words boomed throughout the house. "If it's just the two of us, we can get a toehold a lot quicker; then we can send for them. They'll have fun riding the bus to Baltimore by themselves. I know things ain't been good 'tween me and your young'ns, but they'll learn to love me."

There was silence for a few minutes; then Wendy heard her mother scream, "NO, LESTER! I won't leave my girls! I WON'T! I..."

Grace's words were cut off when Wendy heard a slap. She knew well what a slap sounded like. She also knew how drunk her stepfather was by the way he slurred his words, trying to convince her mother of his plan. The sounds and the words coming through the wall flooded her with an instant hatred for Lester. She began to cry until her pillow was wet.

The argument went back and forth between Grace and Lester for a long time. Wendy couldn't help but hear every word, every slap. For what seemed hours, Grace wouldn't give in to Lester. She paid dearly for her persistency with many slaps and backhands across her face.

Only when Lester threatened, "I'll drag both of 'em out of bed by the hair of their heads and whip dem like a dog!" did Grace's firm stance begin to soften.

"I'll go anywhere with you Lester, but, please, please don't make me leave my little girls," her voice begged.

Another period of Lester fussing and cursing passed, and Grace screamed loudly, "I'LL NOT LEAVE THEM! If they don't go, I don't go! I won't leave..."

Then Wendy heard more sounds of her mother being beaten, but the sounds were different because Lester was beating Grace with his fist.

"You're going, bitch!" he screamed. "You're going! You're going anywhere I want you to go! I own you! Bitch! I own all of you! Even if dem girls don't call me daddy, I own all of you!"

Wendy bit through her bottom lip, trying to keep her crying from being heard. Confusion, anger and hatred were very strange feelings for her. She knew she would never love Lester or call him daddy.

Another long period of time passed with few words and a lot of beating-type sounds being heard from Grace's bedroom; then Wendy heard Lester scream, "All right! All right! You bitch! We'll take Emily, but, by god, the other one stays here with my Momma and Daddy. And, if you say one more word, Emily stays here, too!"

Wendy didn't hear a reply from her mother, only her cries. Soon, she finally cried herself to sleep.

The following Sunday morning, when Wendy came out of the bedroom, her mother was standing at the wood stove in the kitchen. Grace turned a little to see who had entered the room. When she saw it was Wendy, she turned her face quickly from her sight.

Wendy saw something that looked different somehow about her mother's face. She ran to her and tried to get around in front of her to see it again, but her mother kept her face hidden.

About that time, Lester came into the kitchen from the back porch with an armload of stove wood. And, when Grace turned toward the door, Wendy saw that her right eye was swollen shut. The left side of her face was bruised, and her bottom lip was swollen and cut in the middle and there was a small spot of dried blood in the left corner of her mouth.

Wendy's blood boiled inside, and she quickly grabbed a piece of wood from the wood box beside the stove and whacked Lester across both shins as hard as she could swing. Lester let out a yell and threw the wood into the air. It landed all about the kitchen floor, but Wendy was long gone before the last piece hit the floor.

About an hour later after he recovered, Lester found Wendy hidden under the house behind one of the support pillars.

"Get your little ass from under there!" he ordered, but Wendy didn't budge. And, after several more times of ordering and threats, he crawled under the house on his hands and knees and dragged her out by the hair of her head. Then, he held her down on the ground with his foot across the back of her neck, removed his wide leather belt, and whipped her like he had told Grace that he would do, like a dog. He didn't stop until he was exhausted and had to rest.

Then he dragged Wendy by the hair into the house and to her room. He stood in the doorway and slung her by the hair in the direction of the bed. She slammed hard against the foot of the iron bed and slid down into a little ball of flesh on the floor. But not one tear came from her eyes, not one.

•

The fact that she wouldn't cry must have angered Lester even more. He ran into the bedroom, seized Wendy by the throat with one hand, and lifted her clear of the floor.

While Wendy clawed at his hand for air, he screamed into her face, "YOU LITTLE STUPID BITCH! The next time I'll kill you. You will stay in dis room till I tell you to come out." Then, he threw her almost limp little body onto the bed and stormed out of the room.

Wendy would never forget the sound of the key as it turned in the lock at her bedroom door, and the sounds of her mother being beaten in the kitchen. For many years to come, her mind refused to remember the cruel beating, but she could remember her mother's cries with instant clarity for the rest of her life.

In less than half an hour, it was almost as if the beating had never occurred. Wendy's scalp hurt more than the rest of her body because her hair had been pulled so violently. She didn't know how cruel someone could be until that day, but her education was just beginning.

She didn't think a lot about herself as she waited behind the locked door with her thoughts mostly of her mother and the way her face had looked. She just couldn't believe what was happening to her family. Events were happening much too quickly for a little girl to fathom. She tried to understand why Lester had to go to Baltimore, wherever that was, to find a job. She also didn't understand why he was so insistent upon leaving her behind at his parent's house. She had only seen them a couple of times and hardly knew them. Nothing made any sense in her nine-year-old mind.

The day passed slowly in her seclusion inside the bedroom. Her mother opened the door only briefly to put a slop jar into the room. When darkness came, hunger and thirst kept her from sleeping for half of the night. But, a little after midnight, she finally fell asleep. A short time later, Lester awakened her, touching her between her legs in the place that her grandmother told her "Little boys mustn't ever see."

RED SKY IN THE MORNING 57

When he finally left her room, Wendy lay awake, feeling like she was dirty, wanting to get out of bed and scrub her body. She wanted to run, run anywhere, anywhere her stepfather wouldn't be, but the door was closed and locked and she was too afraid to move.

A lot had happened to her during a twenty-four hour period, more than Wendy's tender, young mind could comprehend. Some of it she would figure out as she got older but most of it she would never understand.

The next day, when Wendy awoke, the bedroom door was open. She jumped out of the bed and ran to the kitchen. It was Monday morning, and she had to get ready for school. Her mother was waiting for her there with breakfast on the table—grits, eggs and a tall glass of milk. It was almost as if nothing had happened and she wondered if that was the way things were supposed to be.

Wendy sat at the table and ate as if she were starving.

Grace told her, "You can slow down and chew your food. You don't have to go to school today."

But Wendy hardly stopped eating for a breath. Her mother left the kitchen, returning with a large brown paper bag. She placed it on the floor beside Wendy's chair; then she stood behind her and brushed her hair.

Wendy knew what was in the bag without looking or asking. She began to cry as she had never cried before. Her mother hugged her head tightly to her breast and they cried for a long time together.

"Please, please don't leave me! Please Momma, please!" Wendy begged.

Her mother didn't answer. There was nothing she could say.

Wendy continued to beg, "You'll get up there and forget me. I won't have anyone. Please, please take me! Tell Lester, I won't eat anything and I'll stay in my room and he'll never have to see me. Please! Oh, please don't leave me. Tell him he can beat me or do whatever he wants to me. I'll even start calling him daddy! Just please tell him to let me go, please."

Wendy's mother knelt beside the chair, took her daughter in her arms, and cried until her tears wet the hair on the side of Wendy's head.

"Please don't cry, my baby. Momma loves you and don't you ever forget it. You are my big girl. Hush now! Hush! I know you can't understand all of this and I don't know if I do either. I promise to the good Lord above that I'll come back and get you," she cried.

All of the crying didn't stop what happened late that afternoon. Wendy and Emily were in the back seat of Lester's car and sat hand-in-hand as Lester drove to his parent's house. Emily hadn't been told what was going to happen but she knew. Wendy wasn't crying until she started. Grace turned around in the front seat, reached her hands around her daughter's heads and pulled both close to her.

"Hush babies, now hush. Please stop crying. Remember, you're supposed to act like Momma's big girls and her big girls aren't supposed to cry," Grace pleaded.

"Y'all shut the hell up!" Lester yelled grabbing Grace by the hair and pulling her away from Emily and Wendy. Fear, hate and anger ran through every bone in Wendy's body. She tried to stop crying but couldn't and neither could Emily or her mother.

"Grace, if you don't knock off the crying, I warn you, I'll leave the other one, too!" Lester said, and Grace put her hand over her mouth to hold back the sound of her sobs.

Soon the car came to a stop, and without looking out of the window, Wendy knew where they were. Her heart felt like it stopped when someone opened the door on the side where her mother was sitting. It was one of Lester's sisters, Alice. She was eighteen. He had another sister named Kaye, who was fourteen, but Wendy didn't see her in the yard.

Grace got out of the car, folded the front seat forward and reached for Wendy's hand, but she drew it back quickly and put it behind her back.

"Come on baby, it's time to get out," her mother said, pleading softly.

Lester opened his door, got out quickly and slammed the seat forward on his side of the car. The seat hit the steering wheel and recoiled backward. He grabbed the seat again and moved it firmly forward, yelling, "If I have to get back there and get you out, by God, I will!"

He made a move as if he was about to get into the back of the car and no more encouragement was necessary for Wendy. She jumped from the car, grabbing her mother around the legs. She began to beg again, but her mother didn't answer, for all she could do was cry.

Lester's mother came out of the house and walked across the front yard to the car. She greeted Grace but seemed not the notice the bruises on her face.

Mrs. Flanders pulled back on Wendy's shoulders to try to loosen the hold she had on her mother, but Wendy held tight.

"Please don't leave me Momma!" Wendy cried. "I won't have anyone to love me here. I'll never get to see you again. I just know it! Please don't leave me!"

Mrs. Flanders kept trying to pull Wendy away from her mother, but she held tightly onto the tail of her mother's blue dress.

"Oh my poor baby, please stop crying!" pleaded Grace as she tore Wendy's hands free and wiped Wendy's tears with the hem of the dress. "Mrs. Flanders is your grandmother now and she'll take good care of you and love you, too. You'll even have two big sisters now."

"I don't want another Grandmomma or big sisters. I want you and my little sister. Please don't leave me!" Wendy begged, crying even louder than before.

Emily began to scream and tried to get out of the car, but Lester grabbed her by the hair and snatched her back hard against the back of the rear seat. More hatred for Lester coursed through Wendy.

"Get in the car, Grace!" Lester yelled. "Get in the damned car, NOW!"

Emily was still screaming. Lester grabbed her by the throat and yelled into her face, "Shut up or I'll beat you to an inch of your life!" Emily was frightened into total silence. She sat and her entire body trembled.

Wendy was detracted some while her attentions were on Emily, and Mrs. Flanders finally managed to pull her away from her mother.

"If you're gonna go, then go! She'll settle down in a little while. Go on! Git!" she said to Grace.

"You might take her to see her brothers. That should make her feel better," Grace said. "Would it baby? Do you want to see Tom and Bill?"

Wendy didn't speak. She just nodded her head up and down.

"Do you know where they live?" Grace asked Mrs. Flanders.

"Yes, but she'll be okay after a bit. Just as soon as you all leave and she stops crying. It'll be okay. Now go on!" replied Mrs. Flanders.

"GRACE!" Lester yelled from inside the car where he now sat behind the steering wheel. "Don't make me have to tell you again!" He grabbed his door handle and acted as if he was about to get out of the car again.

Grace knelt beside Wendy and placed the paper bag on the ground. Wendy looked at her mother's bruised face, and wrapped her arms around her neck.

"Please baby, you've got to be strong and let me go now. I promise I'll be back to get you as soon as school is out for the summer. That's in two more weeks. You wouldn't want to go with us and fail your grade, would you?" she said into Wendy's ear and kissed her on the cheek.

Wendy didn't care about school or making her grade. She wanted to tell her mother what had happened during the night, but when she looked over her mother's shoulder and into her stepfather's eyes, fear kept her silent that day. Shame kept her silent later in life.

Mrs. Flanders pulled while Grace pushed and Wendy's hold was broken. Grace got into the car and they drove slowly away.

Wendy reached down and picked up the paper bag that held all of her belongings and waved goodbye in silence. She wanted her mother to turn so she could see her face once more, but she didn't. She tried to run after the car and bring them back, but Mrs. Flanders held her firmly by the shoulders.

Just before the dust of the dirt road obscured the car, Wendy saw Emily waving goodbye through the egg-shaped rear window. The two sisters waved at each other until a cloud of dust hid the car; then Wendy was alone.

5
"A TORMENTED SUMMER"

Wendy stood in the Flanders' front yard for hours after the car carrying her mother and sister drove away. She was confused and didn't know why her world had suddenly crumbled. For the first time in her life she didn't feel love around her. She didn't feel she belonged. She had no way of knowing how difficult the summer ahead would be, or, for that matter, the remainder of the year of 1956, for a little girl, a little girl almost ten but going on fifteen.

It was late in the afternoon when Alice came out of the house to get her. She tried to talk to Wendy, but Wendy kept turning with her back to her. Finally, she grabbed Wendy by the shoulders and turned her firmly toward her.

"Wendy," she said, but Wendy tried to turn her face from her. "Listen to me, girl! Turn around here and listen to me! I'll be your friend if you'll let me! You'll need a friend around here. I'll try to be like a real sister to you while you're here, but you've got to help some. You've got to let me be your friend."

"I don't want you for my sister or a friend! I've got a sister, and she's my friend!" Wendy snapped back at her.

"I didn't mean it like that, Miss Spitfire! I just meant that I'd be like a sister and your friend until Emily comes back. She'll be back before you know it. Would it be so hard to let me be your friend? Would it?" Alice replied with gentleness in her voice.

She knelt on one knee, took Wendy into her arms, and hugged her. Her voice began to crack just a little, as she continued, "We'll play games if you want, and I'll show you how to put on lipstick and makeup like a big girl. Would you like that?"

Wendy nodded her head up and down, and Alice reached to take the brown paper bag from her hands.

"Don't touch my stuff!" Wendy replied sharply, jerking the bag behind her back.

"Okay! Okay!" Alice said, as she stood and began walking toward the house with her arm across Wendy's shoulders.

"I just don't want nobody messing with my stuff," Wendy said in an apologetic tone.

"It's okay," Alice answered. "You can carry them yourself and put them in my room. That's where you'll sleep, okay? No one will mess with your things while they're in my room."

Alice moved her arm from Wendy's shoulders and took her hand into hers. Wendy smiled up at her and they went into the house.

In time, Alice and Wendy got along well together, but Kaye seemed to be her enemy from the beginning. Mrs. Flanders wasn't a friendly person, either. She didn't go out of her way to be friendly to her own daughters, much less Wendy. She seemed cold and unfeeling but tried to keep her feelings hidden.

Wendy knew from the beginning that Kaye didn't like her. She could almost see the hatred in her eyes as she walked into the house for the first time.

Mrs. Flanders held the screen door open as Alice and Wendy entered the living room. She said, not showing the least hint of warmth in her voice, "I'm glad to see you've stopped crying. I had heard about as much of that as I could stand for one day. You can go with Kaye. She'll show you where everything is."

Daniel Flanders was seated in a chair by the fireplace. Kaye stood beside the chair with her hand on her father's shoulder like she was the heir to the royal throne. She grinned from ear to ear when her mother said Wendy would be her charge. Not a smiling grin, but a cold one that didn't say, "Welcome to our home," but rather, "Can I play with it before I eat it?"

Wendy's first few days went smoothly, more or less. She missed a day of school Monday, but caught the school bus Tuesday morning with Alice and Kaye. Alice was a senior and Kaye was somewhere between three grades, the eighth, ninth and tenth. She was taking subjects in three grades.

It became evident to Wendy on Tuesday morning that Kaye would try to dominate and rule over her.

Alice boarded the school bus first, and, when Wendy raised her foot to climb into the doorway following her, Kaye grabbed her by her hair and yanked her from the doorway. Wendy was forced backward to the ground and she sat on the dew-soaked grass along the shoulder of the dirt road. She sprang to her feet and followed Kaye into the bus, trying to brush herself off. She could hear laughter coming from the rear of the bus.

Alice stopped momentarily beside the driver and neither saw what Kaye had done to Wendy. She took a seat directly behind the driver. He was a young boy who, Wendy found out later, was Alice's boyfriend. Kaye passed by the seat where Alice was seated, and Wendy soon followed. Alice reached out and took Wendy's hand as she passed and pulled her into the seat beside her.

Wendy was crying, rubbing her head and squirming around on the seat. Her panties were wet from the dew, and the scalp of her head hurt badly. It was already very tender from the hair-pulling episode with Lester.

Alice whispered to Wendy, "What's wrong?"

"Kaye made me fall in the grass, and I got my panties wet," Wendy answered with a whine to her voice.

Tattling on Kaye would prove to be a big mistake, she would discover, for when she got on the bus after school for the ride home, she saw Kaye seated on one of the back seats with a group of girls. All of them were smaller than Kaye, a lot smaller. Kaye was tall and big. She was much larger than her older sister and larger than most of the senior boys. No matter the crowd she was with, she always looked out of place. She was much too big for kids her own age and much too immature with kids her own size.

Wendy was in a good mood that afternoon. She had seen Bill and Tom that day at school and took a seat where she sat that morning, thinking of her brothers. Alice wasn't there yet nor was the driver. She figured they would be together and would soon come.

She soon heard whispers and laughter from the rear of the bus. She wanted to turn around in the seat to see why everyone was laughing, but she soon learned when everyone on the bus began to chant: "PEE PANTS! PEE PANTS! LITTLE MISS PEE PANTS!"

She almost joined in the chant but remembered her wet panties from the morning. She wanted to crawl beneath and hide, praying for God to let Alice come soon.

However, before Alice or the driver arrived, Kaye came to the front of the bus, grabbed Wendy from behind by the hair, and said, "Come with me, Little Miss Pee Pants!"

Wendy screamed and fought as she was dragged backward by the hair to the back of the bus and slammed into a seat.

"I'll pull every dirty, kinky strand of your hair out if you don't shut your mouth! Let me tell you something else, you little NIGGER!" Kaye snarled. "That's what you are you know, a NIGGER! You say your skin is tanned because your grandmother is an Indian. But my daddy said Indians are the same as NIGGERS! You're nothing but a STUPID LITTLE NIGGER BASTARD! Cause you don't have no Momma or a Daddy no more and that makes you a BASTARD! A LITTLE FUCKING NIGGER BASTARD!"

Kaye used the four-letter f-word often when none of her family was around to hear her.

Some of the kids laughed and chanted, "NIGGER! NIGGER! NIGGER!"

Wendy hid her face with her hands as she continued to cry. Kaye still had a hand full of hair and pulled hard.

"I TOLD YOU NOT TO CRY!" she screamed through gritted teeth. Then, she bent over and screamed into Wendy's ear,

"DIDN'T I? DIDN'T I?" Each time she said a phrase, she yanked down hard on the Wendy's hair, pulling her head into her lap.

Holding Wendy's head down, Kaye leaned forward and whispered into her ear, "If you ever tattle on me again like you did this morning, I'll kill you and drop your body in the well in the back yard! Nobody will even miss you. Nobody cares whether you live or die, anyway! Cause...Cause, you're a nigger and we don't care about niggers 'round here, no how!"

Kaye released the hold on Wendy's hair, grabbed her by the shoulders, and threw her from the seat and into the aisle. Freed, Wendy ran back to the front of the bus with the jeering and chanting beginning again and didn't stop until Kaye and the others found something hateful to do to someone else.

When Alice and the driver finally got onto the bus, Wendy wanted to tell her why she was crying. However, just one glance over her shoulders toward Kaye convinced her otherwise.

During the next few weeks, Wendy began to figure out the unwritten rules of the Flanders household. Mr. Flanders' voice sounded like he had a mouth full of rocks. It made her skin crawl. He didn't have very much to say to anyone, but when he did speak, everyone listened, except for Kaye. Wendy could tell, even at her age, that there was a strange kind of relationship between Kaye and her father and that special relationship extended somehow to include Lester, for his name was nearly spoken in reverence by Kaye and her father.

It seemed each time Wendy did the least little thing, Kaye ran to her father and told on her. Wendy wasn't in the house a week before she was getting spankings almost daily. Mr. Flanders used his open, bared hand most of the time, making Wendy lay across his knee while he lifted her dress tail over her back. Between each slap of his hand on her buttock, he would sort of rub in a circular motion. Sometimes, he even pulled her panties down and rubbed her bared bottom.

In two weeks the spankings turned to whippings with a switch cut from a hedge and the whippings soon turned into beatings with a razor strap.

Wendy tried to avoid Kaye, but it was almost impossible. Everywhere she turned, Kaye seemed to be there, watching. She knew Wendy was afraid of her father, and Kaye used it against her. Kaye had her way with everything and would threaten to tell her father more lies if Wendy didn't go along with each and everything she said or did. Kaye had her own little, white slave.

She didn't call Wendy by her name most of the time, only "STUPID" or "NIGGER" or a combination of the two with the f-word.

Wendy never unpacked her belongings from the paper bag. As she wore them and they were washed, she put them back into the bag. It remained safe in Alice's room. She prayed every night that her mother would come for her and she wanted to be ready to leave, fast.

However, week after week passed, school ended and the summer began. She wasn't able to see Bill and Tom at school and felt more alone than ever. She hadn't heard a word from her mother since she had left nor did her brothers visit her.

Wendy's tenth birthday passed in June without anyone seeming to know she was alive. She waited all day for someone to say "Happy Birthday," but no one seemed to even notice her.

When Wendy could get away from Kaye, she waited out by the mailbox for the postman to come, hiding in the ditch so Kaye couldn't see her from the house. Kaye would call and call for her, but she would crouch lower and lower and wouldn't answer.

Kaye found her hiding place one day and beat her for not coming to her when she called. She beat her with her fist until she fell and then she kicked her in the stomach.

She dared her to tell anyone of the beating and screamed, "NEVER GO TO THE MAILBOX AGAIN! If you do and you ever get a letter, I'll tell my daddy to burn it in the fireplace!"

Later that evening, as everyone sat at the table for supper and before everyone started to eat, Mr. Flanders asked Mrs. Flanders, "Any mail come today?"

Wendy almost felt her heart stop beating when Kaye answered, "Wendy stole the mail from the mailbox and burned it,

Daddy! She stole it right out of the mailbox, carried it in the house and burned it in the fireplace. I saw her with my own eyes, Daddy."

Mr. Flanders never asked Wendy whether she did or didn't. He simple said, "Is that right? Kaye, fetch my razor strop from the back porch. It's hanging on a nail above the wash basin."

Then, to Wendy he ordered, "Git up from the table, raise your frock and shed dem drawers, young lady."

Without an argument, Wendy did as she was instructed while Mr. Flanders pushed his chair away from the table; then, with Wendy's naked bottom across his knees, he beat her with the two-inch wide strap of leather until the blood came to the skin and no one at the table said a word. After that, he made her go to the living room and sit in a corner on the hard, cold floor without letting her put her panties back on. She sat there until the others finished supper.

Wendy could hear Kaye say to her father, "If Wendy don't start behaving herself, we won't let her see her brothers if they come out here again, will we, Daddy?"

Mr. Flanders answered, "That's right, baby!" Both spoke loud enough for Wendy to hear clearly.

Wendy's heart leaped inside her chest at knowing that her brothers had been to see her. She had almost lost hope of anyone caring whether she was dead or alive.

Kaye told Wendy the next day when Wendy asked her if Tom and Bill had been out there to see her, "They come a couple of times, but me and my Daddy told them that you didn't want to see 'em. You might as well forget about your family. You are going to live here the rest of your life. That is, if you live that long. My Daddy and me might decide to kill you. Nobody will care. Remember the well behind the house? Well, it's still there just waiting for us to drop you in. I heard my brother, Lester, tell my Daddy that they were never coming back to get you. Lester don't love you and never will. He loves only me. Even your own Momma don't love you. She don't want you no more neither! My Daddy and me may decide to put you in an orphanage; then you'll never see your precious family again. That would be better than dropping your body in the well. You can suffer every day then. We own you now, my Daddy and me. We can do anything we want!" Kaye went on and on and on.

In time, Wendy began to believe the things she was told. She knew she was a child, and believed she had no rights. She believed adults could do anything they wanted because they "owned" little children. Her stepfather, Lester, had said almost the same words to her when he came to her room during the night.

Wendy lived in fear from day to day, fear at living under the same roof with Mr. Flanders forever and of being murdered by him and Kaye. She was also afraid for another reason. She believed Mr. Flanders would steal into her room the way Lester had.

The very next day after the postman put the mail in the mailbox and drove away, Kaye ran to the road. She made Wendy wait on the porch. Wendy saw her take a letter from the mailbox and walk toward the house. She stopped about halfway, opened the envelope and looked straight at Wendy, grinning.

Wendy knew it was a letter from her mother, she just knew it. She begged Kaye to let her see it, but Kaye held it in Wendy's face and tore it in half then went into the house, took the matches from the mantle above the fireplace and burned it while Wendy begged and cried.

Then and there, Wendy began to make plans to run away. She didn't know where she would go, but she knew she would go somewhere. She couldn't take it any longer. She had to try and find her brothers, her family. And, if it was true and they didn't want her either, she would just go somewhere else, anywhere. Anyplace, as long as Kaye, Mr. Flanders or Lester weren't there.

Alice had told Wendy jokingly the first night she came to live with them that Kaye was a little sick in the head. She may have been only been joking, but what had been happening to Wendy wasn't a joke. In Wendy's eyes, Kaye wasn't a little sick but a lot sick. She was extremely cruel and very unstable sometimes, acting like she was only five or six years old.

Another month passed and Wendy resolved not to let Kaye's words make her cry anymore. She began to make plans of how she would escape from the house she now thought of as a prison. She knew her brothers were in Conway but didn't know how to get to them. She knew where she went to school and how to get there and back. It was to the left on the dirt road in front of the house. She didn't know whether the road to the right would take her to Conway. She didn't know where it would lead her. The only thing she knew for certain about the road to the right was that it was the direction her mother and sister were taken away from her. Wendy prayed it would take her to Conway or maybe even to Baltimore.

Then, one Sunday afternoon, Mr. and Mrs. Flanders planned to visit Mrs. Flanders' sister who Kaye said lived two or three miles down the dirt road to the left of the house. Kaye didn't want to go with them so she stayed at home with Wendy. Alice wasn't there. Wendy had seen very little of her since the school term ended. She spent a lot of time at Myrtle Beach since her graduation. The beach was only about fifteen miles away.

Mrs. Flanders must have seen the fear in Wendy's eyes when Wendy knew she would be left alone with Kaye. It surprised her when Mrs. Flanders told Kaye, "You can clean up the kitchen by yourself and when you're finished, play a game with Wendy. You better not tease her neither, you hear!"

Mr. Flanders overheard what was said and came into the kitchen red-faced, and yelled, "BULL SHIT, old woman! Leave dem girls alone. You'd think Kaye was trying to kill the little scamp or something. Leave them alone, Kaye knows what to do."

Wendy's entire body became rigid and began to tremble. She perceived what Mr. Flanders had said as guidelines to carry out the plan to kill her and throw her body into the well while they were away. That was all it took for her to make up her mind that this was the day she would make her escape.

The car wasn't out of sight before Kaye ordered Wendy into the kitchen.

"You stupid nigger!" she screamed. "You get your black ass into that kitchen and clean it until it's spotless!"

When Wendy passed her in the doorway entering the kitchen, Kaye screamed, "Stupid! You stupid little fucking nigger bastard!" into her ear and hit her squarely between the shoulder blades with her fist. It hurt but Wendy gritted her teeth and went into the kitchen.

Later when Kaye thought Wendy should have been finished, she went into the kitchen inspection. Satisfied, she ordered Wendy to the front porch.

The heat and humidity that day were almost unbearable. The front porch faced east so it was in the shade in the afternoon and somewhat cooler. Only one oak tree was in the yard and it was in the front, out by the dirt road. The farmer who rented the land from Mr. Flanders planted corn up to the very edge of the yard on three sides. The rows of corn ended within twenty feet or so of the house. The back yard was the same except for four rows where the well was found. The well was actually 100 feet inside the cornfield. The four rows of corn stopped at the well. The house looked like it sat in a valley of corn. No air could get to anyone unless they were in the front of the house, either on the porch or under the lone oak by the dirt road.

It was scary for Wendy to go to the well after dark. One of Kaye's favorite tricks was to wait until after dark and pour the water from the bucket on the back porch and then tell her father that Wendy was the one who used the last of the water. Most of the time, Mr. Flanders would then whip Wendy with the razor strap and make her go to the well in the darkness to fill the bucket without anything to light her way.

Wendy didn't want to go to the front porch where Kaye was waiting. She just knew Kaye was going follow what she had thought were Mr. Flanders' instructions, kill her and drop her into the well, so she delayed as long as she could.

First, she went to the well and drew a fresh bucket of water for the back porch and one for the kitchen. Thinking ahead to her possible death, she dropped the well bucket back into the well when she finished instead of placing it back on the hook next to the handle for the wooden wench. She figured if Kaye didn't kill her, she could climb up the rope to get out. Mr. Flanders had beaten Wendy once for doing the very same thing. Kaye had been the one who left the bucket in the well, but she told her father, "It was Wendy, Daddy! I seen her with my own eyes!"

She told Wendy later, "I did it because I love to see my Daddy beat you!"

After filling the buckets that Sunday afternoon, Wendy went toward the outhouse, though not out of necessity. The outhouse was on the left side of the house, facing the dirt road and ten rows inside the cornfield. It was a very hot, foul-smelling place and it was a fly's heaven. However, Wendy was desperate to find a place to hide. She believed she had to stall somehow until someone came back home.

Going across the rows of corn was like walking through rows of razor blades. The sharp edges of the blades of corn cut the skin on her arms and neck and made her itch. She tried to keep her eyes always looking forward to push the blades of corn aside but couldn't because she also had to watch where she stepped.

Hardly anyone used the outhouse because of the stench, the flies, and the spiders. Consequently, the furrows between the rows of corn were filled with human feces and wads of catalog pages. It was like walking through a minefield.

Alice had warned Wendy when she first came to stay with them not to use the outhouse. However, Wendy figured it would be a safe refuge for her that day and the last place Kaye would search for her. But when she opened the door, she couldn't make herself go inside. The stench was unbearable. Even thoughts of drowning in the deep dark well itself wouldn't force her to enter.

She closed the door and went around to the rear to hide, but the smell there was even worse. The entire area reeked with such a foulness it nearly made her throw up. She was holding her nose, gagging and running deeper into the cornfield when Kaye saw her and ordered her to the front porch. Wendy obeyed and walked slowly back across the rows of corn.

"You sit your stupid little ass right there on the steps!" Kaye yelled as soon as Wendy had her foot on the bottom step. "I'm going to play Jacks, and you are going to sit and watch, stupid. That way, if Momma asks, you'll have to say I played a game with the little nigger!"

Kaye began to bounce the red ball with Wendy setting where she had been ordered. She didn't know where Kaye had gotten the game. She had never seen it around the house before.

Soon, Kaye handed Wendy the ball, and, as soon as Wendy's hand touched it, she withdrew the ball, and said, "You missed, nigger! My turn now!" Kaye tried to mock the voice and antics of a little girl. Wendy thought she had finally lost her mind. Regardless, she was relieved to know Kaye wasn't going to kill her, at least, not yet.

Kaye was up to her sevens and missed at least a half-dozen times, but Wendy only grinned and said nothing. She didn't move unless ordered to retrieve the ball when it bounced into the yard after a miss.

When Kaye bounced the ball to begin her eights, she suddenly grabbed at her stomach and bent over almost double. The ball hit on the edge of the porch and ricocheted out into the yard. Wendy jumped up and ran after it without being ordered. When she picked it up and turned around, she saw Kaye was still bent over at the waist.

At first Wendy thought it was all part of the Kaye's game, but, when Kaye began to rock back and forth and moan, Wendy began to think that maybe it was real. Then, Kaye screamed an ear-piercing scream and vomited all over herself and the porch.

"Wendy!" Kaye said in an authoritarian voice. "Go get help!"

Wendy watched as all the color drained from Kaye's face, and replied, "DIE! DIE, you bitch! I ain't no nigger and I ain't stupid neither. So, damn you, DIE!"

Kaye looked puzzled, as if she couldn't believe Wendy's audacity and boldness or her language. Wendy had learned how to curse from some good teachers.

Kaye's voice suddenly became very humble as she begged, "Please, Wendy, please run and get help! Please!"

Wendy hated Kaye with all a ten-year-old knew how to hate, except of course, the hatred reserved for her stepfather. She stood, looking at Kaye, not knowing whether she was sick and not caring one way or the other. But she had never heard her beg for anything before and the tone of Kaye's voice awoke something inside her. A gentleness that felt strange and made her think of her mother. She knew she didn't want Kaye to die, not really.

"What's wrong? Are you sick?" asked Wendy.

Kaye pointed down the dirt road in the direction that Mr. and Mrs. Flanders had gone, and said, "There's a house a little ways down the road. Please Wendy, run and get help. Please!" Then she fell over to one side and was silent.

"Oh, shit!" was all Wendy could say. She thought Kaye had just keeled over and died. She spun around on her heels and ran crisscross from where she stood, cutting the corner of the yard. She ran down into a four-foot clay ditch and popped out the other side hardly missing a step. The tail of her dress stood nearly straight out in back as she ran faster than she had ever run in her life. She knew she could run because she could outrun Alice or Kaye even with their long legs, but she didn't know she could run as fast as she was running that day.

The distance was at least a mile and it seemed to pass in a snap. When she reached the house and ran into the yard, she saw a man on the front porch and started screaming and waving her arms. He got out of the swing and had started down the steps when she reached him.

She was completely out of breath and couldn't say a word that made any sense. All she could do was point in the direction of the Flanders' house. The man made her sit on the porch steps until she had enough breath to tell him about Kaye.

"Go git in the truck over there," he drawled to Wendy and pointed toward an old truck parked beside the house. He went into the house, and returned in moments with two bed pillows and a blanket. He ran across the porch, jumped off of the corner, and ran to the truck.

When they drove back to the Flanders' house, Kaye was still slumped over on the porch and, to Wendy's relief, she was alive.

"Now you stay here at the house," the man told Wendy as he was bundling Kaye up. "So's you can tell your folks what has happened. Tell 'em I've taken her to the hospital in Conway, okay?"

"Yes sir," Wendy answered, but the only word she heard was Conway. She saw the opportunity as a chance to escape and was going to take it.

Wendy quickly ran into the house, had the brown paper bag in her hand and was out of the kitchen door before the man hardly lifted Kaye from the porch.

She crouched down low and ran to the truck on the side away from the house; then crept along the side until she was behind the rear wheel. She dropped to her knees and peeked around the wheel to see where the man and Kaye were. He was about halfway between the porch and the truck, looking in the direction of the truck's cab and carrying Kaye so that the top of her head was toward Wendy.

Wendy wanted to jump into the back of the truck but was afraid he might see her. She remained on her hands and knees and waited until he reached the truck and raised one foot to the running board. He rested Kaye on his knee for a second, opened the door, and put her inside the cab.

Wendy saw her chance. She believed it was now or never. She made her move as the man laid Kaye's head on the pillow.

The truck wasn't a pickup; it was a truck with big duel rear wheels and a bed made of wood, commonly called a flatbed. The bed was about even with the top of Wendy's head when she stood. If it wasn't for a trailer hitch bar, welded low onto the rear frame, Wendy couldn't have climbed onto the back. Lady luck was on her side for once in her life. She threw her bag onto the bed, and with a foot on the trailer hitch, she bounded up onto the bed without a sound.

The sides of the flatbed were made of wood with spaces between the slats. The rear of the cab, where a window should have been, was covered with a large piece of plywood. There were a few rectangular-shaped bales of hay, covered with an old piece of canvas. Wendy grabbed her paper bag and slid beneath the canvas with her heart pounding in her ears. It beat so loudly she thought the man might hear. She was afraid to even breathe, so she didn't. She held her breath until she heard the man shut his door then took a slow quiet breath.

The engine began to crank over and over, but it wouldn't start. Wendy's chin dropped when she heard the door open again. She knew her luck had run out and she wouldn't get to Conway to her brothers. She figured it wouldn't be a total loss if Kaye were really sick, sick enough to die. She hated her just that much.

Wendy heard the hood hinges squeak as the man opened it, then a tapping-sound followed by the hood slamming closed. The truck door opened again and closed. She prayed the engine would start, and when it finally did, she thanked God and begged to be forgiven for what she had thought about Kaye.

The truck backed out into the road; then went forward. Wendy peeked from under the canvas and knew they were going in the direction for her freedom—to the right, to Conway.

It seemed to take hours for the truck to finally come to a stop again. She peeked from under the canvas to see that they were parked at a hospital emergency room. She could read the lighted sign: Conway Memorial Hospital Emergency Room Entrance.

The man left Kaye in the front seat and went inside, returning a short time later with other people. Wendy could hear their voices as Kaye was given a cursory examination.

One of them said, "It looks like appendicitis." Wendy wondered what that was.

It seemed to take forever for them to finally load Kaye onto a gurney and for their voice's to fade away. Wendy remained hidden under the canvas, waiting her chance for freedom. She waited until she didn't hear anyone then eased from underneath the canvas and jumped out of the back of the truck and was gone.

She ran as fast as she could until she couldn't run another step. She paused for a moment, sat the paper bag on the ground, and, with her hands on her knees, stood in the middle of the dirt street, panting for air. Her side began to hurt and the first thing that came into her mind was that God was getting even with her for thinking what she had about Kaye. She thought she had appendicitis, too, whatever that was.

But, with her side hurting or not, she started running again. She figured appendicitis wouldn't kill her because Kaye hadn't died. The most it could do was hurt and she knew hurting wouldn't kill her as she held tightly to the paper bag and ran.

Soon, she had no idea of where she was. All of the streets looked the same to her, but still she ran. She could read the street signs under the dim streetlights, but that didn't help. The only street she knew by name was Powell Street. One by one the names passed, but no Powell.

Finally, around 10 o'clock, she rounded a corner and saw the church and the funeral home. She knew where she was then and the way to get to where she had once lived, the house where her brothers would be. One block went by, then two, and three, and before she knew it, she saw what she believed was the house. There wasn't a streetlight nearby, but she was sure she was finally home.

She wanted to run onto the porch and into the house like she always had, but she wasn't sure whether it was where her grandmother still lived. She walked very slowly into the yard and up the short walk, hoping to see someone at a window or hear a voice she would recognize. When she was almost at the front steps, she heard a voice. It was Tom. She knew she was finally with her real family after the longest and most hell-filled summer she had ever lived through. Little did she realize, her real hell was just beginning.

6
"THE REUNION"

The reunion of Wendy with her brothers that hot August night helped to make the long day worthwhile. After the initial greeting, Mrs. Tanner had Mr. Tanner bring a basin of warm water into the living room. While the Wenslow kids talked, she held Wendy in her lap as she sat in the wheelchair and began to wash away some of the dirt. Wendy was drenched with sweat and dirt was caked on her bare feet and legs. After hiding under the old dirty canvas, Wendy's face was almost as dirty as her feet. Her grandmother attempted to remove some of the dirt but it was hopeless. She did her best, deciding the rest could wait until morning.

Wendy wanted to stay awake all night and talk with her brothers, but Mrs. Tanner made the three of them go to bed. A pad of quilts was made for Wendy alongside Tom and Bill's bed. However, the Wenslow clan didn't go to sleep right away. They talked some, and their conversation made Wendy restless throughout the night.

She discovered that her brothers had tried to visit with her at the Flanders' house and were told that she didn't want to see them. Also, her mother had indeed written while she was in Baltimore. She sent Tom and Bill postcards and had said in Tom's that she had mailed one to Wendy. Tom told her that her mother had even sent her a birthday present—a Jacks game.

Wendy told her brothers some of the things that had happened at the Flanders' house, but Tom thought her recollections sounded a little farfetched. She told him of how Lester had beat her and their mother, but Tom found that difficult, as well, to believe.

He said, "Momma's postcard didn't say nothing about no beating before she left here."

"I kind a doubt that Momma would have written that on a postcard that Lester could have read, Tom," replied Bill. It was easy to tell that he believed every word his sister told them.

Wendy wanted to tell them about Lester coming into her room the night before they left and that he had touched her where he had, but she didn't think Tom would believe her. She decided she wouldn't risk the possible ridicule and made up her mind then and there not to make another accusation about Lester or anyone else unless she had proof.

The doubt shown by Tom hurt her feelings, and Wendy began to cry. Tom got out of the bed, lay down beside his sister and held her close until she went to sleep.

Tom's mind was changed the following day when he went to the hospital to see if Kaye was there. He found Alice in the lobby and talked with her for a long time. She confirmed enough of Wendy's story for him to know his sister must have been telling him the truth.

However, it was still difficult for him to believe that Lester had beaten his mother. He couldn't understand how someone could hit her, let alone, beat her, for she was such a gentle person.

Grace was about five and a half feet tall and may have weighed 100 pounds. She was a very slim woman and looked almost brittle. Her shoulders were stooped a little and she always seemed to be looking at her feet. She rarely looked anyone in the eyes when she talked and didn't have a lot to say whenever she did.

She had the facial features of the Cherokee: high cheekbones, a slim narrow nose and a sharp chin. And, like her mother, her complexion maintained a deep tanned look throughout the year. Her shiny black hair reached to her waist when loosened from the restraints of the bun she wore low on the back of her head. Her eyes were bright and clear with pupils as black as an onyx stone. Her very thin lips hid straight white teeth not often seen unless she laughed, and she hadn't done a lot of that lately. Her thin hands had a gentle touch even though they were red and cracked most of the time. However, a touch from her hands wasn't necessary for someone to feel her gentleness, for a kind of pleasantness came from just being near her. To her children, her almost hidden smile was like a warm fire on the coldest night of the year. Her beauty was something they could feel rather than see.

Two weeks after Wendy was with her brothers again, Grace, Emily and Lester came back from Baltimore. Immediately, Tom noticed something was somehow different about his mother and so did about everyone else. Mrs. Tanner tried to find out exactly what the problem was but was told nothing.

One day, Tom asked his mother about Wendy's accusations that Lester was abusing her and Wendy, but he got no satisfactory answer. She would only confirm that Lester had slapped her a few times, and added, "Even your father did that, Tom."

After talking with his mother, Tom's suspicion that something was wrong was confirmed. He couldn't exactly put his finger on it, but he knew that there was something, for she didn't look right, and he refused to pass it off as stress from the trip.

Lester hadn't worked a day since he left South Carolina. The so-called-job in Baltimore turned out to be exactly that—a so-called-job.

Wendy also sensed something different about her mother, but somehow it didn't matter. All she knew was that the family was together again, and that she was a happy little girl. She knew her mother still loved her and felt that she really did belong.

Lester started half-heartedly looking for a job as soon as he got back to Conway, but none of the construction companies or builders in the area would hire him. His history of being a drunk and laying out of work finally came back to haunt him, but those who shut him out, shut out an innocent family, too. Grace hadn't known this about him before they were married. Now, it was too late.

Lester found a house about fifteen miles outside of town and, about a week after they returned, they moved. The move was accomplished in one trip with Lester's car and Mr. Tanner's pickup truck. They had very little before the Baltimore episode and now had even less but, somehow, enough was put together by friends and family to give them enough furniture and a little food and clothing to start again. Grace called upon some of the Wenslow family members for help, but none would.

The house Lester found wasn't a house but a shanty, a shack. It was a square wooden structure divided into four small equal-sized rooms. There were no glass windows, just wooden shutters. The rooms didn't have wooden doors, only sheets of burlap made from fertilizer sacks suspend from wires across the doorways. Even though there wasn't a door to Wendy's room, she could still hear the hollow sound of a metal key turning inside a lock. As she stood looking at the sheet of brown fabric, she felt dirty, and unclean. Old fears began to slowly fill her mind.

There was an old well behind the house, but they didn't have to draw water from it ordinarily, to Wendy's delight. There was a pump on the little back porch though it never held its prime and water from the well was necessary.

There wasn't a front porch or front steps. A block of wood about a foot and a half tall functioned as steps. Wendy and Emily could manage their first step, but Emily had to be lifted the rest of the way, for there was still a good foot and a half to the threshold of the front doorway.

The house wasn't wired for electricity nor was there an outhouse. If anyone had to go, they had to walk across a cotton patch full of cockleburs, sand spurs and beggar lice to get to the pine thicket about a hundred yards behind the house. If they made it through all of that, they still had to constantly fan their behinds to ward off hordes of giant mosquitoes.

About the only thing Grace had to say about the house was, "It's home."

It was for Wendy, too, because she was again under the same roof with her mother and her sister. She could see the stars through that roof but that mattered little to her. Such as it was, she was happy, except for her wish to have her brothers living with them again, and of course, her fear of Lester.

Lester didn't lift a finger to do anything. All he did was fuss, cuss and bitch! Everyone tried to stay clear of him. He swatted at Wendy a few times during the day, and she dodged most of them. She was fast and was getting good at dodging. Her luck ran out once when she got a little to close.

He caught her with a firm backhand to the side of her head, adding, "That'll teach you ta run from your ole Pappy!"

Her ear rang for hours and blood was on her pillow the following morning. She believed it was worth it.

It was nearly dark before the few furnishings were placed where it suited Grace and Bill and Tom returned to Conway. There was hardly any food so Grace gave Lester a dollar and a half that she had saved and kept tied in the corner of a handkerchief. He left the house about 6:00 p.m. to go to the little country store not far down the road from the house to buy a loaf of bread and some bologna and cheese to make sandwiches for supper. He didn't return until after 9:00 p.m., drunker than he had been when he left. He had a half-pint of whiskey in his back pocket and screamed at Grace, demanding his supper. Grace built a fire in the stove and did the best she could with what she had, but all of her efforts didn't prevent Lester from beating her later that night after he thought Wendy and Emily were asleep.

It was difficult for Wendy to sleep after Lester came back for Baltimore. She was afraid he would keep his promise and again come to her bed during the darkness of the night. So, she heard every blow.

The next morning it was difficult to see the visible signs of the abuse. Lester had learned to hit Grace in places that wouldn't show, but even though Wendy couldn't see the marks, she had heard what had happened.

A new school year began shortly after the move. Wendy and Emily had nothing to wear that wasn't old or patched or faded. Wendy knew that almost every other girl would be probably be wearing something pretty and didn't want to get on the bus that first morning wearing something that wasn't store-bought and new.

Bravely, she took Emily's hand and escorted her onto the school bus and to school that morning in clothes that weren't as new as the others, but were clean, starched and ironed. Wendy's dress was made of the material from her mother's favorite dark-blue dress that she had worn to Wendy's father's funeral. In fact, it was one of only two dresses that her mother possessed.

Wendy began the fifth grade that year. Her ten-year-old body hadn't grown much during the summer. She paid little attention to the teacher that day. Her mind was on recess, and the time when she would see her brothers. She found Bill during the first recess, but not Tom.

Bill told her, "Tom ain't gonna come back to school no more. He's working full-time at the concrete block plant with Granddaddy Tanner."

Wendy carried the news to her mother and Grace was furious. She begged Lester, "Please take me into town this very minute so I can talk some sense into him!"

Lester was drunk as usual and didn't answer. She begged him until they went to bed that night and every day for a week, but he wouldn't take her into town. Finally, on the last Sunday of September, Lester took the family to church, and Tom and Bill were there.

Grace tried to talk to Tom to persuade him to go back to school, but he wouldn't listen.

"Your Daddy would roll over in his grave if he knew you had quit school!" she told him in a stern voice. "That was one thing he made me promise before he passed away, to make sure you youngens got an education. He only went to the third grade and could hardly write his own name. He didn't want y'all to go through what he had to."

"Momma," Tom reply, looking his mother in the eyes. "I can write my name, and I've learned about all out of books that I can learn for now, I reckon. I've got to work. I've got to pay mine and Bill's way in this world."

"Please, Tom," Grace begged. "If you won't go back to school for your Daddy, go back for me, please?"

"I'm sorry, Momma," Tom answered, his voice quivering a little. "I've never disobeyed you, at least, not in anything worth mentioning, but I won't go back to school. Please don't try to make me, okay?"

"Promise me that you'll make Bill stay in school, okay?" she pleaded. "Will you promise your Momma that?"

"Yes, ma'am," Tom replied, reaching to hug his mother.

***

The social security check for Emily and Wendy came the first of October. It was barely enough for Grace to pay the rent for a month and to buy some staple items like flour, sugar, salt, salt-pork, lard, corn meal and coffee.

She still took in washing for others and made a few dresses. She used a peddle-type Singer that a woman from town brought to make her a dress. In payment, the woman left it there for a while for Grace to use. With the leftover pieces of material, dresses for Emily and Wendy were sown. But even with the extra money she earned, times were still difficult.

Lester couldn't or wouldn't work. He managed to get a day's work here and there but never brought any money home. If he earned seventy-five cents, he bought a half-pint of cheap whiskey or wine. If he earned more, he bought a larger bottle. Soon, he stopped looking for work and just stayed drunk.

Grace hid what little money she could from him, but, if he found it, he beat her. If she said she didn't have any, he beat her. If she gave it to him, he beat her for not giving him enough.

When the social security check arrived the beginning of November, Lester stole it from the mailbox, cashed it, and stayed gone for days. When he finally came home and couldn't find any more money, he began to beat Grace with his fist until Wendy stepped between them. His anger then directed toward her, he removed his belt and whipped her with the buckle end until the blood ran from the many cuts on her back, buttocks and legs.

Three days later Lester returned with his tail between his legs, begging forgiveness. The rent didn't get paid, but that didn't matter to Grace. If she'd had another check to give him, she would have done it to prevent him from whipping Wendy the way he had.

It was a very tough month for food. People from the church helped some, but mostly they survived off of biscuits, cornbread, collards and turnips given to them by farmers nearby. Grace sent word to her family for help and again appealed to the Wenslow family, but no one could or would help. It seemed everyone had forgotten them.

A week before school turned out for Thanksgiving, Wendy found out what was different about her mother when Grace sat her down for a little talk.

Grace told her, "Momma's gonna have a baby."

If she had not told anyone, it was doubtful anyone would have known. She had gained very little weight.

Wendy became violently sick to her stomach and ran outside to puke. She had learned from Kaye how children were conceived, and the thought of Lester and her mother together that way made her sick. She hadn't thought of her mother in Lester's arms until that very moment. She only thought of Lester or any other man as someone who sat around, drank whiskey, beat women, and hurt little girls. From that moment on, she hated the child inside her mother and added it to the hatred for its father.

Wendy's Aunt Mary, Grace's sister, and her daughter, Sandy, moved in with them the following day. Sandy was about Emily's age. Emily was excited to have someone closer to her age to play with. Grace looked like she would bubble over with joy.

Mary was a year younger than Grace, and they seemed to never stop talking to each other that day. Wendy had never heard her mother talk so much or act so happy. It meant two more mouths to feed and the house more crowded, but Wendy was happy they came to live with them. She was for anything that made her mother happy. They were about the same size, so her mother would have more clothes to wear.

The landlord came by that afternoon to get the November rent money, and when there wasn't any, he ordered, "Well, y'all will have to move by the end of the week!"

"Oh please! Please don't make us move. I'll come up with the fifteen dollars somehow, some way! I promise I will," Grace begged. "If you could just see your way clear to wait until the December checks come for my girls."

"Nope," the man replied, spitting chewing tobacco juice into the fireplace. "By then I can have me a family of niggers in here. Nope! It's fifteen dollars by Friday or y'all gotta be out of here."

Lester never said a word while Grace begged the landlord. He just sat by the fire with his feet up and rolled another cigarette from a red Prince Albert tobacco can.

Grace even told the landlord the truth about Lester having stolen the checks, but it didn't sway him. However, she paid dearly for her forthrightness, for and as soon as the landlord drove away, Lester charged across the room and slapped Grace hard on the side of the head. The slap sounded like a firecracker exploding; then grabbed her around the throat with both hands and squeezed until the veins bulged on the backs of his hands.

"You don't blab and run your mouth 'bout what goes on in dis hare house!" he snarled through clinched teeth. "I'll choke your liver out, you bitch!"

Mary grabbed Lester by the shoulder and turned him toward her and away from Grace. Lester was no more than a shell of a man, weighing at the most 115 pounds.

"Don't hit her again!" Mary yelled at Lester. "If you got to beat on somebody, why don't you try hitting me? I'll get the money for the rent somehow and some for you to buy some more damned whiskey. Just don't hit her again. She's gonna have your baby in a month or so. You worthless bastard, do you want to kill her and the baby?"

Wendy was surprised when her aunt stood up to Lester and the language she had used. From that moment on, Wendy thought of Mary more as a friend than an aunt.

Lester just grinned through teeth the color of tea, and said, "You better git dat whore'n ass of your'n busy, bitch! You ain't got but two days left in dis here week, and your ass'll be on the street with ours."

Mary loved men and what they could give her—money. She left the house that afternoon when a man in a pickup truck pulled up in the front yard and honked the horn.

"Got to go honk a horn," she said as she ran out of the door. When she returned in about half and hour, she handed her sister some money. From that day on the men who came to call for Mary were called "honkers."

Grace knew what her sister had done to earn the money but didn't say anything to her about it. Even as young as Wendy was, she knew, too. The only thing Grace had to say was to chastise Mary for cursing in her house.

"Lord knows!" she exclaimed, standing with one hand on a hip. "You used words that I have never heard before, or, at least, not from a woman. My little girls, and Sandy for that matter, will have plenty of time in life to learn such words, but, Mary, it will not be in my house! Do you understand what I am saying?"

Mary replied, "Yes, ma'am," matter-of-factly and went on about her business. Two days later, the rent was paid, food was on the table and Lester had enough to get drunk again.

Mary was on welfare and received a small check each month. Her husband was in prison for murdering one of Mary's honkers, though no one spoke of it. She found it easier to tell everyone her husband was in the Army and stationed in Korea. The check she received wasn't very much by itself, but once added to the social security check, the household budget grew some.

The Thanksgiving school break came and somehow there was enough money to have a nice holiday meal and to give Lester enough money to stay drunk for a while. As long as he had money to buy whiskey, he was away from the house and that suited just about everyone, even Grace.

Tom and Bill came by to spend the day and to eat. Mary left the house with a honker later that afternoon. They occupied a lot of her time in those days and no one seemed to mind.

The first few days of December the weather was bitterly cold. It was so cold in the drafty old house the water froze in a bucket that was in the kitchen. The pump handle froze, as well, and couldn't be moved until it was thawed.

Each day after school, Wendy and Mary gathered dead limbs from the woods until it was dark. They tried to gather enough so there would be enough to cook and have a fire through the night.

The checks came and the rent was paid, no thanks to Lester. He still didn't have a job and stayed drunk or was gone most of the time. Wendy prayed each time he left the house that he would die somewhere and never return, but he always did and seemed to grow meaner by the day.

When Saturday came, the weather warmed up like it was September again. Grace opened the shutters to let in the fresh air. Mary and Wendy moved the mattresses outside to air and began to clean the yard. Lester had been gone since that Thursday, and a lighthearted atmosphere had prevailed around the house.

About mid-afternoon, after the mattresses were back inside the house, Mary and Wendy took a break from cleaning the yard and walked to the little country store down the road. Wendy had walked to the store with her before and knew why the trip was necessary. Sure enough, as soon as they got to the store, a red pickup truck drove up and honked.

Mary told Wendy, "Now, if you promise me that you'll stay here until I return, I'll give you a nickel to buy candy." Wendy nodded a reply; Mary gave her the money and was gone.

After two hours of waiting and with the money and candy gone, Wendy decided she would disobey her aunt and walk home. About halfway home, she kicked at a paper bag alongside the road and heard the jingle of money. She picked up the bag and in it she found three quarters. It was the most money she could remember holding in her hand at one time. She almost went back to the store to buy more candy but decided she should first ask her mother if she could keep the money.

She was a happy little girl as she quickened her pace and continued her walk home, thinking of all the things the money would buy. She approached a house with a long lane and saw a short, old woman walking toward the highway. She wasn't much taller than Wendy. Wendy noticed a mailbox on the other side of the road and figured she was coming out to get the mail.

Wendy walked past the end of the lane, waved and the woman nodded her head as a reply. Wendy continued toward home, and had gone only a short distance past the lane, when she heard the sound of tires skidding behind her. She turned her head quickly, thinking a vehicle was about to hit her, when she saw a red pickup truck hit the old woman.

The woman's body, from her knees up, smashed into the bumper and grill of the Ford truck. Her head impacted the front of the hood dead center between the "O" and the "R" of the word "Ford" across the hood. Parts of her skull, blood and brains splattered the windshield. The lower halves of her legs were severed almost as cleanly as if they had been surgically removed.

Wendy stood frozen in her tracks as the truck skidded past. Blood splattered on her face and clothing. It all seemed like something unreal, like a story from a book or newspaper. It was so horrible and something inside Wendy's mind switched everything "off" like one would turn off a lamp.

The pickup finally slid to a stop about seventy-five feet down the road from where Wendy stood. A door opened on the passenger side, and Mary got out and ran back to Wendy.

Wendy came to her senses a short time later and found that she was sitting in the back seat of the Horry County Sheriff's car on the way home. Mary sat alongside, trying to wipe some of the blood from her face. Wendy's hand was also bloody. She had squeezed her hand so tightly the quarters had cut into her palm.

Mary tried to force her to open her hand, but Wendy kept it tightly closed.

If the things in Wendy's life hadn't been the way they were, the tragic death of the little old woman that she had witnessed might have affected her more than it had. But as it was, there was hardly room in her heart for her own hurt.

7
"THE WHORE AND THE HOE"

It was nearly dark by the time the sheriff's patrol car pulled into the front yard. During the drive home while Mary tried to wipe the blood from Wendy, she begged Wendy's forgiveness for leaving her at the store alone. She cried until she had the sniffles, but not one tear came to Wendy's eyes. The horrible accident seemed not to bother her. She would remember the day, although for a different reason.

Grace had heard the sirens wail earlier in the afternoon. The sound came from the direction of the store, and she was on pins and needles with worry, sitting and waiting on the block of wood at the front doorsteps to her home while Emily and Sandy played in the yard nearby.

When the car entered the driveway, her heart leaped inside her chest. She jumped to her feet and ran to it before it came to a stop and saw Wendy and Mary in the back seat. A big smile came across Grace's face as she, peered inside, saw Wendy's smiling face. Then she saw the blood.

Grace screamed and began beating on the glass. Wendy saw and could hear her mother. She tried to open the door, but the door handle was missing from the inside. Panicking, she approached hysteria. All of the emotions and fears of the day's events seemed to pour out of her. Mary tried to hold her to keep her from clawing at the window while the sheriff jumped out of his side of the car and ran around to open the door.

Mary attempted to explain to Wendy why the door wouldn't open, and to Grace why Wendy had the blood on her, but the noise made by Wendy and her mother blocked out everything she said, nobody could understand anyone.

Mary had her hands full dealing with Wendy. The inside panel of the door took some abuse but Mary took the most, for Wendy fought like someone possessed trying to reach her mother.

Grace could easily have opened the door from the outside but the thought never crossed her mind. Her hands clawed at the window from the outside while Wendy clawed from the inside.

When the sheriff finally reached the other side of the car, he pushed Grace away so he could open the door not realizing what he was about to loose. He opened the door and didn't allow enough room for the little hellcat to exit.

Wendy's head was at exactly the correct height to catch him squarely in the groin as she charged from the car. The only word he had time to say just before Wendy's head rammed into him was "SHIT!" He fell backwards like a falling tree. It took a few moments as he crawled to the rear bumper, pulled himself to his feet, retrieved his hat and half-smoked cigar from the dirt and dusted himself off.

Mary was still in the back seat and was doubled over laughing at what happened to the sheriff.

When he flopped beneath the steering wheel, he yelled, "Get the hell out of my car!" without looking over his shoulder.

Mary stopped laughing as quick as you could snap your fingers, looked straight into the rear view mirror, and asked, "Pardon?"

The sheriff looked into the mirror, and sheepishly replied, "Please, Mary." She got out of the car in her own good time and soon the sheriff was gone.

The accident had been ruled just that, an accident. No fault was fixed to the honker who drove the red pickup truck. The sheriff gave him a stern talking to at the scene when surrounded by others who were old enough to vote. A few days later Wendy recognized the rather large body of the Sheriff of Horry County as he sat behind the steering wheel of another pickup truck that stopped in her front yard and honked the horn for Mary.

Reunited again, safe and quieted down, Wendy began to tell her mother about the money she had found. Her mouth seemed to be running ninety miles a minute. If Mary hadn't been there to interject clarifications, Grace wouldn't have made heads or tails of what had happened, for Wendy's story contained nothing of the old woman.

Wendy gave the quarters to her mother, and she put them into the pocket of her apron for safekeeping. Grace was busy wiping more of the blood from Wendy's face and hands when a car stopped on the road in front of the house, and Lester got out. He staggered into the yard as drunk as a skunk, as usual, taking a zigzag path to where the others were.

Grace lifted Emily and Mary lifted Sandy up and into the front doorway while Wendy scampered inside unassisted; then Grace placed herself between the door and Lester's approach. Not needing to be told, the girls ran to their bedroom. Emily and Sandy slid under the bed, and Wendy ran to a corner of the room that had become her place of solitude during the past months.

There were no closets in the house. A piece of strong wire was fastened about three feet out from a corner and strung across to the other wall, making a small triangle. Hang-up clothing was hung on the wire and another piece of wire was suspended in front of the hanging clothes. A curtain of sorts, made from bleached cotton flour sacks, hung from this wire to hide the makeshift closet.

In the darkened corner, behind the hanging clothes, Wendy could hide from the world. She hid from Lester when he came home drunk and on a rampage. She felt safe and secure as soon as she made herself into a tight little ball and wedged herself deeply in the corner, interlocking her fingers behind her head and drawing her arms down tightly so that her forearms were across her ears to block out the sound.

At other times when she hid there, Lester would yell so loudly it sounded like he was right behind her. When that happened, she recited through her multiplication tables or sang. After having done all of that, she could still hear nearly every word he yelled at her mother in the front yard.

Lester told Grace, "You wouldn't give me no money and I ran out of gas! Damn your soul!"

He staggered toward her, yelling, "I had to walk nearly five miles!" and slapped her across the face.

"I told you that I don't have any more money, Lester!" Grace pleaded, wiping the trail of blood that oozed from the corner of her month.

"You lying bitch!" he yelled and backhanded her on the other side of the face; then forced her against the front of the house and held her around the throat with one hand.

"You and that whore'n sister a your'n have been hold'n out on old Lester! I'll show y'all who's the boss 'round hare!" he exclaimed.

With her back held firmly against the wall, Lester slapped her with an open palm to one side of her face; then reversed his swing and hit her with another slashing backhand. Mary tried to get between them, but Lester hit her and sent her flying across the yard.

Lester's hold loosened a little on Grace's throat while hitting Mary and she slid down the side of the house to the ground, causing Wendy's quarters to spill from the apron pocket onto the ground. The three pieces of shiny silver seemed to gleam in Lester's wild eyes.

Grace saw the quarters and tried to cover them with her hand, but he stomped on her fingers and twisted his foot as if he was mashing out a cigarette butt.

Wendy heard the fight—every word, every slap, and every cry. She tried to make herself smaller so she could get deeper and deeper into the corner. She wanted to make herself so small she would disappear.

She pushed harder and harder on her ears with her forearms, and sang "Jesus Loves Me" as loud as her voice could but still she heard her mother's cries of pain, and Lester's cursing.

Something inside of Wendy told her, "Go help your mother!" but something more powerful told her, "RUN! Run away from the house! HIDE!"

She silently eased from behind the curtain, saw the open window in the bedroom, ran to it and jumped out into the yard, intending to run as fast as she could, as far as she could. She wanted to be anywhere, away from that house, away from her stepfather.

When Wendy and Mary had been cleaning the yard before they went to the store, Wendy had hated what they had been doing, but her mother wanted the yard cleaned before Christmas. In those days, every blade of grass had to be hoed from the yard. Even if it was already dead from the frost, her mother told them, "Hoe it up, sweep it into a pile and burn it."

They didn't own a regular garden hoe. The only hoe they could find was one used to mix mortar. The face of the hoe was about five times the size of a garden hoe and had two large holes in the blade. It belonged to Lester and had been used when he was employed as a mason.

Mary had worked hard to sharpen an edge on it with an old file. It was all Wendy could do to chop the grass with it, but she made it work. They didn't have a yard rake, either. Mary cut some small branches from a crepe myrtle bush, tied them together in a hand-sized bundle, and made a broom.

Wendy ran toward the cotton field and tripped over the handle of the hoe where it lay near the well. When she scrambled to her feet, she saw it and lifted it into her hands, slowly turning and looking toward the house. Her hands trembled so violently she could hardly hold onto the handle.

She began to walk toward the house with one thought on her mind: to kill Lester. Not to just stop him from beating her mother, but to chop his brains out, to put an end to his days. The more that she thought about what she wanted to do the faster she walked. Soon she was running and screeching Lester's name to the top of her voice.

Lester had put the quarters into his pocket by then and had lifted Grace to her feet by her throat. He was beating her again when he heard someone shriek his name. He thought it was Mary. However, he discovered differently when Wendy rounded the corner of the house with the hoe raised above her head.

He saw her out of the corner of his eye, turned, and looked into eyes that glared at him with an icy stare.

Suddenly, he began to grin, as if daring Wendy to do anything, like she wasn't even there; then he turned his head and began beating Grace again.

Wendy stood stiff-legged, not knowing what to do next. Her anger had brought her to that point but something else was needed to move her the rest of the way. Then blood splattered on her face from her mother's busted lip. The hoe held above her head began to tremble with the taste of her own mother's blood. It was the missing ingredient she needed to carry out her plan.

The anger within her seemed to feed on the tiny droplets of blood. She knew then that she could kill the man she hated; the man who was hurting her mother; the man whose look made her feel dirty and unclean.

She didn't say his name again; she didn't say a word. The look in her eyes and the hoe raised above her head spoke for her.

Slowly the heavy hoe began to move downward. Lester saw the movement out of the corner of his eye. He wanted to run, to move, to get out of the way, but his drunken legs would only tremble.

"NO!" he cried, but the word never reached Wendy's ears, or was it really her? Was this the helpless little ten-year-old girl he had beaten and molested? The face looked like his stepdaughter's, but the eyes didn't. They stared at him and looked almost evil, and he felt a cold shiver run up his spine.

Things looked like they were in slow motion to him. The hoe seemed to hang in the air at a slight downward angle. The two large holes in the blade looked liked eyes guiding its course to its mark. He wanted to scream again for her to stop but his mouth was so dry that his lips stuck to his teeth, his dirty yellow teeth.

He felt his muscles become rigid as the hoe began to fall slowly. He could see the red glow of the sunset reflecting from the sharpened blade, but still he couldn't make his body move. His eyes traced the wooden handle downward to the eyes of his stepchild, and again he saw those hate-filled eyes.

All the things he had done to her flashed through his mind. She was the same little girl he had held down with his foot and whipped like a dog; the same one he had dragged by the hair of the head and slammed against the foot of an iron bed. He tried to close his eyes to try to stop the things he was seeing but couldn't. He managed only to turn his face from Wendy, but out of fear, not out of shame.

The blade passed very quickly in front of his eyes, causing them to cross. It came so close to chopping him in the forehead that it nicked the end of his nose and cut away a small piece of skin. The heavy hoe, propelled mostly by its own weight, continued downward and caught the top of the Prince Albert tobacco tin in his shirt pocket, tearing it from his pocket and it fell toward the ground in slow motion.

The hoe was again being raised into the air before Lester could turn his head toward Wendy. He tried to make his head move fast, but it wouldn't. Again, he tried to make his feet move, but they still wouldn't obey. It was like they were nailed to the ground.

Wendy had made the correction in distance as the hoe reached the top of its swing again and slowly began its downward movement. It looked to Lester like it was the size of a car door. He tried to turn his face away from what he knew would be the last thing he ever saw, but his head still refused to move. He closed his eyes and waited his end.

Lester didn't hear Mary when she screamed Wendy's name as she ran between them and grabbed the handle of hoe.

"Wendy! No! Wendy!" she yelled.

Lester's eyes slowly opened in time to see that Mary was now holding the hoe in her hands.

"No! No, baby!" Mary repeated in a very firm voice. "Don't kill the bastard! Don't kill the worthless piece of shit! Don't you do it, baby! No baby, not you, not you! Let me do it! I want to be the last person he every sees! There ain't a court in this world that would convict me!"

She turned toward Lester and began to swing the hoe back and forth in front of his face like a sickle.

WHOOSH! WHOOSH! it said to Lester as the air rushed through its eyes.

Lester's eyes crossed and they followed the arc of the hoe in front of his face. He wanted to run as before but nothing seemed to work below the waist except his bladder. Water ran down his legs as he began to urinate.

He saw the blade coming toward his face again and managed to raise his left arm as he turned his face away.

Teary, angry eyes and Lester's last second turn made Wendy's chop a little long. The fading light of day made Mary's swing a little short, but the blade came so close to its mark that the button on the cuff of his shirt was cut off without tearing the fabric.

Before Mary could swing the hoe again, Grace stepped between her sister and Lester.

"Stop!" Grace pleaded, "Don't! Don't do it! Stop!" She held her hands up to try to stop the hoe if it was swung again.

Lester stood behind her with a dazed I don't believe what's happening expression on his face. Blood dripped from the tip of his nose and splashed in the puddle of urine at his feet. His bloodshot eyes were so widely opened they literally glowed in the twilight.

Slowly Mary let the blade fall to the ground. The rage in her eyes frightened Wendy as she watched her throw the hoe under the house.

She wiped the blood from the edge of her mouth, and said, "This time, this time, damn your drunk soul!" She pointed her finger at him and yelled, "This time Grace was here to stop me or you'd be laying down there in your own piss, dying! The next time, she might not be around, you piece a shit!"

Lester moved to one side so Grace would be between him and Mary, but Mary sidestepped a little and spit a mouth full of blood and spittle into his face.

"You worthless piece of shit!" she said to the top of her lungs. "If you hit Grace again, if you even touch her again, you'll go to sleep one night, you bastard, and I'll kill you! Do you hear me? I will kill your already damned soul!"

Lester moved stiff-legged and very slowly from behind Grace, then crab-like out to the dirt road and soon disappeared in the dusk.

Wendy's legs felt like jelly, and she couldn't move, couldn't speak, but she didn't cry a tear—not one.

The three stood in the front yard, looked at each other and didn't say a word for a long time. It was as if they had been spectators at a movie. Finally, Mary pointed to the red tobacco can in the puddle of yellow urine and began to laugh; then Grace; then Wendy.

***

Things began to settle down some around the house that evening after the incident with the hoe, and peace and quiet prevailed. Emily, Wendy, and Sandy took their baths before supper in the kitchen by the dim light of an oil lamp while Grace prepared the meal. After all had eaten the girls cleaned and polished their shoes while Grace starched and ironed their dresses. Lester had promised to take the girls to town for church the following morning.

Grace was counting on his promise regardless of what had happened and carried on like tomorrow was just another day. Wendy and Mary just looked at each other in amazement. Wendy's insides still trembled with fear and hatred.

The wood stove in the kitchen was used to cook and heat. There wasn't enough wood to keep fires in the stove and the fireplace nor was there enough kerosene to burn more than one lamp. The hardships seemed to make Grace stronger and the household more united.

The day's warmth and sunshine ended as soon as the sun sat. The temperature dropped to near freezing. Extra wood was put into the stove. Grace heated the iron and talked of old times as she ironed. The girls sat on the floor in front of the warm stove, and listened to the stories as they cleaned their shoes.

Grace's superficial display of happiness to hide what had happened was betrayed by her physical appearance. She looked as if she would drop from exhaustion before she finished ironing. A rocking chair had been moved into the kitchen during the cold snap, and when she finished ironing, she collapsed into it.

She looked haggard and worn, and her face had a gaunt appearance. Her eyes sank into her head and the large black crescents beneath them gave her slim face a hollow look. She was exhausted from the happenings of the day. But surprisingly, her face wasn't badly bruised. Her bottom lip had been cut but it had stopped bleeding and was barely swollen.

Emily managed to climb into what little remained of her mother's lap. Grace now carried her soon to be born baby very low. Mary sat in a straight-back chair and Sandy crawled into her lap. Grace rocked back and forth while Mary simulated the same in the straight chair. Wendy sat cross-legged on the floor, held her mother's feet in her lap and rubbed them with witch hazel. Grace was only thirty-one, but the varicose veins showing in her feet and legs made her legs look like they belonged to someone sixty.

Soon, the rocking and the long day caught up with Emily and Sandy and they nodded off to sleep. Mary carried Sandy and Wendy struggled with Emily as she walked to the bedroom, half asleep. As soon as they were tucked into bed, Wendy and Mary returned to the kitchen.

It was 10:30 p.m. and normally Wendy would have been made to go to bed, but that evening neither her mother nor her aunt treated her like a little girl. Wendy didn't feel like a little girl either; somehow she felt like she belonged with the other women of the household.

Fireworks seemed to be going off inside her young body. She felt strange inside. The day before, Wendy would probably have tried to get into her mother's lap as soon as Emily was out of it, but for some reason that night, she felt she didn't belong there anymore. She stood beside the rocker and rubbed her mother's slim hand as it lay on the arm of the rocker.

The two sisters sat in the kitchen and talked about everything under the sun except what had happened earlier with Lester. Wendy stood silently by, looking at her mother as they talked. She wore a brightly colored yellow blouse and Wendy could see tiny spots of blood down the front. Wendy's heart hurt as she rubbed her mother's hand and looked at her.

Their hands were nearly the same size. Her mother's fingers were longer but for the most part, the hands were a mirror reflection of the other. Her mother's fingernails were worn into the quick. The skin on the back of the hand was red, cracked and chapped. It was rough to the touch, yet it felt warm and comforting to Wendy. Something unseen seemed to radiate into her hand and it seemed to calm her.

However, Mary was still very much agitated from what had happened in the yard and would not settle down or be kept from speaking her mind. When Grace stopped talking, Mary began.

"Grace, you can sit there and pretend like nothing happened this afternoon, but that low-life piece of shit woulda killed you and probably Wendy if I hadn't been here. That man's dangerous," Mary said, trying to keep her voice calm.

Grace just sat there, closing her eyes in silence. She laid her head against the back of the rocker and rocked while her sister unloaded her feelings.

You could have heard a pin drop for a long time after Mary's outburst; then Grace said, "He didn't mean it, baby." She opened her eyes, looked at Wendy, and continued, "It's just the whiskey. It makes him do them things. There's another person inside of him that can be good and kind. It's the whiskey, not Lester." Then, she closed her eyes again and rocked.

Wendy looked at her aunt and saw that Mary was shaking her head.

"Grace," Mary finally said. "You can't believe all of that horse shit! The bastard's worthless! He ain't worth killing! Why don't we just leave him, Grace? Why don't you take these two girls and leave?"

The rocker stopped and Wendy felt her mother's hand grip the rocker arm. Her body leaned forward a little as she opened her eyes, and said harshly, "Mary, I've let you have your say and didn't say anything about what you were saying or the words you used, but that'll be enough of that kind of talking. I've told you before, you can speak as you like in your house, but as long as you're in mine, you'll not talk like that. I've heard as much of it as I'm going to hear this day."

Wendy had never heard her mother use such a harsh tone of voice before except when she was arguing with Lester about Baltimore.

As if Grace hadn't said a word, Mary kept talking, but without saying another curse word. She hammered away with her statements, trying to make her point.

Finally, she paused for a moment, and Grace said, "Mary, I married that man before the eyes of the good Lord in heaven. I said I would stay with him through better or worse. I can't and I won't leave him. He's my husband. The only way I'll leave him is if I die."

She stopped talking for a moment, looked at Wendy, and continued, "He'll be different when the baby comes, Wendy. You'll see, you'll see. He'll be just like a real daddy."

Mary shook her head and answered, "If you live that long. Grace, I can't believe you mean what you're saying! Can't you see what's going on right before your eyes? I believe he means to kill you and that baby!"

Wendy wanted to speak. She found confidence in her newly acquired status. She wanted to reinforce the point her aunt was trying to make by telling what Lester had done to her, but something told her she was still a little girl.

Then, just before she had gathered enough courage to opened her mouth to speak, her mother said, "Mary, that's enough now! Leave it lay!"

"But," Mary replied, and Grace said sternly, "I said, leave it lay!"

Mary didn't say anything else. Instead, she folded her arms across her breast and exclaimed, "Huh!"

Wendy didn't try to speak again. She went around to the back of the rocker and pulled the long hairpins from the bun of hair on the back of her mother's head. She let it drape over the back of the rocker and began to brush the long silver and black ribbons of hair. The thought of her mother's gentleness brought a lump into her throat and tears came into her eyes, but she didn't cry—at least, not outwardly.

She thought of the unborn baby inside her mother, Lester's child. With each stroke of the brush through her mother's long hair, she became more enraged. She thought of the baby inside her mother's belly and wished it to die, die before it was ever born. She hated the unborn baby and its father.

Finally, Grace said, "Baby. You're brushing too rough. Please stop. It's been a long hard day for all of us. Kiss your Momma and go on off to bed, please."

Wendy kissed her mother on the cheek, kissed her aunt, and went to bed. Mary followed her to the bedroom, tucked her in and returned to the kitchen.

Wendy's head had hardly sunk into the pillow before she was asleep. However, the torment of the day wasn't over yet, for while she slept, her stepfather came home and crept into her room, again.

She was shocked into wide awareness by his hand over her mouth. His other hand was where it had been before, her private place. She could see him clearly for he had been so bold as to have brought an oil lamp into the room and it sat on the floor beside the bed. She could smell the kerosene. Its upward projected glow gave Lester's face an evil look.

Wendy tried to make a noise and move so that Emily, who slept beside her, or Mary, who was now in her bed and asleep a few feet away, would awaken. She tried to wiggle her body, but she couldn't. The more she wiggled, the more Lester pushed down with one hand over her mouth and nose, smothering her. The other elbow held her knees.

Wendy stopped wriggling and gasped for air. When she was still, Lester released the downward pressure a little, allowing her to breathe. She tried to wiggle free again and make some sound come from her mouth, but her body was forced down into the cotton mattress, making the springs creak. Finally, when she was smothering again, she stopped fighting and he released the pressure once more. Emily never moved, nor did Mary stir. Both slept soundly.

Lester leaned over the bed so his mouth was near Wendy's ear. The stench of his breath and the urine on his clothing made her gag. She tried to turn her face away from the odor, but the hand at her mouth grabbed her chin and turned her face toward his.

Shock and fear rushed into her mind as the tip of a finger invaded her tiny body, again. It burned like a hot rod as it bore inside her, causing her muscles to stiffen and cold beads of sweat to pop from her forehead.

"Do you remember what I told you the last time?" he whispered with his face within inches of hers. His eyes looked wild in the golden lantern light as his finger began to move.

She hadn't heard him clearly and didn't answer.

"Do you? Do you?" he hissed with his face coming nearer to hers.

She didn't know how to answer a question that she hadn't heard, so she shook her head. But, when his brow wrinkled, she nodded, hoping that was the answer her stepfather was looking for, hoping it would satisfy him enough for him to stop but he didn't. She could still feel his finger moving inside of her.

The first time he molested her, she didn't really know what he was doing but now she did, thanks to what she had learned from Kaye, and anger began to flood her thoughts. She felt sick and thought she was about to vomit but swallowed hard and let her anger assume control. She wanted the hoe in her hands again.

Lester's lips touched the end of her nose as he said; "I just saw something in your eyes, little lady. The same look I see'd in the yard when you had dat hoe. Y'all thought you could gang up on ole Lester, on your ole Pappy. I showed your Momma who's da best one 'round dis here house and I can damned well show you!"

His wet words hissed and a fine mist of his spit fell on Wendy's face. She tried to wiggle her body to resist him in any way she could, but he pushed down harder. The hurt was worse than anything she had ever felt and an involuntary whining sound escaped her mouth.

"Shut up!" he jeered into her face. "Or I'll drag your lit'l ass out of dis bed right dis here minute and beat you to an inch of your life!"

His voice got louder and louder as he spoke and Mary stirred a little in her bed. He heard her movement and froze until she settled down again.

When his glaring eyes moved back to Wendy, a cold chill ran down her spine and sweat ran into her eyes although it was cold inside the bedroom. She could see each breath her stepfather took.

Lester lowered his mouth again to Wendy's ear and whispered, "If you ever say a word ta anyone 'bout dis, I'll beat yo Momma and dis time I'll kill her! Do you hears me? I'll kill her! I will! I swear, I'LL KILL HER!"

The dimly lighted room highlighted a grin across his face as he continued, "Ain't nobody can stop me, neet'r! Y'all's mine! MINE! You hears me? You're mine and I'll make you love me," punctuating each strong word with his burning finger.

Fear and hatred gripped Wendy and her mind shut everything out and everything went away; she fainted.

When reality returned a short time later with her consciousness, Lester had left her room. She wondered if it had been a dream. She reached down, found her panties were pulled down to her knees, felt the hurt inside her body, and knew it had really happened to her; it had all been real.

She jumped from the bed and ran to her hiding place in the corner of the closet, her secret place, the place she knew Lester wouldn't be, her hiding place behind the bleached cotton flour sacks.

She bit down on her lip to keep from crying and trembled with fear. Only a faint whine was heard as quiet tears of anger and fear rolled down her face. She didn't know what to do or how to stop what her stepfather was doing to her. She felt anger, hatred, fear and confusion.

***

Emily didn't find Wendy beside her when she awoke Sunday morning. She looked for her all over the house; then she remembered the place she had seen her go the day before when they hid from Lester. She found her curled into a little ball deep into the corner and asleep. Emily shook Wendy until she awoke, and asked her, "Why are you hiding?" but Wendy didn't answer.

Wendy dressed that morning trying to cover every inch of her body with clothing. She wore shoes, knee-high socks, a pair of Bill's old jeans, a long sleeve flannel shirt, a kerchief tied over her head, and a pair of socks on her hands for gloves. She felt ashamed of her body. She believed it was dirty, and she didn't want anyone to look at it. She wanted to tell someone about what had happened to her, but she didn't want her mother beaten again or murdered nor did she want Emily to go through what she had.

She was confused and wondered if all little girls were treated the same way. She wanted to ask someone if her stepfather should be doing the things he was doing, but she was ashamed to speak of it. She began to feel guilt, as if somehow it was her fault and determined then and there to keep her body covered when she was near him.

Everyone was up and stirring when Wendy came out of the bedroom. It was cold that morning and beginning to mist, a big change from the sunny day before. The floors in the house were like sheets of ice and bare feet didn't stay bare for long. Grace thought Wendy was bundled up the way she was because of the weather.

Lester was in the kitchen and acted really nice to everyone. He was spooning hot oatmeal into bowls on the table when Wendy came into the kitchen. The very sight of him sent shock waves through her body and made her sick to her stomach. She could not fathom how things could appear so normal and again wondered if things were really the way they should be, the way normal families lived.

She couldn't eat while Lester flipped around, carrying on as if nothing had happened. Grace was all smiles at the change in him and rushed around the house like she was on cloud nine, like she was in a dream world. She hurried everyone through breakfast and to get ready for church. Lester was already dressed in a suit, white shirt and a tie.

Wendy had never seen him dressed up. She wanted to grab the necktie and choke him to death. She couldn't stand to look at him. Her insides rolled. She ran out of the kitchen and behind the house where she puked pure bile from an empty stomach. The misting rain felt good on her face and helped to settle her nerves. She squatted with her head between her knees, but she didn't cry—not one tear.

Wendy could hear everyone in the house getting ready to leave for church. She heard her mother call to her several times but she didn't answer.

Finally she heard Mary tell her mother, "Grace, she probably doesn't feel good. I don't feel well either. It's my turn to ride the white horse. Why don't you just let her stay home with us? She can help me clean up the house and start dinner and you can lie down and get some rest. You look like you're about to drop that baby any second."

Grace agreed, but wondered what could be wrong with her daughter.

Tom and Bill were supposed to come home with them from church. Wendy made up her mind to tell Tom, now fifteen, what Lester had done to her. She wasn't sure how she would put it into words, for she had never heard anyone speak of such things. Just thinking about it made her feel ashamed.

As soon as Lester's car pulled away from the house, Wendy returned to the kitchen. Grace had already gone to her bed and Mary was washing the breakfast dishes. Wendy didn't say a word to Mary nor did Mary try to talk with her.

Wendy left the kitchen for a moment and returned dragging a big washtub. There was some hot water on the stove and Mary carried the kettle to the porch to thaw the pump; then she helped pump enough water to heat and fill the tub.

Wendy could smell the nauseating odor of Lester on her body. She could smell the whiskey, the urine and the kerosene. When Wendy removed her panties to get into the tub, she saw blood in them. She quickly wadded them up in her hand, but Mary had already seen them. She thought Wendy was spotting from her first period. Little did she know that Wendy's first period was three years away.

Mary helped her scrub with lye soap until her skin was cherry red. Wendy never spoke a word to her aunt, nor did Mary encourage a conversation.

Everyone returned from church around noon and Grace was in the kitchen, cooking dinner for her family. It had been a long time since the family sat together for a Sunday dinner, a very long time. Just the thought of it made her sing. Laughter and joy filled a house that had been filled with cries and hatred the day before. Wendy still couldn't believe everyone's attitudes.

Grace loved to cook and Wendy believed she was the best cook in the world because no matter what she prepared, it tasted good. No matter the meagerness of what was in the cupboard, she put a banquet on the table. One skinny little pullet fed the whole family that Sunday.

The day came and went without Wendy telling Tom what had happened. She waited and waited for the right opportunity, but that chance never came. Lester seemed to always be near her. It was almost like he was making a special effort to be close to her and acted like the best of stepfathers while Tom and Bill were there. His attentiveness made Wendy sick to her stomach.

Mary noticed how he was acting and told Wendy, "The bastard acts like butter wouldn't melt in his mouth!"

When Bill and Tom were getting ready to go back to Conway, Tom took Wendy's hand and walked her out to the pickup. Lester didn't follow. Instead, he stood in the doorway following her with his eyes.

"Momma said the reason you didn't go to Sunday school was because you're sick or something," Tom said to her, and added as he turned her toward him and took her other hand in his, "Is everything all right now? Do you feel okay now?"

Wendy looked at Lester and his eyes looked like they would burn holes into her. Fear gripped her in an embrace she had never felt before. All the color drained out of her face and she began to tremble.

Tom put his arms around her, and said, "You really are sick, aren't you? Let me walk you back in the house. It's chilly out here."

She wanted to tell Tom why she acted the way she did, but the words wouldn't come out of her. She still remembered the standoffish way he had acted when she first told him about Kaye and the Flanders. She was afraid of the doubt he might show again. But, the real reason she didn't speak was because of what Lester had said he would do. Even with all the hate she had inside for him, it couldn't overcome that fear, fear not necessarily for herself, but fear for her mother and sister.

Later that evening while everyone was still up, Lester found Wendy in her room, and asked, "What wus you'n Tom talk'n 'bout today?"

Wendy didn't answer him and he started to press the question, but Mary came into the bedroom.

"Did you lose something?" she snapped at him.

He didn't answer but turned and left the room.

After Mary went to sleep that night, Wendy climbed into the bed with her and Sandy. She did the same thing for many nights to follow. Mary never asked why she was in her bed in the morning.

Beginning that Sunday, something caused Lester to change. He drank very little and began looking for a job in earnest. Whatever the driving force behind the change, it was welcomed. The change made Grace happy.

She told Mary, "I told you. I told you."

Mary tried to warn her sister that it was only an act, but Grace would not listen. Mary whispered into Wendy's ear, "Horse shit! Pure horse shit! You can saddle a jackass but he's still a jackass."

When Wendy came home from school in the days to come, Lester actually went into the woods with them to help gather wood. It was getting very difficult for her and Mary to gather enough wood in the afternoons to keep the house warm at night. There were only so many dead limbs on the ground, and they needed Lester's help to cut some trees down. Mary welcomed it. She manned the other end of the crosscut saw and pushed and pulled, stroke for stroke with him.

Wendy didn't want Lester's help. She told her aunt, "I'd rather freeze to death than have him around me."

Mary asked her why, but Wendy didn't answer. Mary said, "Well, if you won't think of yourself, think of your Momma."

Days were getting shorter and there wasn't a lot of daylight remaining after the school bus brought them home from school. Lester proved to be a pretty good worker and with his help enough wood was gathered for the stove as well as the fireplace. Regardless of what her aunt had said, Wendy still hoped a tree would fall on him. He must have sensed how she felt, for he remained well clear of her when she had the ax in her hands.

The social security checks arrived in early December and the rent was paid. Some food was bought, but not much. However, thanks to Mary and the honkers, the family didn't go hungry. The house was cold, dark and drafty, but at least it was a roof over their heads. The food wasn't much, but such as it was, it kept the stomach from hurting.

Emily and Sandy were beginning to get excited about the coming of Christmas, as was Wendy. At ten, she still believed with all her heart in Santa Claus. One afternoon after school recessed for the holidays and they were gathering wood, Lester cut the top out of a little pine sapling and said it would make a good Christmas tree. It didn't look like a Christmas tree to Wendy; at least not like the ones she remembered seeing. Lester dragged the little pine to the house, nailed it to a board, and it was placed on a small table at the window in the living room.

The next day was Saturday and the girls were allowed to stay up late to decorate the tree. They worked for hours stringing popcorn but the string only seemed to grow by inches. It was Monday afternoon before the string was long enough to wrap around the tree once. They had plenty of time to decorate the tree, for they had little else to do. Grace sent them into a cornfield across the road to get some corncobs and into the woods to find little pinecones.

The corncobs were dyed different colors with food coloring. Little pieces of cotton from the field behind the house were also dyed; then glued along with dyed chicken feathers to the pinecones and corncobs to make ornaments. Some of the cotton was dyed; then twisted into long strands. When everything was placed on the tree with little strips of colored cloth, it finally looked something like a Christmas tree. A single candle was placed on top but it wasn't to be lit until Christmas Eve night.

A day or so before Christmas everyone loaded into Lester's car and went to Conway to look at the Christmas lights. Grace made Lester drive by the house on Powell Street to pick up Tom and Bill to ride with them. Lester protested but Grace would have it no other way. Lester had almost become a different person since the day of the mortar hoe episode. He still didn't have a steady job, but he was looking. The only work he could find was helping some of the farmers gather corn. It only paid two dollars a day, but he brought home what he earned.

They rode around town for hours singing Christmas carols and looking at all the Christmas lights. The lights were strung from lamppost to lamppost and along the fronts of the stores downtown. There were more lights than Wendy had ever seen. They drove into the neighborhoods of the so-called rich and looked at the Christmas trees lighted in the yards. Wendy didn't understand why others had so much while they had nothing. She didn't understand why so many trees on the lawns were decorated with so many lights while their tree at home had only a single candle.

"Momma?" she asked from the back seat where she sat in Tom's lap so she could see out of the window. "Why do all these people have all these lights when we don't have any?"

A moment passed, and her mother answered, "Baby, we wouldn't have no place to plug them in. They have to have electricity."

A time passed in silence, and Wendy asked, "Will Santa have anything left for us when he leaves Conway?"

Silence again fell over the car for a moment; then her mother answered, "He will baby, but probably not very much."

Not a word was said for a long time. They were on the opposite side of town from the Tanner house and it took some time to drive Tom and Bill home. The three little girls in the back seat appeared to be asleep. Wendy was still in Tom's lap, and Emily was in Bill's lap on the other end of the seat. Sandy was in her mother's lap in the middle of the seat.

Wendy's head lay back on her brother's chest and her eyes were closed, but she wasn't asleep. She was too excited to sleep. Her thoughts were of Christmas and all the presents she thought Santa would bring her.

Tom leaned over and whispered into Mary's ear, "Has anything been bought for these kids for Christmas?"

The word "bought" seemed out of place and surprised Wendy. She almost jumped up and asked, "Bought what?" but she lay quietly and listened as her dream of Santa Claus was shattered.

"I don't think so," Mary answered. "When Lester took Grace to the health clinic the other day for her check up, he tried to get something on credit while they were in town, but they didn't come back with anything. They won't give any credit to somebody who ain't got no steady job and nobody around here wants to hire him. Tom, there ain't a cent of money in the house. There ain't even enough money to buy kerosene for the lamps. There's only enough to burn one lamp a little while at night. Lester's made a little money, and I give your Momma every cent I get my hands on, but Tom, that ain't enough to buy Santa Claus for them. There ain't hardly enough money to buy food to eat."

"Why in the world didn't somebody tell me before now? I could have helped a little. I don't make much, but I can help some," said Tom.

"Tom, are you blind? You've been there, didn't you see what was going on? Didn't you see how we have to live from day to day?" Mary replied.

Tom didn't answer. There was nothing he could say. He wasn't looking to see things like enough food in the house and felt guilty at having filled his stomach at his mother's table.

"He wouldn't have asked you of all people," Mary continued to whisper. "He hates you, Tom. He had rather see these kids go without and wake up Christmas morning with nothing beneath the tree than to admit to you that he can't buy anything for them. It's bad, Tom, real bad and your Momma will have that baby in another week or so. She's worried about everything until she's made herself sick, and she was sick enough already. She's not getting along too good."

"What did the doctor tell her at the health clinic?" Tom asked.

Mary answered, "He said she needed to be in the hospital right now, but she won't go until it's time for the baby. The doctor said the county would have to pay the bill but that ain't it. Something's wrong, Tom, and she ain't telling me everything. I just know it." She was crying when she finished speaking.

Wendy felt Tom's chest when his lungs filled with air as he sighed. She felt his body tremble and she opened an eye to peek upward at his face. The street was lighted and she saw tears running down his cheeks. She wanted to cry along with him but she held it inside.

She hated Christmas. She didn't understand why adults told children about Santa Claus when there wasn't any such thing. There were a lot of things she was just learning about adults. Her education was just beginning.

The following day Wendy wanted to tell her mother she didn't want anything for Christmas, but she didn't.

With every day that passed drawing nearer to Christmas, Wendy became more depressed. Emily kept telling her all the things Santa would bring her and Wendy kept telling her not to expect very much. She watched as her mother turned her back every time someone mentioned Santa Claus. She saw the hurt in her eyes and it almost tore her insides out.

Then finally, Christmas Eve arrived. It was an absolutely miserable day for Wendy. Emily and Sandy's excitement nearly drove her up a wall. The two of them must have moved each ornament on the tree fifty times. When darkness came, they could hardly control themselves until Grace lit the lone candle. It had hardly started burning before the two of them wanted to go to bed so Santa would hurry and come. Grace nearly had to sit on them to keep them still long enough for her to read the story of the birth of Jesus from the bible.

Tom and Bill were there, as well, and sat with Mary on the sofa. Grace sat in her rocker and Wendy, Emily and Sandy sat on the floor at her feet. Lester sat by himself near the fireplace.

Wendy stared at the flame of the lone candle on the top of the tree. She wanted to look at her mother but she knew if she did, she would cry.

After the story was completed, Tom, Bill and Mary left the house. Emily and Sandy ran to the bedroom and jumped into bed. They had to be threatened with a spanking before they would get out of bed and say their prayers. Wendy didn't want to go to bed but Grace made her anyway. Wendy said her prayers and begged God to have Santa leave something underneath the tree for Emily even though she knew Santa was only a myth.

On Christmas morning, Emily woke long before sunrise. She then woke Wendy and Sandy and tried to get them to go into the living room with her to see what Santa had left them. Wendy didn't want to go. She knew there wouldn't be anything there for either of them. She knew it would break their hearts and tried to tell them again not to expect much.

As soon as it was light enough to see, Emily and Sandy could be contained no longer. Wendy finally told them to, "Go! Go!"

They ran to the doorway and stood peeking around the side of the curtain. Wendy heard both girls gasp for breath; then they turned and ran back to Wendy's bed saying in unison, "Oh boy! Oh boy! Oh boy!"

They took each other by the hands and jumped around and around on the bed in a circle above Wendy repeating, "Oh boy! Oh boy! Oh boy!" Then they jumped off the bed and ran through the curtain and into the living room.

Now it was Wendy who couldn't wait any longer. She had to see what all of the excitement was about. She got out of bed and ran through the curtain herself. She found Emily and Sandy were correct. There was a stack of gifts beneath the little pine Christmas tree.

Emily and Sandy stood in front of the tree in total amazement, shifting their stance from one foot to the other. The floor was freezing. It was so cold Wendy's bare feet couldn't take it; so, she ran to a chair near the tree and sat with her knees drawn under her gown, trying to keep her legs warm. Mary was on the couch and played like she was asleep, but Wendy saw her smiling.

Wendy heard soft footsteps behind her and when she turned she saw her mother. Grace's hands covered her face and she was crying. A lump that felt the size of an orange came into Wendy's throat. She hadn't cried in a long time, but this time she couldn't hold it inside. She jumped out of the chair, ran into the kitchen and out onto the little back porch.

It was freezing but she didn't feel the cold. She sat on the floor with her back against the wall as the emotions penned inside erupted into tears.

Grace followed Wendy out of the living room and into the kitchen and stood just inside the kitchen door with her back against the wall, putting her opposite her daughter, through the wall. Tears streamed down their faces, but this time, a mother's cries made no sound.

8
"ONE COMING; ONE GOING"

Wendy sat alone in the cold on the back porch that Christmas morning. She was torn between believing in Santa Claus and remembering the conversation between Tom and Mary. She cried until she heard someone in the kitchen attempting to start a fire in the wood stove. She cracked the thin layer of ice that had formed overnight on the bucket of water on the washstand on the back porch and the cold water felt good as she splashed it on her face. She went into the kitchen where her mother met her with a towel. Grace hugged and kissed her and she ran back into the living room.

Emily and Sandy were having the time of their lives. Torn wrapping paper was scattered about the floor. A fire was burning in the fireplace and the room had warmed. Mary sat on the floor wrapped in a blanket, nearly in the hearth of the fireplace, feeding wads of paper into the flames.

Wendy wanted to see the gifts she had under the tree but first she had to warm herself. She was chilled to the bone and her teeth were chattering. She ran to the fireplace and her aunt pulled her down into her arms beneath the blanket.

"You're frozen, baby," Mary said as she began to rub Wendy's hands between hers.

Grace came into the living room and went to the fireplace. She stood beside Mary and Wendy, and asked, "Wendy, did you see what Santa brought you?"

Wendy answered by shaking her head, still looking at the fire.

"Go on," Mary prodded, and added in a begging way, "Go on baby, look." But Wendy wouldn't. Mary took hold of her shoulders and turned her entire body to face the tree, and ordered, "I said look!"

Sandy jumped to her feet with Wendy's gifts to her hand and placed them in her lap.

Wendy looked up at her mother and asked in a questioning way, "Momma?"

Tears were streaming down Grace's cheeks. She lifted her apron, wiped her eyes, and replied, "Santa Claus, baby. It must have been Santa Claus."

A great big smile filled Wendy's face from ear to ear. She knew it wasn't really Santa. She knew the gifts had to have come from Tom but somehow knowing he had bought them with money he had earned made them even more special.

Wendy's gifts were a little red truck, a big red and white striped candy cane, an apple and a set of jacks with a little red ball. She probably received other gifts but she only remembered the red things.

As soon as the girls were alone, Wendy gave the jacks to Emily, saying, "Santa made a mistake. This was meant for you."

It was a very happy morning around the house that day. Grace found a great big box of groceries on the kitchen table. It contained everything needed to fix a big breakfast and Christmas dinner. She began to cook Tom's Christmas present to his mother. She sang Christmas songs as she worked at the store and seemed to float around the kitchen even though one only had to look at her to know she was very sick.

Every minute, it seemed one of the girls ran into the kitchen, exclaiming, "Look at this!" or "Look at that!" Grace took time with each of them as she sang, cooked and cried most of the morning.

Lester didn't come out of his bedroom until mid morning. He didn't say a word to anyone as he went out of the front door. He got in his car and left for a while, returned, and immediately went to the woodpile in the back yard. He began to cut and split wood in the freezing cold. He didn't come into the kitchen for breakfast nor did he come inside when Tom and Bill came for Christmas dinner. He ate both meals while sitting on the back porch steps.

He didn't talk to anyone nor would he allow anyone to talk to him. Grace tried to find out what was bothering him when she went to get his empty dinner plate, but he turned from her, went back to the woodpile, and continued chopping wood. Emily and Sandy went outside to show him their dolls, but he ignored them.

After dinner, Tom took Emily, Wendy and Sandy into Conway to their Grandmother Tanner's house. Tom still didn't have a driver's license, but drove all the time anyway. Grace didn't go into town nor did Mary. Grace said she had to lie down for a little while and Mary stayed with her.

As Tom backed the pickup out of the driveway, he saw the reason Lester stayed by the woodpile all day. Tom saw him raise a quart mason jar to his mouth and knew the clear liquid wasn't water.

The three girls filled up on sweets at their grandmother's. Mrs. Tanner gave them each a doll she had made from socks and a paper bag filled with fruit, nuts and candies. The best part of the trip to her house was watching the television she had received as a gift from Mr. Tanner. It was the first television the girls had ever seen outside of a store window.

Tom drove the girls back home before dark. They carried their gifts from their grandmother and Tom carried a chocolate layer cake that his grandmother had baked for Grace and Mary.

Lester was in the living room by the fire when they came back from Conway. He looked like he was drunk and didn't turn around when they entered the room. Tom didn't stay long and went back to Conway. The three girls took their baths, ate supper, along with a large slice of chocolate cake, and went to bed. It had been a very long day for them. It was a day they would remember for a very long time. Wendy was afraid Lester's drunkenness would bring him to her bed that night, so she slept with her aunt again.

Christmas day passed, and, for a few days that followed, it was like one long Christmas Day for Emily and Sandy. They took the tree down and put it back up again, acting out Christmas morning over and over again. Wendy played the game a few times but was soon bored. She began to follow her mother.

Wendy was under her mother's feet everywhere she went. She could tell she wasn't feeling well. If she needed something lifted, Wendy was there. If she needed something moved, Wendy was there. If she went to pee, Wendy was there. Wendy was so close to her mother that she began to get on her mother's nerves.

"Will you please find something to do, Wendy, that's not right under my feet?" she finally said. Wendy heard her, but she didn't listen, for the little shadow remained.

Lester was gone from the house most of the time following Christmas. He helped a farmer haul pine straw to burn off tobacco beds. However, he kept plenty of wood split and piled beside the stove and in the living room beside the fireplace.

Everyone knew he was drinking again, but he didn't fuss, fight and curse as before. In the evenings, he ate supper after everyone else was finished. If everyone was in the living room, he was in the kitchen. If they were in the kitchen, he was in the living room.

Mary told Wendy that Lester's pride was hurt. Wendy didn't care what was wrong with him. She was glad she didn't have to look at him nor did he come to her again in the night. But, just in case, she continued to sleep with her aunt.

One morning Grace got out of bed and started trying to clean the house. Mary and Wendy tried to help her, but she told them, "I'd rather do it by myself."

She must have wiped the oilcloth on the kitchen table a hundred times. Mary finally told her, "I'll swear, Grace, if you wipe that tablecloth one more time, you'll wipe the red squares off of it."

Mary knew what was about to happen. She knew the baby would be born soon. She tried to explain it to Wendy but she didn't quite understand. Wendy only knew her mother looked like she was in pain, and instead of sympathizing, Wendy blamed Lester for causing the pain and added it to the already long list of reasons she hated him.

Grace began cooking supper early that afternoon. She prepared everyone's favorite: fried chicken, biscuits, big white lima beans and rice. She sat at the table to roll the biscuits instead of standing at the waist high counter beside the stove.

Wendy sat in the chair across from her and watched every move she made. "Momma?" she asked.

Her mother didn't look up as she kneaded the dough, but answered, "Huh."

Wendy got on her knees in the chair, placed both elbows on the table and, with her chin in her hands, asked, "What makes your biscuits so good, Momma?"

Grace continued to work the dough, and replied, "Oh, nothing special. Just a little secret ingredient."

Wendy looked puzzled, and replied, "What secret? I've watched everything you done, Momma, and I ain't seen no secret stuff."

Her mother smiled, and responded, "Oh, you can't see it, baby. You must feel it."

Wendy reached across the table and touched the dough with the tips of her fingers. Grace looked up with a smile on her face, and gently said, "Not with your fingers, baby. You have to feel it with your heart. You have to feel it down deep inside your heart."

Wendy moved her hand to her chest above her heart.

"No, baby," her mother said, laughing. "It's inside your heart." Wendy's forehead wrinkled again as she gave her mother a puzzled look.

Grace rubbed her hands together to brush off the flour, wiped her hands on her apron and reached across the table and took Wendy's hands into hers.

"It's love, baby," she said. "A pure and simple love just like Jesus loves all of us."

Wendy understood a little of what she was saying, and she asked, "Love?"

"Yes, baby, love," Grace answered. "If you put a little inside everything you do, like I do these biscuits, cause I love you, then everything will always turn out to be good. Love feels good and makes everything taste good."

Grace began to roll the biscuits in her hands and placing them on the baking pan. Wendy watched without speaking. She was trying to understand what her mother had said and, as she looked into her face, her eyes began to tear and she wiped them on the sleeve of her dress.

Grace heard Wendy when she sniffled and looked up to see the tears in her eyes. "You are Momma's oldest girl," she said, reaching to touch Wendy's hand again. She had to swallow a few times and wipe her eyes again before she continued.

"You're a big girl now, and you got to be strong. You've got to be able to love. Momma knows how things have been around here, but baby, you can't hate people. You can't hate Lester. The Lord says you have to love people. You got to love him. That's my recipe for making biscuits and it's God's recipe for living."

Wendy made no reply to what her mother had said. She was thinking of Lester and what he had done to her. She knew she hated him regardless of what her mother said. She couldn't and wouldn't believe that her mother knew what had happened and would still ask her to love Lester. She had to believe that one thing above all else. Otherwise, love made no sense to her. She wouldn't believe her mother wanted her to love the man who was causing so much hurt in her life.

"I'll need your help a lot when I come home from the hospital with the baby," she told Wendy as she began to knead the dough. "It will be fun to have a little baby around. You've never been around a little baby that you remember. They're so soft and warm. You'll love it as much as you do your brothers and Emily."

Wendy thought about what her mother said but she couldn't visualize ever loving the baby, not Lester's baby. However, she didn't say this to her mother. She tried to look into her mother's eyes as she spoke but she couldn't. Instead, she stared without speaking at her mother's hands as they rolled the biscuits.

While everyone ate supper that evening, Grace took a bath. She came into the kitchen just as they were finished eating with a small suitcase in her hand. Wendy turned to look at her and saw the prettiest woman she had ever seen. Her mother's face seemed to glow. She smiled more than Wendy had ever seen her smile, even her teeth showed. She seemed to be bubbling over with joy and happiness. She wore her pretty yellow blouse, the same one she wore the day Wendy had seen the blood speckled down the front.

Emily left the table and ran to her mother. Lester came into the kitchen and took the bag from Grace's hand. Everything was all happy and smiles until Wendy saw the grin on his face.

Grace stooped as much as she could, hugged and kissed Emily. She explained what was about to happen, and added, "I'll be back in a day or two and you all will have a brand-new baby to play with. You girls be good, mind your Aunt Mary, and remember that I love you more than anything in this whole wide world."

She walked around the table, kissed Wendy on the top of the head, and said, "Come on Lester. Let's go and we had better hurry. I think my water's about to break."

The following morning they hadn't heard a word from anyone as to how things were at the hospital. Wendy probably asked her aunt a hundred times if everything was all right. Mary's standard answer was: "No news is good news."

Mary cooked supper and everyone ate and had their baths before dark. Still they hadn't heard a word of news. She had been worried all day. Mary had tried not to show it, but as soon as it became dark outside, she couldn't help herself. She must have opened and closed the front door twenty times.

"It looks like somebody could come out here and at least tell us whether it was a boy or a girl. It ain't like we live on the other side of the world," she said as she slammed the door.

It was about 8:30 in the evening when the headlights of a vehicle finally pulled into the drive. Mary ran to the front door as the three girls came running in from the kitchen. Tom and Bill came into the house and Wendy saw her brothers were crying, and all hell broke loose. Wendy knew what was wrong before Tom told her. Aunt Mary did, as well.

Wendy stood to the side of the door, her lip began to tremble, and her eyes burned like fire. She asked very calmly at first, "What's wrong?" When no one answered, she cried, "MOMMA!"

By then, Emily knew something was wrong with her mother and began to scream at the top of her lungs. "Where's my Momma? Where's my Momma?" Wendy and Emily asked nearly in unison.

Mary held Tom in her arms as he cried, then Tom knelt to one knee, and Wendy ran to his open arms. Wendy clutched Tom's neck as he lifted her clear off the floor. Mary knelt and held Emily in her arms.

"Momma's gone to be with Daddy," Tom said, sobbing with every word.

Tom took what remained of his family back to Conway later that night. "We're still a family and we are going to stay together," he told Mary when they walked out of the door. They cried all the way to town. Tom tried to tell them funny things about their mother and they laughed, a little. Their emotions were left with only two choices, to laugh or to cry. They laughed some and cried some.

Realizing all that had happened and believing it wasn't possible for her mother to be dead, Wendy asked, "She just can't be gone. God wouldn't let that happen, would He?"

Tom didn't answer and Emily hadn't stopped crying. "She just can't be dead! She just can't be dead!" Wendy repeated over and over again. The more she repeated it, the madder she got.

"You and Bill are boys and you are old enough to take care of yourselves, but what's going to happen to me and Emily? God wouldn't do this! Would He? Would He?" she cried.

"I don't have any answers," Tom finally said. "But I do know one thing. We are going to stay together. Nobody's gonna split this family up again, and I mean it."

Wendy hadn't thought of what her brother had just said, but now she wondered what would happen. She had heard horror stories in school about families being torn apart, but even after what had happened since her father died, she just couldn't believe anything else bad could happen.

She tried to imagine what life would be like without her mother. Her mother's love was the only thing she had in her life that could be counted on. It had been the only thing that kept everything together. Now what would happen, she wondered, and cried deep tears.

The following morning when Wendy awoke at her grandmother's house, she didn't want to open her eyes for fear it all had been true. She knew it was morning. She could hear voices in the house. She began to run the events of the last days through her mind to try and make some sense out of the utter chaos. She tried to picture her mother's face but the only face she could see was Lester's.

She believed Lester had killed her mother just as surely as if he had put a gun to her head and blown her brains out. She believed it would have been more merciful than her tortured death.

Tom had told Wendy on the way to Conway the night before, "When Lester took Momma to the hospital to have the baby, and he just left her standing outside the emergency room entrance and just drove away. He didn't even go into the hospital with her. Momma died with no one around her that she knew or that loved her."

Wendy didn't think there was any way she could hate Lester any more than she already did until Tom told her the rest of what he had found out and tried to explain it again and again so that her young mind could understand.

"The doctor had warned Momma and Lester while they were in Baltimore not to carry the baby to full term. He told them, if it wasn't aborted, Momma's chances of living through the delivery would be slim, very slim. The doctor said her heart couldn't withstand the strain of childbirth."

"Momma didn't have the chance to decide for herself whether she wanted to have the abortion or not. Lester made that decision for her. He wouldn't allow it. The doctor at the health clinic also warned them about the childbirth. It was too late for an abortion by then. He was worried about Momma's heart condition."

As Wendy lay in bed at her grandmother's house and thought of Lester that morning and what Tom had explained her, layer after layer of anger and hatred began to fill the tiniest crevasses inside her. She began to cry loudly and tremble nearly to the state of convulsions.

Tom ran into the room and lifted her into his arms. Wendy's body felt icy cold to him, yet her clothing was soaking wet. Tom kissed and hugged her until she settle down some and began to relax in his arms; then she began to cry again. All the pent-up tears she held back for the past months flooded out of her. Tom tried to get her to stop, but she couldn't.

Finally her grandmother came into the room, and said, "Leave that baby alone. Let her cry if she wants to. I'm hurting too much to cry, so let her cry. Let her cry for both of us."

She took Wendy from Tom's arms, and added, "You go ahead and cry, baby. You cry all you want. You've got a right to cry. You've lost your Momma, and...and I've lost my precious, precious little girl."

Then, the tears her grandmother couldn't cry came rushing out of her as the impact of losing her daughter crashed down. She took Wendy into the living room, got out of the wheelchair and into her rocker and they began to rock and cry together. Emily and Sandy soon came into the room from the kitchen, and both of them began to cry, followed by an equal amount from Bill, Tom, and Mary. They all had a good cry for at least an hour.

It was a little past noon when Wendy and Emily went on the front porch and sat in the swing together. Sandy sat on the front steps and played with a cricket that Tom had tied to a string. The day was sunny and warm, almost like a spring day. Soon, a long black hearse stopped on the street in front of the house. Emily jumped out of the swing and ran into the house followed by Sandy. Wendy kept her seat until the hearse backed to the front porch steps and the men opened the back door and began to pull out the casket.

Then, she went inside and stood in the doorway between the living room and dining room and watched as the men carried the copper colored casket into the house. They placed it on a stand in front of the two large living room windows. Wendy watched as they opened half of the casket lid and draped a pretty piece of white lace over the opening; then the men unloaded flowers from a panel truck and placed them around the room.

Wendy wanted to go up to the casket after they had left to see if her mother was inside, but she couldn't make herself move. She turned, went through the kitchen and out into the back yard. She walked around the house to the front porch and took a seat again in the swing.

She sat there for nearly the entire afternoon and watched as people came and went. Most of the people she had never seen before. Almost everyone who came spoke to her but she didn't greet them. The men tipped their hats and most of the women touched her hand or rubbed the top of her head.

Tom, Mary and others from the Tanner family were beside the house, talking late that afternoon. She heard Tom ask Mary, "Does Emily or Wendy have anything to wear to the funeral?"

Mary answered, "Tom, I brought the best clothes Wendy had when I came back from home this morning, and she's wearing the best dress now. Emily's wearing one of Sandy's dresses. They are about the same size. They don't have anything, Tom, and neither did your Momma. I told you when we were looking at the

Christmas lights that they didn't have anything! Lester never bought them anything. He never spent one red cent on anything except to buy whiskey, the worthless bastard! I wish he was in that cold box in there with his toes pointed up instead of my sister. Damn him! Damn him to hell!"

Another of Wendy's aunts said, "Don't hold back, Mary. Tell it like it is, child! Like they say, if it walks like a duck and talks like a duck, the bastard's a duck!"

Everyone laughed at the sarcasm, and when they stopped, the same aunt added, "Tom, I know your Momma didn't have anything so I bought a dress, and I took it to the funeral home. She's wearing it now. When I went out there with Mary this morning, I looked through the closets. I didn't see anything I wanted my sister to wear the last time I looked at her. I should have asked you before I went and bought the dress. I'm sorry. I can't believe that man made them live like that! They didn't live in a house! Tom, that place ain't even fit for mules!"

Wendy didn't laugh when the others had laughed. She didn't catch the sarcasm. The statements she overheard were true and she didn't see anything funny about them. Lester never brought anything into the house but pain. She didn't know how she would get even with the man who had taken her mother from her and who had hurt her.

She knew she should be thinking of her mother and her death as she swung the swing back and forth, but she couldn't. All she could think of was Lester. She hadn't thought of the baby until that very moment. No one had mentioned anything about it. She hoped it was dead.

As was the custom of the times when a death occurred, a setting-up took place. Almost everyone who came to the house to pay their respects and give condolences to the family brought a covered dish of food. Some who brought food stayed to eat. Some who didn't bring food also came to eat. Others stopped by the house and used the event as a kind of social gathering. They saw old friends they hadn't seen since the last setting-up. The women gathered in the kitchen and spread the latest gossip. The men stood around outside mainly because it was a more convenient place to smoke, chew their tobacco and spit. Some brought along a taste, as they chose to call it, because it sounded better than its actual name, whiskey.

Consequently, oftentimes segments of people's memories were marked by funerals around Conway. Someone might ask another if they had seen old So-and-so, the answer often would be, "Hadn't seen him since we buried old What's-his-name."

Not that they didn't respect the dead—on the contrary, the passing was forever immortalized. For example, one might hear, "What's-his-name was buried the same day the war ended," or "Boy, So-and-so shore did get some kind a drunk at old What's-his-name's setting-up."

As soon as everyone had their fill of eating, gossiping, drinking their favorite beverage, or genuine mourning; the crowd thinned out at the Tanner home. Those with heavy hearts had time to themselves to remember the things they wanted to remember about Grace Tanner Wenslow Flanders.

Wendy must have looked into the living room a hundred times that afternoon from the window on the front porch. She knew she had to go inside sooner or later and look into that cold box. She knew her mother was dead. However, she figured she wasn't, not really, unless she actually looked at her face.

Wendy believed that as long as she kept her mother alive inside of her heart, her world was still intact. That one single thought kept her together throughout the day, but she knew inside she would have to face the truth before she slept that night.

***

Wendy's grandfather and Tom were on the back porch talking to the preacher. Her grandmother, Mary and some other women were in the kitchen, talking over coffee. Emily was somewhere playing with Sandy, and Wendy sat on the bed in Tom's room alone with her thoughts.

She thought of the pretty yellow blouse that her mother had worn and how beautiful she looked in it when she went to the hospital. She wasn't thinking of the bad times her mother went through or remembering the savage beating given to her at the hands of Lester. She wasn't even remembering how badly she hated the man who had hurt her mother. None of that, because she was remembering her mother's soft voice, her gentle touch.

Wendy's mind slipped back to when her father was alive and they were truly a family. Her mind began to ease forward in time, but only seeing the good things. She remembered when her mother came back to her from Baltimore, held her in her arms and told her she still loved her. She remembered the biscuit dough, how her mother smelled and how her lips tasted when she kissed her.

And, oh, how she remembered her mother's smile. She saw again her mother's thin lips just barely curled upwards at the corners, the tiny dimples in her fair cheeks, and her eyes. Oh yes, her eyes, for that's where her mother's smile came from, her beautiful dark eyes. Eyes that spoke and said, "I love you, baby." Eyes that made the bad things go away. Eyes that made Wendy feel warm inside.

Before Wendy confronted what she knew she must, she knelt beside Tom's bed and prayed, "Dear Lord, now you've got my Momma there with you and you've got my Daddy. Heaven must be a pretty place with them there. Please, take care of them and tell my Momma that I love her."

There was more she could have said, but her heart was just too heavy. Tears rolled down her cheeks, but they were silent tears.

Wendy got up from her knees, dried her eyes, fixed her dress and went into the living room. She walked to the side of the casket and stared through the white lace at the white satin cloth on the inside of the open lid. She stood quietly for a moment as her knees trembled; then she let her eyes move slowly downward until she saw her mother's face. She was beautiful, more beautiful than she had ever seen her and looked like she was sleeping peacefully. The dress she wore was her favorite color. It was royal blue with a tiny white lace collar.

Wendy's eyes moved down the length of her mother's body until she saw her hands. She tried to make herself close her eyes, to shut out the sight of them but her eyes would not obey. Her mother's hands looked pitifully small and frail. They were rough and worn. No fingernails extended beyond the tip of her fingers.

Wendy reached inside the casket and touched one of her mother's hands; then she drew her hand back quickly as if she had touched something hot. However, her mother's hand felt icy cold to the touch. Wendy knew then that her mother was gone. She moved her hand inside the casket again and placed it on top of her mother's hand; then she began to cry, "Please don't leave me again. Take me with you. Please Momma! Please!"

Wendy wiped the tears from her eyes with her other hand and reached it inside the casket and touched her mother's cheek. A teardrop from her hand was transferred to her mother's face, and Wendy took a corner of the white lace draped over the casket and wiped the tears from her mother's face and thought she saw her mother smile.

Someone touched Wendy's shoulder and she jumped in fright. She turned to face the one person she wanted least of all in the world to ever see again—her stepfather, Lester. Anger seemed to touch her very soul. She wanted to speak, to yell, to scream at him but her jaws seemed to be locked. She wanted to hit him, to have the hoe in her hands once more. She wanted one more chance to end his days on earth. She trembled. She felt naked and ashamed. She felt dirty as his eyes looked into hers.

"I wus wondering how you wus," he slurred meekly.

Wendy could smell the scent of whiskey on his breath and felt nauseated. Memories of his hands touching her made her gather the collar of her dress around her neck, trying to hide her flesh from his eyes. She stood as if frozen in front of him.

Suddenly, he reached out, took Wendy's hand, turned it upward and laid two tightly rolled ten-dollar bills in her palm.

"That's to buy you and a...a...your sister a pretty new dress," he said, stammering and almost falling.

That was the straw that broke the camel's back, for Wendy threw the money into his face, and jeered threw gritted teeth, "Her name is Emily! My sister's name is Emily!"

She threw the money into his face and flew into him like a windmill. The fingernails of her right hand lashed out like a cat. The two middle fingernails slashed two bloody strips down the left side of his face. Her left hand went straight toward his eyes, but he blocked her thrust with a raised forearm. Both of her hands tore at him like something wild. What the big mortar hoe didn't do, she tried to do with her fingernails. If left alone, she probably would have reaped her revenge, but her grandfather and Tom came into the living room and pulled her off of him.

"What in the hell are you doing here?" shouted Tom at Lester.

He held back Wendy's flailing hands with one hand and pushed hard into Lester's chest with the other. Lester was forced backward toward the front door.

"Get out of this house!" Mr. Tanner added as he stepped between Tom and Lester.

"He tried to give me money!" Wendy said, and continued, while pointing into Lester's face, "Where was that money when we needed it?"

Blood drained from the scratches on his face as he stood, swaying back and forth with his mouth half-open. He looked like he had been drunk for days.

"You never gave them anything but heartache and pain!" yelled Tom. "Why do you try to give them money now, you bastard? Why did you come to this house drunk?" he continued, angrily stepping around his grandfather.

Tom poked his finger roughly into Lester's chest, forcing him backward hard into the door facing. Tom was a fair-sized fifteen-year-old young man. His work at the concrete plant had turned his youthful muscles into those of a man.

Wendy tried to get to Lester again, to finish what she had started, but Mrs. Tanner hurriedly positioned her wheelchair between them and grabbed Wendy by the arm, pulling her into her lap.

"Y'all take all of this in the yard! This ain't no place for all this! Tom, don't you cuss no more in my house! Lester Flanders, you ain't welcome here! Leave!" Mrs. Tanner said, speaking loud and very sternly.

Wendy yelled, "Why didn't you spend that money to buy my Momma a new dress when she was alive? Her sister had to buy a dress for her to be buried in. Money can't ever make up for what you done to her, to me and this family. I hate you Lester. I hate you and that baby more than anything in this world. I hope both of you die deader than hell!"

Wendy tried to get away from Mrs. Tanner to get at Lester again, but her grandmother held her tightly. Tom grabbed Lester by the muscle of his upper arm and lifted that side of his body so that his toes barely touched the floor. Lester had drunk so much whiskey in the past year that his body had wasted away to almost nothing.

Tom opened the front door with his other hand and pushed Lester out onto the front porch, down the front steps and he fell headlong into the front yard.

Two men that were standing near the steps lifted Lester to his feet. Tom headed down the steps toward him, but his grandfather stopped him.

"That's enough Tom. Settle down, now!" Mr. Tanner ordered as he stepped between Tom and Lester.

With Mr. Tanner's hand in the middle of Tom's chest, Tom yelled at Lester, "You get your drunk, sorry ass away from here. There will come a day when you'll have to answer for all you've done to my Momma and this family. That day might come sooner than you think. You'll pay. I promise you Lester Flanders, you'll pay."

Wendy wanted her big brother to jump on Lester and beat him the way she and her mother had been beaten. She wanted

Tom to throw Lester to the ground, put his foot on his throat and whip him like a dog. She wanted her brother to kill the one person on earth that she hated. She wanted to watch as Lester drew his last breath, but her stepfather turned and staggered away into the darkness.

The funeral the next day was about as sad as funerals get. Wendy didn't remember very much about it in the years that followed. She remembered the song that the congregation sang, "No Tears in Heaven." She wouldn't walk past the open casket with Emily, Bill and Tom. The last time she saw her mother's face, she thought she had seen a smile, and that's the way she wanted to remember her.

***

An event was marked by Grace Flanders' funeral that day in Horry County, South Carolina. It was New Year's Eve, but that wasn't the reason people remembered.

Some coon hunters were gathered before a night hunt at a little country store not far from Conway a few days after the funeral. The conversation ranged from old hunting stories to bullshit gossiping.

One of the old timers who was just along for the ride and the stories commented, "Did any of y'all see that cement truck out this a ways late the other night?"

No one spoke, only the nodding of heads were their answers.

A period of silence passed with the same old timers asking, "Has anyone seen Lester Flanders lately?"

One of the other hunters scratched his whiskered chin, and answered, "Hadn't seen hide nor hair of old Lester since the day they buried his wife, Grace."

***

It was very quiet around the Tanner home the first day of 1959. Bill stayed mostly to himself. Wendy and Emily seemed inseparable. Mrs. Tanner stayed in the kitchen with Sandy. Tom and Mary left the cemetery together after the funeral and neither came home until just before daylight. Both slept well into the afternoon. Some family and friends visited throughout the day, but not many and none stayed for long.

Bill and Sandy went back to school when it began again following the Christmas and New Year breaks. Tom and Mr. Tanner went back to work at the concrete block plant. Emily and Wendy were left alone at home with their grandmother. They didn't return to school. Wendy didn't know why they weren't made to go back to school but she didn't ask any questions. She hated school and didn't care if she ever went back again.

A family meeting of sorts was held the first weekend in January between members of the Tanner and Wenslow families. Their discussion concerned what was to happen to Grace and Francis Wenslow's children, primarily, the three youngest—Emily, Wendy and Bill.

It was decided Tom would remain in Conway with the Tanners. He had a job and could look after himself. Tom and Mrs. Tanner wanted to keep the family together, but things didn't work out that way.

The children still received the Social Security checks. The four checks, when combined, would have made a sizable financial contribution to a family's budget, but, even with the money as an incentive, no one would assume the burden of four children to rear. So the Wenslow children were split apart.

Bill, thirteen, would move to Alabama to live with an uncle, his father's brother. Emily, seven, would move to Charleston to live with another uncle, Grace's brother, but it wasn't the same uncle who had been the drunkard and had joined the Army. Wendy, ten, would move to Myrtle Beach to live with another of her father's brothers. Regardless what Tom had promised, the little family that began on Powell Street was being torn apart again.

Tom took part in the family meeting and was the one selected to tell his brother and sisters what was about to happen. He assembled them into a group on the front porch steps. It was the middle of the afternoon and the weather was chilly but the sun shone brightly. He tried to be the big brother and not cry, but he couldn't hold back the tears when everyone began to hug each other and cry.

Wendy and Emily were playing in a tire swing under a chinaberry tree in the front yard about midday on Monday following the family conclave weekend. A car came to a stop in front of the house and Wendy saw it was Uncle Clarence, the uncle from Myrtle Beach. She remembered him from the funeral. She had sat beside Mary during the services, and she pointed out some of the people to her. Uncle Clarence was one of them.

Emily ran into the house as soon as her uncle got out of the car, but Wendy knew it was no use in running. He was an adult and she believed he owned her now and could do anything he wanted with her. She believed she had nothing to say about anything. She found it difficult to believe all that had happened to her and her family and wondered when she would wake from the dream that was more like a nightmare.

Uncle Clarence entered the front yard and walked to where Wendy sat in the swing. His face looked kind. She didn't necessarily blame him for what had happened. He tried to talk to her, but she fiddled in the dirt with her toes and didn't say a word. Finally, she stared at him as she slowly got out of the swing. Without a word, she looked down at her feet and walked to the house.

Mrs. Tanner, alarmed by Emily, sat in her wheelchair in the living room. A large brown paper bag was in her lap, and Tom, Bill and Emily stood around her. Wendy hadn't thought much about leaving until she saw the paper bag. The sight of it felt like someone reached inside her chest and tore out her heart. She thought she had become immune to hurt and pain, but she was wrong.

The four children stood speechless and looked at each other. Words weren't needed nor would they have helped. Begging hadn't helped in the past and Wendy knew it wouldn't help them now. Neither would more tears, but everyone began to cry anyway, except for Wendy. Not a tear fell from her eyes.

Emily and Wendy stood apart for a moment and held each other's hands. Wendy looked into Emily's red and swollen eyes and her bottom lip begin to quiver. The walls that she had begun to build around her emotions began to quake, but they held. The two sisters hugged and held onto each other for as long as they could; then it was time to go.

Wendy didn't want to leave any of her family but least of all Emily. She wondered if anyone would love and watch after her. She wondered how anyone else would know the things that frightened her or the things that made her laugh.

She held her little sister close one last time and Emily whispered into her ear, "I love you." Wendy tried to answer and tell Emily that she loved her as well, but she didn't.

Wendy began school the following day in Myrtle Beach, but it wasn't until she was in the tenth grade that her life began again when normal things began to happen to her for a change. Things like boys and dates. After the Christmas break, a substitute driver drove her school bus several days a week. She usually sat with a friend on the seat just behind him. She didn't know him very well, but she didn't like him. She only sat behind him because her friend thought he was cute and had a crush on him, but the driver sat with his eyes glued to the road ahead and never gave her friend even a casual glance.

He was a senior and never talked to anyone on the bus. Wendy thought that he must have thought that he was too good for her. However, neither knew fate had stepped into both of their lives. The bus driver was Jack Jackson.

By then, Wendy lived with her cousin, Clara, and her husband, Sammy. In the summer before Wendy's junior year, Sammy was offered a job in Charleston, and before school began again, the family moved, and Emily and Wendy were reunited before school began.

Wendy went to work after school at a drugstore snack bar. She made friends with a girl named Dianne who also worked there. She was dating a sailor who was stationed aboard the USS Howard W. Gilmore (AS-16).

Dianne had a date one Saturday night during the Charleston County Fair. Her boyfriend's car wouldn't start, so a friend brought him to the drugstore to pick up Dianne. They were supposed to give Wendy a ride home before they went to the fair, but, instead, she decided to go with them.

The friend's name was Jack Jackson. Wendy remembered him, and she still didn't like him. Jack remembered her as the skinny girl who sat with the girl who ran her mouth from the time she got on the bus until the time she got off. Jack didn't like or dislike Wendy. He was only doing a favor for a shipmate, but fate had other plans.

9
"THE ABDUCTION"
(SEPTEMBER 1997)

Wendy Jackson was isolated from the other deputies at the football game that Friday night in Thomasville, Georgia. There were only two deputies with her at the stadium. The two deputies weren't full-time officers but members of the Thomas County Sheriff's Posse that functioned much as an auxiliary force, augmenting the regular force of deputies during football games, parades and other events when assistance was needed. This helped to keep certified officers from being diverted from their assigned duties and patrol areas.

During the game, a rash of incidents began to happen in Thomas County—several house fires, two armed robberies, and a four-vehicle pileup involving a semi truck on US-19 just north of Thomasville. The game began with six regular deputies in the vicinity of the stadium, but before the fourth quarter started, only the two Sheriff's Posse members and Wendy remained.

Wendy was assigned an area between the bleachers and the south end zone at the end of the field that bordered Jackson Street. One of the posse members was assigned the end zone at the opposite end of the field, and the other was assigned to the rest room area beneath the bleachers of the home team, the Bulldogs.

Wendy watched the game during the middle of the fourth quarter and was enjoying herself. The score was tied between the two teams. Hardly anyone was seated in the bleachers behind her.

Everyone was either standing, jumping up and down, or crowded around her. She asked some men to help her keep the spectators off of the field, but as soon as they were moved back behind the white line, the very next play of the game brought them into the end zone area again.

A little boy with flaming red hair and freckles pulled on Wendy's pants leg, trying to tell her something. She looked down and could only see his mouth move because the noise around her was nearly deafening. However, the boy was persistent and kept pulling on the leg of Wendy's trousers. Finally, she knew that he wasn't going away and knelt next to him.

She moved her ear to his mouth and heard him scream, "There's a man beating a woman in the parking lot!"

Wendy didn't call either of the Posse members on the radio that was clipped to her belt to alert them that she was leaving her post. Instead, she ran out of the gate used for vehicles to enter the football field when work was done. She carried only her radio and her courage—no flashlight, no baton, no sidearm.

She could barely see her hand before her face when she ran into the parking lot, for the bright lights of the stadium made her night vision nearly useless. So, with her arms and hands extended in front, she began to move slowly through the parked vehicles until she saw the faint outline of two people. Their silhouettes were almost in front of the school's gymnasium, which had a 35-foot bulldog painted on the towering front wall.

Wendy had parked her car in front of the gym when she arrived at the stadium. Now that area of the parking lot was very dimly lit. She strained her eyes to see and moved zigzag between the vehicles with her hands dragging along the sides of them until she was within a row of where the shadowy figures had stood; by then, she could only see one of the figures and couldn't tell if it was a man or a woman.

"Hey you!" she yelled at whoever it was but could hardly hear her own words. The uproar from the stadium behind her nearly masked all sounds.

Suddenly, someone grabbed her from behind and lifted her clear of the pavement. A long, bony arm encircled her upper body, pinning her back and shoulders against an equally bony chest. Her arms were pinned at her sides then almost simultaneously, a hand with long thin fingers clasped tightly across her mouth and nose.

Surprised at first, Wendy began to fight back as she saw a figure run at her out of the darkness and drew a cloth bag over her head; then, a gentler and softer hand pushed the larger hand from her mouth and a piece of duct tape was placed over her lips. The black hood was then tied tightly around her throat.

Wendy couldn't see anything inside the hood, but she could feel that she was being carried somewhere. Her upper body was trapped against the chest of the person carrying her and her legs dangled freely like a string puppet.

Wendy began to kick her feet frantically. One of her kicks caught the person carrying her squarely in the groin, and judging from the groan, she thought it was a man.

The target found, she continued to kick backwards until someone grabbed her ankles and tied them together. She heard a clicking sound as the bonds around her ankles were drawn tightly, and judging from the sound, she believed the device was an electrical tie-wrap. The Sheriff's Department kept them in inventory to be used for crowd control.

Wendy's car keys and handcuffs were attached to her belt with the radio. She felt a tug at her waist as they were ripped away, then she heard the keys jingle and a 'pop' sound as the trunk of a car was unlocked and opened. She was lowered so that her feet touched the ground and her wrists were handcuffed very tightly behind her back with her own cuffs.

Wendy felt herself being lifted into the air and thrown into the trunk of the car. The car rocked as the trunk lid was slammed shut. She heard the engine start and the car begin to move. She felt what she believed were speed bumps as the car moved through what she knew was the parking lot at the stadium. She felt the movement of the car pause for a moment, then the weight of her body shifted to one side as the car accelerated and turned left.

She knew Thomasville well and knew the car had turned left and was headed east on Jackson Street. Soon, she felt the car stop again and believed they were at the intersection of Jackson and Pine Tree Boulevard, normally a very busy intersection. She wormed her body downward so her feet would reach the side of the trunk and began to kick with her tied feet. Immediately, she felt the car surge forward.

Wendy mentally tried to track the movement of the car but in the darkness and fear, she lost track. There were many left and right turns and many stops and starts; then the car traveled a short distance around several sharp turns at a high rate of speed. Not being able to anticipate the turns and stops, her body was rolled around and banged from side to side in the trunk compartment.

In the darkness, Wendy tried to figure out what was going on. Was it a dream, a nightmare, what? Why was she being treated this way?

Her mind raced trying to think of possible answers, until she realized from her work with law enforcement that a sick mind didn't necessarily need a reason. She tried to make her mind hear the voices of those who had crossed her path, but it wouldn't.

Finally, the car slowed and turned off a paved surface and onto a bumpy road. A few minutes later it stopped. Wendy heard the doors of the car open and slam shut. She heard a key being turned in the lock of the trunk. The trunk opened and she could see a bright light through the black fabric of the hood. It was a directed beam that she believed to be a flashlight.

The light caused her eyes to burn and hurt. Hands touched her and she jumped and struggled in a vain attempt to escape. However, there was no place for her to go. She remembered her secret hiding place in the corner of a long ago closet and wished the bleached flour sacks could hide her again.

A voice, sounding strangely muffled and very difficult to understand, said in a soothing way, "Easy now! Easy girl!"

Wendy's body was gently but firmly rolled onto her side. Soft fingertips began to rub her upper arm. Suddenly she felt a sharp pain in the muscle. She knew it was a hypodermic needle being pushed into her arm. The tape across her mouth stifled her moan of pain and fear.

"Stop! Stop!" she tried to say, but the pain continued. It changed slowly to a burning sensation as the contents of the syringe were pushed into the muscle. The needle was withdrawn, and the soft fingertips rubbed her arm again.

The soft-sounding muffled voice said, "Easy, honey, easy, just relax."

"Don't pamper the bitch! Get the hell out of the way!" another harsh-sounding muffled voice yelled. The bright light was turned off and the trunk lid was closed very hard.

Wendy felt her head begin to swim. She knew she was going to sleep. She had felt the same feeling before when she had been given a shot for pain in the hospital after hurting her back. She heard more voices, but they seemed far, far away and echoed in her head. She thought she heard car doors slam and an engine start. She waited for the car she was in to move again, but the movement never came. She was soon unconscious.

She never knew her car didn't move. It remained the entire night in a wooded area near the airport about six miles outside of town. All she knew for the next six hours was silence, a cold, black, total silence.

She began to float into dreams. First, she dreamed of her husband and their lives in Thomasville; then she dreamed of her loneliness when Jack was in the navy and gone from her. Slowly her dreams drifted back to her childhood, and she felt the cold dampness of her father's bare feet as she touched them when he was dying. She saw Kaye playing jacks and herself in the bottom of a deep well. She saw three shiny silver quarters in her mother's outstretched hand.

Her mind wanted to relive the past, but new things began to flash among those of old. She saw her mother rocking on Jack's favorite twisted-vine rocker. She saw Emily, Bill and Tom playing in a tire swing in a chinaberry tree alongside the ivy-covered walk of her dream house. She saw herself standing in her deputy's uniform, dirty, tired and cold on the front porch of her grandmother's house, playing with a cricket on a string. The door opened and Jack took her into his arms, kissed her and told her he loved her. She saw herself try to repeat the same three words, but her mouth wouldn't form the words. Instead, she heard Emily say them as her two brothers gathered around a wheelchair.

Wendy couldn't remember ever having said those three little words, not even to her husband. Each time she tried to say them, she only thought of Lester.

It seemed only an hour passed, and Wendy heard a key turning the lock of the trunk again. A bright morning sun parted the mesh of the black hood. Her head began to swim. She tried to clear it and concentrate on what was happening around her, but everything seemed to be hidden behind a blanket of fog. Her head spun.

Suddenly, hands touched her neck and she jumped as if shocked by electricity. Other hands grabbed roughly at her feet as she was jerked up and out of the trunk's sunken well. Her back was dragged across the lip of the trunk, and she felt her skin tear. She whimpered with pain, but no one seemed to hear.

Her feet were dropped to the ground and she was placed in a standing position. The electrical tie-wrap securing her ankles had been very tightly drawn and had restricted the circulation and her feet were numb. Her legs, having been cramped in one position for a long time, seemed like jelly as they wobbled under her weight.

Wendy's knees suddenly collapsed and she began to fall forward. Someone stopped her fall by grabbing a handful of her hair through the black hood, and she was yanked upright and held by her hair like a headhunter's trophy. She tried to stand on her tiptoes to relieve some of the pull on her hair but couldn't. She couldn't feel her feet.

Wendy's mind flashed back briefly to the time Lester dragged her from beneath the house by her hair. The very thought of her stepfather caused her to tremble.

"I thought you said her husband, Jack, would be here this morning!" the muffled voice of a man said angrily. Hearing Jack's name snapped Wendy's mind back to the present.

"Like last night, I guess!" the same voice continued. "You didn't know she was going to that football game, either. This could've all been over last night. It would have been prettier in the dark. We wouldn't be here now if you had known. Shit! You don't know a whole hell of a lot about anything, do you?"

Wendy thought for a moment that the man with the muffled voice was talking to her but soon knew he wasn't.

"No matter. No matter," he added. "Fetch me that...that thing. Hand me that button thing, damn it, and roll that hood up so she can see. I wouldn't want her to miss this!"

The black cloth hood was loosened from Wendy's neck and rolled upwards exposing her eyes to glaring rays of the morning sun. It was very bright and burned, causing them to water. Her vision was cloudy, and her eyes wanted to close. She blinked them rapidly and held them open. Her feet were regaining some feeling and she was able to stand on her own. She felt the hands that had steadied her as they let her go.

"Wendy," the man's muffled voice called out softly from behind her.

The sound of her name being spoken surprised her and she tried to turn her head, but a hand reach from behind, seized her chin, and kept her head from turning.

"You're standing in the yard of your house," the voice said.

"Take that tape off her mouth," he ordered, and it was ripped violently from her lips and thrown to the ground at her feet. Her body cringed with pain and she tried to bring her hands up to rub her lips but they were still handcuffed behind her back.

Moments passed and Wendy's eyes began to focus. Out of the cloudy haze, she began to realize that she was standing on the side of the yard where Jack's workshop was. A white pickup truck was between her and the west side of the house. She was near the rear tire of the pickup looking over the bed. She could see her car parked near the house.

"Wendy," the muffled man's voice spoke again. His voice had an almost evil sound. "Do you see your house?"

Wendy didn't answer, and the man behind her grabbed her hair, and yelled, "I said, DO-YOU-SEE-IT?"

"Yes! Yes!" Wendy replied.

The man replied, "I want you to watch very carefully."

He let go of Wendy's hair, and asked, "Did you make that phone call like I told you?"

Wendy questioningly thought, "Phone call?"

Then a voice answered, "Yeah! Just did it." The voice was also muffled. However, Wendy was almost sure it was the voice of a woman, the same who had given her the injection.

"Great little invention, that cellular phone," the man's muffled voice answered.

"But...hadn't we better hurry up?" the woman's voice asked from behind Wendy.

"Shut up! You just do what you're told!" the man's voice snapped.

"Look closely," he added, but Wendy wasn't sure whether he was talking to her. However, just then, the man placed his hand on her shoulder and squeezed. Her body began to tremble at his touch.

Then, she heard a telephone ring in the direction of the house but it didn't sound like one of their house phones. It sounded more like her cellular phone. Before it stopped ringing, she saw a bright flash of orange light inside her kitchen. It looked to her to be the same color as a road flare, which it was.

The thought of Jack suddenly flashed before her eyes. She wondered where he could be, and why she hadn't seen Earnhardt in the yard, for he always challenged vehicles when they came into lane.

Moments passed with no one speaking. Fear gripped her insides, and she wanted to cry out, for she knew something was very, very wrong.

"Where's Jack?" she said to herself, or at least she thought she had said it to herself; however, she had said it to the top of her voice.

Suddenly the kitchen seemed to explode before her eyes. She screamed, and the man behind her laughed and his hand squeezed her shoulder, again. Almost instantly, the intensity of the fire rapidly grew, engulfing the kitchen within seconds.

Wendy heard the muffled man's voice behind her saying, "Yes! Yes! Oh yes!"

Seconds ticked away and the flames began to eat through the kitchen ceiling making a hissing sound like the forked tongue of a mythical dragon.

The kitchen windows blew outward with a WHOOSH, and Wendy felt the searing heat against her skin. The hot air from the explosion rushed against her face as the flames gushed from each kitchen window. She tasted the licking white-red flames as her mouth gasped in fear and the hand on her shoulder pushed her down behind the bed of the pickup truck just as shards of glass and wood peppered its side and the front of Jack's workshop behind her.

"JACK! JA...!" Wendy cried as she was held down, and someone put the tape again over her mouth and rough hands yanked the black hood down over her face.

Someone suddenly grabbed her underneath the arms as another took her ankles. She was lifted and hurriedly carried a short distance; then someone laughed as she was swung back and forth like a hammock.

"One—two—three," a muffled voice counted in English. "*Uno—dos—tres*," a muffled Hispanic voice counted at the same time. At the count of "Three" and "*Tres*," she was thrown into the air and landed headfirst on a very hard surface, knocking her unconscious.

The first cellular telephone call the woman made was to the Thomas County Sheriff's Department, the call Deputy Jamerson relayed to Sheriff Young. The second call ignited the road flare.

***

It was nearly an hour before Wendy regained consciousness enough to know what was going on about her. She heard the sound of a vehicle door slam, causing the hard cold slab she lay upon to vibrate. She heard what she thought was the creak and slam of a wooden door. It sounded distant somehow but similar to the sounds when she was in the trunk of the car. However, she knew she wasn't in the trunk of a car for she had room to move her legs.

It was difficult for her to think. Her head hurt with a throbbing pain. It pounded like a drum and everything seemed to be spinning around. She lay quietly for a moment, trying to listen, to figure out where she was. Ten minutes passed and the only sound she heard was her own breathing. She tried to make herself think but everything seemed to be jumbled together.

The things that stuck out in her mind were the ringing of the cellular phone that came from her kitchen, the fire, and a man's muffled voice that called her name. She also remembered someone counting. One voice had sounded Hispanic, and the other, well, his dialect sounded very strange. She tried to connect a voice with a face for the other male voice she had heard, but Jack's face was the only face her mind would see.

She heard the wooden door creak again. A moment later, she heard a door or something open at her feet. A pair of hands grabbed her ankles and began to pull. She felt a hard ridge pass beneath her back. It tore at her skin again, and her muscles tightened in pain as her feet were suddenly jerked into the air. In an instant, her body was snatched feet-first and she fell three feet downward.

Again, her head hit first; then her shoulders and her back. She thought for sure that her skull had been cracked. She saw flashes of light before her eyes as the air rushed from her lungs like a smithy's bellows. She tried to open her mouth as she struggled for a breath of air but the duct tape held it closed.

She tried to kick her legs, fighting for a breath of air, but couldn't. Her feet hadn't been dropped with the rest of her body. They were still held high in the air. Someone yanked her feet hard and dragged her for a short distance, over another ridge that tore at her back again. Her raised feet were turned to the left and she was tugged a short distance farther; then her feet were dropped and she was left alone for a time.

Slowly she began to get air back into her lungs. Her head began to clear some and it stopped spinning so violently.

A hand touched her shoulder, causing her to jump as a muffled voice asked, "Do you have to use the toilet?"

Wendy eagerly nodded, for she felt like her bladder was about to burst but hadn't thought of it until it was mentioned. Now, it was all she could do to keep from wetting on herself.

The tie-wraps were cut from her ankles and she could feel a tingling as the blood began to circulate freely again. Someone grabbed her by her shoulders, helped her stand and began leading her.

"Just walk where I lead you," the muffled voice ordered.

For the first few steps that Wendy took, her feet felt numb and she would have fallen if not for the hands at her right and left supporting her. But with each step, the feeling slowly began to return to her feet.

A muffled voice said, "Wait while I unlock the door." Then, a sound that Wendy believed was a deadbolt.

"Well, what's the problem? Open it," another muffled voice asked.

"It's stuck," a muffled voice answered.

"Kick it!" the other voice ordered.

Wendy heard the kick that was applied to the bottom of the door and felt the fresh air on her face when it opened.

The hands that helped to hold her upright urged her forward again. It was still difficult for Wendy to walk the hands kept her from falling, hands that more or less dragged her from the cabin and to an outhouse behind the cabin.

Wendy could tell where she was just by the odor. It had been long ago, but her nose remembered.

"Wait outside," a muffled voice said and Wendy heard the wooden door and hinges creak. Her uniform trousers were unfastened and pulled down to her knees along with her panties. She hoped the person helping her was the woman, but at the time, it didn't really matter.

Afterwards, she was helped back to the cabin and placed in the same room where she had been. The handcuffs were removed; she was placed in the sitting position at the foot of a bunk bed and tied—hard and fast—to the corner post of the bed.

Wendy heard footsteps as they walked away. One set fell heavily on a hollow-sounding surface that she believed had to be wood. They made a tapping or clicking sound like the metal taps on a dancer's shoes. The other set fell softly, almost daintily, as if the feet wore gym shoes or were bare. The soft-falling feet belonged to the woman who had helped her to the outhouse.

Some time passed, but Wendy didn't know how long because everything seemed to be all jumbled up. She heard the soft footsteps approaching her. Someone touched her arm and she jumped in response. The person began to rub Wendy's arm and Wendy knew what was about to happen. She tried to move away, and began to beg behind her taped lips, "Please don't do that again. Please! What do you people want?" But her pleas were only mumbles as the burning needle was pushed into her arm.

"You bastards!" she sneered beneath the tape.

The soft footsteps walked away and soon she heard two muffled voices, but Wendy couldn't make out what was being said. An engine started and she heard a crushing or cracking sound. Not like the sound rock or gravel made when a vehicle's wheels roll on them, but kind of like the sound she remembered hearing when she parked her car under the oak trees at work.

The wooden door opened and shut again. Wendy heard the soft footsteps again, but no one spoke. She was left alone with only the sound of her heart pounding in her ears. She was exhausted and frightened, very frightened. Her eyes grew very heavy and her tired, sore body seemed to float. Soon, all the pain was gone and she was unconscious again.

***

A plume of red dust followed a white Ford pickup truck as it rattled along, headed due west on Metcalf Road. Sunday church services were just ending when it passed through the little sawmill town of Metcalf, Georgia, located on a narrow county road about ten miles south of Thomasville.

Metcalf Road connects Metcalf and Beachton, Georgia. Beachton is a little community on US-319 twelve miles southwest of Thomasville and about halfway to Tallahassee, Florida. Unless you had a detailed map of southwest Georgia, it is doubtful you would find either of the small towns.

The road between Metcalf and Beachton was made of hard-packed red clay and lined with huge water oaks and tall virgin pines. Most of the land on both sides of the road had been plantation land for the past 200 years or more. Very little of it was still farmed, as it was in olden days; it was used now mostly as private hunting preserves.

Except in a few spots, little, if any, underbrush grew below the stands of pines nor were there many fallen limbs or dead trees. The pristine forests were maintained for the sole purpose of bobwhite quail hunting.

The old truck slowed and turned off the road. It stopped at an iron gate and was engulfed by the red cloud of dust. A moment passed and a man got out of the passenger side, coughing and waving his hand in front of his face. He unlocked the gate and the truck drove past him and stopped. The gate was closed and locked and the truck continued down a narrow-rutted road into the pines.

The road was used primarily during quail hunts for a mule-drawn hunt wagon that carried hunters and their hunting dogs. It meandered through the pines for about a mile and a half, passing through small half-acre plots of brown-topped millet, sorghum and small fields of drying corn stalks that had been planted to serve as blinds and bird-feeding areas. The old truck rattled along the trail with the side of its rusted bed swinging back and forth.

The road gently fell downward to a muddy branch, and a muddy trail continued beyond it for about 300 yards up a small hill toward a thicket of four or five majestic, moss-covered oaks. A small two-room cabin of rough-cut lumber sat in the center of the oaks. The cabin looked old and was one of many scattered throughout the plantation. The families who once worked the fields had lived in the cabins, but now they served as shelters for the hunters in case bad weather or the wagon ride was too rough for them. Some of the cabins were equipped with electricity and plumbing, but this particular cabin had neither.

An old outhouse stood sentinel about a hundred yards behind the cabin as if in defiance of modern times.

A wooden box-like enclosure of weathered heart pine remained around the deep earthen hole of a long abandoned well about twenty-five yards behind the cabin. An eight-inch square oak cross member hung above the well. A large rusty metal pulley and rope still hung as if in contempt to the hand-operated pump that protruded from the earth ten feet away.

The old well, unused for years, had a collection of discarded items at its bottom and only a small amount of water remained. It was only enough to breed mosquitoes, as well as being a haven for spiders and other crawling creatures.

Even though the weather had been extremely dry, the branch that crossed the road was filled with green, stagnant water. It was fed by a natural spring a short distance to the west. The road was passable through the mud, but only by four-legged mules or four-wheel-drive vehicles. The spinning wheels of the four-wheel-drives had caused the branch to become a foul-smelling mud hole. The old Ford wasn't a four-wheel-drive, so it stopped at the mud hole.

Two men staggered out of the pickup, and while one sat on the front bumper, the other leaned against the left fender. Both removed their boots. They seemed somewhat hesitant to enter the stinking bog. Both were laughing as one tried to force the other into the mud. Finally, both men stood at attention, soldier-like, and marched forward into the mud until they stood knee-deep. Both men held their boots high in one hand and a brown whiskey bottle in the other.

One of the men was an average height and build with his hair in a ponytail. The other was short, squat and bald as an onion. One was Hispanic, one was Cajun and both were very drunk and very loud. They staggered through the mud laughing and cursing in their own language or dialect each time either sank into the murky depths of the stinking gray-green mud.

Soon, one man fell; then the other. They crawled the rest of the way to the other side of the mud hole and pulled themselves out. Their language was the only distinguishable difference, for both looked like melted Claymation figures.

They stood laughing and pointing at each other. The only parts of their bodies that weren't covered with mud were the whites of their eyeballs, and the hands that held the whiskey bottles. The boots were as muddy as they would have been if they had been worn. The men saluted each other with the bottles and took a long drink.

Suddenly, a rifle shot rang out and the bottle in the fat one's hand exploded. Both men jumped backward and landed back in the middle of the mud hole. They held their muddy boots high in the air and began to curse as they stomped out of the mud. The Cajun-sounding one cursed in his unique French/English patois, the Hispanic in his broken Mexican/English. The Cajun still held his bottle of whiskey and it was still free of mud.

The fat one yelled, "*Perra! Condenar perra!* You beech!" as he kicked at lumps of wet mud in the ruts of the road. He looked at the neck of his bottle, still held tightly in his hand, and repeated, "*Condenar perra*! Beech!" and threw the short round piece of brown glass in the direction of the cabin.

The cabin door opened and a woman came outside. She stood laughing with her right hand holding the muzzle of a rifle and its butt resting on her hip. She was a large-framed woman, almost the size of a large man.

The long scope on the top of the rifle barrel reached nearly to the front sight. She slowly raised the rifle and sighted down the road at the muddy men, causing one muddy figure to jump left and the other to jump right. She lowered the rifle, laughed, turned, and went back into the cabin.

The two men picked up small, hardened lumps of mud from the roadway and threw them in the direction of the cabin. The fat one kicked at a dried lump with his bare foot, and immediately dropped his boots, letting out a howl. He lifted the foot into the air with his hands and hopped around on the other like he was riding a pogo stick while cursing in an unintelligible language. The other man, with the ponytail, laughed and drank from his bottle, the bottle he refused to share with the fat one.

After more cursing from both men, they continued up the hill toward the cabin. Marble-sized, hard, sharply pointed acorns were hidden under a carpet of brown leaves that covered the ground around the cabin. The two men looked like they were walking over hot coals.

"Ouch! Ouch! Oh wee! Ouch! Shit!" Their words echoed off the front side of the cabin.

Moss hung from a low U-shaped limb of one of the ancient oaks. The one with the ponytail, the Cajun, tore some moss from the limb and began wiping the mud from his face, then his feet. Onionhead, the Mexican, unzipped his pants and began to urinate in the direction of the cabin while pointing his finger down toward his penis, and yelling in broken English, "*Perra*, I brought for you a *pequeno don*. No, no...it is a *mucho grande presente* for you. Come, *senorita*, come see this *grande serpiente*."

The door of the small cabin began to open and the Mexican attempted to run across the acorns to the safety of a moss-covered oak.

"Ouch! Ouch! Oh wee! Shit!" he yelled as he peed all down the front of his trousers, washing away some of the mud from his feet.

The woman came out of the cabin without the rifle and disgust showed on her face. She pointed toward her half-open mouth, exposing a yellow object with a dime-size hole in the middle like the mouthpiece of a football player. A fat muddy head peeked from behind the oak followed by a stumbling, fat, muddy body. He bent down, picked up some acorns and leaves and threw them at the woman while cursing every breath. The woman stepped to one side and the acorns peppered the wall beside her. Some of the acorns went through the open door and into the cabin.

The fat one took a muddy, yellow object from his front pocket and looked at it. The Cajun withdrew another from his pocket and poured whiskey on it to wash away some of the smelly mud. The fat one extended his mouthpiece toward the Cajun, but he only pointed a finger at the fat one's penis, and said, "Water already you got," then turned his back and laughed.

The fat one threw his mouthpiece on the ground in anger and it landed in a small puddle of urine. He began cursing again with his penis still hanging out of the front of his trousers.

The woman reached behind her back, retrieving a nickel-plated 44 magnum from the waistband of her jeans. Her thumbs pulled the hammer back as she brought the sight to bear on the fat one's muddy forehead. To the fat one, the barrel looked a foot long with a bore the size of a hotdog wiener. Instantly, he grabbed the mouthpiece from the ground and crammed it into his mouth—mud, pee and all.

She held the large pistol in a double-handed grip. "Mex," she said very slowly in a muffled voice. "And, you too, Cage. Y'all listen very, very carefully. If either of you morons say another word without them yellow things in your mouths, I will blow your fucking heads off. Is that absolutely clear?"

Mex didn't utter a word but stood grinning, showing the yellow mouthpiece in his mouth and a naked, muddy penis hanging from his fly. His head and his penis bobbed up and down in acknowledgment. Cage was nowhere to be seen.

Wendy was somewhere between awake and asleep when she heard the rifle shot. She was very drowsy at first but soon her head began to clear. Her head felt as if someone was beating it with a large sledgehammer. She tried to move but she couldn't. She was sitting in the floor upright with her back against the foot of one of the bunk beds. Her wrists were still tied with hard plastic tie-wraps to the rough four-by-four legs of the bed; the black hood was still draped over her head; and the tape still across her mouth. Another tie-wrap was around her neck and fastened to a picket at the foot of the bed. Her legs were spread apart and her ankles were tied to the post of another bunk bed that had been moved directly in front of where she sat.

If she tried to move, the sharp edges of bonds cut into her flesh. She found this out the hard way when she tried to bent her knees. Evidence of the struggle showed in the blood around the tie-wraps at her ankles. She now sat almost motionless except for a slight uncontrollable trembling of her body.

She thought it was late Saturday afternoon, but it was actually a day later. There was very little she could recall about the past twenty-four hours, only vague memories of being taken to the outhouse a few times.

As time passed that afternoon, Wendy became a little more aware of what was going on. She could see sunlight through the black fabric mesh of the hood. She had heard un-muffled cursing and talking outside following the gunshot. They were the only un-muffled voices she had heard up to that point, but they were too far away for her to hear what was said. She thought one was the same Hispanic sounding voice that had counted, but she couldn't be sure. Her mind seemed to be in a haze. The other voice was a laughing voice. Wendy didn't think it was the same person who laughed when her house started to burn. She now believed the group who held her numbered at least four.

She was sure one of the people who brought her to the cabin and helped her to the toilet was the woman who had spoken when her house was burned. She believed her soft fingers had rubbed her arm before the shots of the drugs.

Wendy had heard the names Mex and Cage spoken outside, and heard someone say *senorita*. She tried to recall everything that had happened to her and ran them through her mind over and over. She didn't want to forget anything.

Her body ached and was bruised badly. She had been thrown into the vehicle at her house like a sack of potatoes. However, her body didn't hurt outside as much as it hurt inside. She was heartsick, wondering where Jack was and remembering their dream home put to the torch. Her insides felt like they had been torn out. Everything they had was in that house.

Wendy was terrified, terrified not only for herself but also for Jack. Where was Jack? Why had the one she believed was the leader asked about him being at home? Why did they burn their home? These questions and many more crowded into her cloudy, confused mind and nothing made any sense.

"What do they want with me? Why do they want Jack, too?" she mumbled.

Soon, the woman and Mex entered the cabin. Mex stepped on an acorn that he had thrown into the open cabin door and his cursing snapped Wendy back to reality; then she heard his muffled voice say, "My little *palone*, I am here. Your *hombre* is home."

Wendy heard sandy footsteps approach her and stop close by. A hand grabbed at her breasts, squeezing and mashing them hard against her chest. Rough fingers pinched and twisted a nipple through her shirt. She moaned with pain.

"Oh, you like! You love!" the laughing muffled voice of Mex said and violently pinched and twisted her flesh, again.

The sound of Mex's laughter sent chills of fear down Wendy's spine. Old hurting memories were awakened. Memories her mind had tried to shut out for many, many years.

Suddenly, Lester's face flashed before her eyes. She tried to wiggle, to move her body away from his wicked touch, but she was helpless, helpless the same way she had been long ago when her stepfather's heavy hands restrained her.

Her private places were being touched again, the private places little boys mustn't ever see. She suddenly became sick to her stomach and began making gagging sounds behind the tape over her mouth. She swallowed hard and fought to keep from vomiting. Bitter tasting bile flooded into her mouth from an empty stomach.

Mex's face drew near to her ear, and his mouth touched the fabric of the hood. She could smell his foul-smelling breath. She felt like someone had dunked her body into a cesspool. Lester's face flashed before her eyes again.

Mex hissed Spanish words mixed with English and laughter into her ear. She didn't listen to the words. She didn't have to. She had heard the same words before, words whispered by her stepfather, words she hadn't understood, those evil-sounding words that had frightened a little girl, those intimidating words threatening to kill her mother.

The unmistakable scent of urine permeated the black hood and surrounded Wendy's body. Lester was near, for she could smell his scent. He had crept into her room again in the darkness. She could smell his foul-smelling whiskey breath. His loathsome odor filled her nostrils like a serpent's cold breath.

Mex's wicked-sounding laughter sent waves of fear through her body, dredging up old memories from the depths of her soul. Tears ran from her eyes and caused the black hood to cheeks, yet no sound came from her frightened insides. She tried to turn her head away from the repulsive smell. She tried to turn her face from Lester again, but her head was snapped back by a heavy slap across her face, causing her to bite her tongue, the tie-wrap around her neck cutting into her flesh.

The laughing voice left Wendy's ear and towered somewhere above her. She heard the "clicking" sound and thought it was the sound of a tie-wrap, but it was the zipper of Mex's trousers.

Blood oozed into Wendy's mouth, and its taste reminded her of the taste of her mother's blood. It brought back the hurt of the night blood spotted her mother's pretty yellow blouse. She could taste her mother's blood again.

Her ears rang a hollow sound within her skull, awakening the headache again while the lingering smell of urine awoke the anger and hate. Her body shivered—it felt dirty—it felt defiled. She tried to draw her knees upward to hide her body from Lester's stare, but the tie-wraps cut into the flesh of her ankles and blood dropped to the floor beneath them.

She was a child again, surrounded by adults who could do whatever they wanted. She was someone's possession.

The blood began to run freely from the torn skin at her neck and she could feel it trickle between her breasts. The pain of reality began to clear her mind. Now one of the muffled voices had a name and a scent. She would remember him as she remembered Lester. For in her mind, it was Lester who touched her. The one who held a frail little girl down on the bed and pushed a finger into her body. The thought of his loathsome touch again burned inside like a hot iron branding the anger and hatred into her heart, anger and hatred so intense, it began to block out everything happening to her.

More hurting episodes of her life flashed before her eyes, one at a time. Each added more weight to one side of giant balancing scales, the measure of her life. She was a little girl once and couldn't fight back, but now, if she was ever freed, she'd fight back. She'd get even with Mex; she'd even the score with Lester.

Mex held his erect penis in his still muddy hand and began to masturbate. The woman's voice behind him yelled, "Mex! You sick bastard! Get the fuck out of there!"

Mex quickly returned his penis to his trousers, turned and left the room while zipping his fly.

Wendy heard the woman's voice and the f-word. She also heard another laughing voice, one of the same voices she had heard outside the cabin though she couldn't discern the third person's nationality. She had heard the others call him Cage. She was sure his was the other voice that had counted, "One—two—three." He spoke English but it was a form she didn't think she had ever heard.

Suddenly, Wendy heard footsteps of more than one person entering the room. A hand touched her arm and she jumped, causing tie-wraps to cut into her skin. The soft fingers of the woman rubbed her upper arm, and Wendy began to beg through the tape, "No! Please don't, please!"

"Shut up, bitch!" Cage's muffled voice boomed inside the room; then he stomped down hard on Wendy's left thigh with the heel of his western-style boot. Wendy moaned in pain as a giant charley horse rose underneath her trousers.

"Give to me that thing!" his deep sounding voice echoed inside the tiny room.

"No, Cage!" the other muffled voice yelled but to no avail.

Cage grabbed the hypodermic from the woman and plunged the needle deeply into the muscle of Wendy's thigh where he had stomped. The long needle hit the bone and pain cut through her body like a knife. She screamed behind the piece of duct tape and tears ran from her eyes.

Wendy added another name to her list: Cage.

***

Her captors soon left the room and Wendy's head began to swim. The drugs soon made the pain in her body slowly subside. She knew she would be out soon and began to work her right wrist, trying to free herself. That side was away from the area she heard the others most of the time.

She could hear their voices in the other room. She heard the woman's muffled voice say, "He's gonna be pissed when he finds out what y'all did to her today. He told you two not to put your hands on her. He's gonna be mad, and you two had better look out. He's acting very strange. I think he's lost his fucking mind. He acts like a crazy man."

"If he finds out," Cage replied, "You told him. If my ass he gets, your ass I gets, aye-e!"

A few moments of silence, and Wendy heard the woman say, "Did you see him in town this morning?" Wendy listened but didn't hear anyone reply.

"Did he tell you anything?" the woman asked.

Wendy heard Cage reply, "Shore."

There was another short pause in the conversation. Wendy felt herself drifting into unconsciousness again. She bit down on her tongue to keep from going to sleep and heard the woman say, "Well, Cage, what in the hell did he tell you?"

Mex answered, "He say us not get borracho." Cage and the woman stared at Mex, and he added, "Drunk, drunk, not get drunk." Mex and Cage laughed.

Cage added, "Dat too damned late, dat is." Mex and Cage continued to laugh.

After Mex and Cage's laughter quieted some, Wendy heard the woman ask, "Anything else? Did he tell you anything else? Come on guys, it's like pulling fucking teeth to get an answer out of you two."

"Here for us to stay until finished he is with her," Cage answered. The woman was learning to understand him better, but his dialect still sounded phony to her.

"Did he say how long? Did he say what he was going to do with her?" the woman asked.

"Nope," Cage answered, paused, and added, "He say, dat one tough bitch in yonder, she is. Might a long time take, maybe, aye. Maybe we all will have some fun, aye." Cage reached his hand out and pushed on Mex's shoulder. Both men began to laugh again.

Wendy's head fell forward and caused the tie-wrap to cut into the skin of her throat again. The sharp pain kept her awake a little longer. Her mind seemed very cloudy and she fought to keep her senses. She heard the woman's voice speaking again and it sounded far, far away.

"Well, if we're stuck here together, you two get out of here and wash that stinking shit off. Go out back to that pump and wash. Mex, you smell like fucking piss. Get the hell out of here. Both of you," the woman said.

The smell of the two men wasn't the real motive behind the woman's comment. She wanted Mex and Cage outside away from Wendy. Mex and Cage laughed at the woman's statement, and the woman joined in their laughter as she led them out of the rear door of the cabin.

Everything that had happened baffled Wendy. It seemed she became more confused as each event unfolded around her. Her body ached but the anger and hatred she felt inside helped her overcome the pain.

The statement made by Cage was partially true. Wendy Wenslow Jackson was no bitch, but she was tough. That's the way she had been reared. She had to be tough in order to survive. Her captors could shoot drugs into her, hurt her and make her bleed. They could even make tears flow from her eyes, but they would never make her cry.

10
"SILVER-TIPPED BOOTS"

It was late Sunday afternoon before Jack became coherent enough to realize that he was still alive. His tried to open his eyes, but they hurt and his face, head, and hands hurt, as well. In fact, it seemed every inch of his body ached with pain.

First, the right eyelid opened, slowly followed by the left. His eyelids parting felt like the sound a fingernail makes when scraped on a chalkboard. They burned like they were filled with soap; he tried to focus them, but they wouldn't. The pain made him want to close them but he kept them open. Many minutes passed before his vision cleared enough to begin to make out the texture in the ceiling tiles and the fluorescent light fixture above the bed where he lay.

He could feel the two fork-like inserts inside his nostrils and heard a hissing sound. He was aware of each and every breath he took as his lungs expanded and pain ripped through his chest. He slowly rotated his head to search his white-looking surroundings so his hazy vision could help figure out where he was; however, it wasn't his eyes that told him where he was, it was his nose. The smell of the place told him he was in a hospital.

He tried to sit up in the bed, but as his head lifted from the pillow, the room seemed to spin around, so he lay back down for a moment to clear his head. He tried to grab hold of something with his hands to steady himself and try to rise again but they did not seem to work. He raised his arms a little with a struggle and looked at them. He was reassured to see that he still had hands at the ends of his arms, or, at least, there was something where the hands should be. Both hands were wrapped in gauze and looked about the size of soccer balls.

With great difficulty, Jack slowly rose to a half-sitting position, more or less. He paused for a moment, resting his weight on his elbows. His body hurt so badly he thought he would cry. Usually, when he was hurt, had the flu, or just generally felt badly, he called for Wendy. Somehow, she made things all better.

His mind wasn't warned as his heart made his mouth say "Wendy." The sound of her name felt almost soothing to him. Some forgotten, dormant, unused source of strength filled his heart with a warm feeling that caused goose pimples to rise over his body. He remembered the same goose pimples rising on his skin when Wendy answered, "Yes" to his question, "Will you be the wife of this sailor?"

In the silence of that night in his old Chevy, he had cried for the first time in a very long time. Wendy hadn't seen or heard him in the darkness, but he had cried just the same. It had felt good and his happiness had sought out the least point of resistance to escape his heart: his tears.

Jack loved Wendy. He always had, though she had never told him that she loved him. But to Jack, hearing her say those three little words wasn't that important. What was important was the way she made him feel when he was near her. How her hair smelled after she got out of the shower; how she still hid her body from his eyes even after all the years they had been married; how her face had retained all the beauty it had when she was young.

Wendy told her friends about the first time she saw Jack driving her school bus, saying, "He never even noticed me!" but Jack knew that wasn't true. He had noticed her long ago. He remembered the skinny tenth grader who once sat behind him on a school bus. They never talked, but he remembered her. He remembered the strong defiant look that was always on her face, the go-to-hell look that said, "If you want to talk with me, fine! If you don't, that's fine, too!"

However, Jack never knew how much he loved Wendy until he opened his eyes in that hospital room, alone. His body hurt, but not as much as the feeling of loneliness inside his heart. He felt like a little child needing to be comforted by his mother. He felt like he was lost.

"Whoa, old boy," Jack said in a hoarse voice that was no more than a whisper. "You'll fall off the deep end if you don't get a grip on yourself," he said to himself and tried to smile. His inward humor hid the fact that he was very seriously burned and in a very bad state. He wasn't aware that he had spent the first twenty-four hours in the hospital in the intensive care unit. The insides of his lungs were burned badly. But even his badly burned condition couldn't completely hold back the strength he always summoned with his humor.

He straightened his back, pushed hard with his bandaged hands and sat upright in the bed. His shoulders stooped like he was a hundred years old. The pain was excruciating but he was in a sitting position. His skin stretched to accommodate the movement, and his entire body felt like it was covered with burning hot grease yet he wouldn't lie down again.

A cold clammy feeling came over his body and beads of sweat the size of pinto beans popped out on his forehead. The sweat running into his eyes felt like hot wax.

He raised his hand to wipe them, and mumbled, "One hell of a handkerchief," as he looked at the wad of gauze on each hand. He tried to laugh but his chest felt like it was on fire. "You're one sad, sorry looking human," he said and his secret weapon, his humor, began to slowly take control. It had protected his emotions before, and he needed it to rescue him from the pain outside and inside his body.

Painfully, Jack swung his legs over the side of the bed and sat with them hanging. He could almost hear the skin stretch. It was extremely difficult for him to breathe.

The open door to the bathroom was directly in front of him. He didn't realize he needed to urinate until he saw the toilet. He didn't know how he would reach it, but his bladder told him he better try and fast.

The bed was about four feet above the floor and high enough for him to look into the mirror above the sink in the corner of the room. He looked at the reflection of himself—at least, he thought it was Jack Jackson.

His entire head was covered with a greasy gauze-like hood except for holes cut for his eyes and the oxygen tubes in his nose and his mouth. His eyes were as red as his old bloodhound's eyes. For a moment, he thought of Earnhardt and wished he could scratch him behind his ear. He looked at his hands, smiled and felt the skin on his face move in pain.

Jack looked down at his feet as they dangled two feet from the floor, but it may as well have been twenty feet. He knew he needed help.

"Nurse!" he tried to call. His throat felt like he had swallowed a mouthful of chili powder. He tried to call again, but his tongue refused to make understandable sounds. He began to move it around in his mouth to stimulate saliva to moisten his mouth, but there wasn't any.

He tried to pick up the nurse's call button with one hand but couldn't. He wedged the button between his two bandaged hands and finally managed to lift it. He tried to push the call button—nothing. The red light above the bed didn't flash. He raised his hands and tried to push the button with his tongue but couldn't.

Jack tried to improvise. He put the button assembly, about the size of a pack of chewing gum, into his mouth. He moved it around until his tongue found the button and pushed until he saw the red light come on above the bed.

"May I help you?" a female voice asked. Jack tried to speak, but the call button was still in his mouth. While he tried to spit it out, the light went out.

"Man!" Jack grumbled more or less to himself. He waited a few moments, thinking someone was bound to come and check on him, but after five minutes, with his bladder expanding every second, no one came to his rescue.

Jack put the call button back into his mouth and went through the entire process again, but this time, as soon as the red light came on, he spit the button out like a watermelon seed.

"May I help you?" the voice asked again. He tried to talk but his tongue was stuck to the roof of his mouth. He mumbled and moaned a few times, and the light went off again.

"If you want something done, you do it yourself!" Jack grumbled to himself. He was left with two options—either he managed to get to the toilet or he would pee all over everything.

There was a plastic IV bag hanging at the top of a vertical tee-shaped post that stood on the right side of the bed. A plastic tube for the intravenous fluid ran down to his right forearm. A small blue box to monitor the IV fluids was mounted about halfway up the vertical post.

Using both of his wrapped hands, Jack was able to remove the oxygen tube from his nose and the elastic band from around his head. The very next time he inhaled, he knew he shouldn't have removed his oxygen supply for it was extremely difficult and painful for him to breathe. He repositioned the IV tubing tangled around his right arm and began to stretch his right leg toward the floor.

"Pain! Pain! Oh, pain!" he mumbled as he inched closer and closer to the floor.

The thought of holding onto something hadn't crossed Jack's mind until the white hospital sheet began to slide over the plastic-covered mattress of the bed. His speed of descent increased and the blue box began to beep. Soon he was sliding from his lofty perch at a very high rate of speed. He reached out his hands to grab something but they were useless.

"Oh shit!" were the only words he had time to say before his feet met the floor. His knees collapsed immediately under his weight and he fell headlong toward the bathroom. He tried to grab something, anything, to stop his fall, but his hands only waved around mid air and looked like two-thirds of a pawnshop sign.

Somehow, Jack managed to get his left hand in front of him, hoping it would break the fall. His right hand was entangled in the plastic tubing and pulled backward as he fell forward. However, as the floor approached his face at a very high rate of speed, his right arm and hand charged forward, bringing down the IV pole, blue box and all.

His right hand went straight into the toilet like a laser guided it there. Water, which wasn't ejected from the toilet, soaked into the gauze wrapped around his hand like a giant sponge. The IV post lay across his back and the blue box beeped almost as fast as Jack's heart was beating.

Jack took a moment to try to compose himself, and then began the struggle to retrieve his hand from the toilet. It felt like it weighed fifty pounds.

"Pain! Pain! Oh, pain!" he said again.

After a very trying minute or so, he managed to withdraw his hand and get to his feet. He stood before the toilet with nothing on his body that wasn't hurting, trying with all his might just to breathe.

However, even with all that had happened—the pain and the terrible shape he was in—he began to smile. It caused his face to hurt even more, but he still smiled.

There he stood needing desperately to urinate and wondering just how he was to accomplish such a feat. A laugh escaped his burned lips as he looked down at his sorry state. He wore a hospital gown tied in the back with no opening in the front. His hands were even more useless than before—one he could hardly lift, and the other a ball of gauze.

"It's a good thing I don't need to pick my nose!" he said and another laugh escaped, causing even more pain in his chest.

Jack had come far and wasn't to be denied. There was only one sensible solution. As unmanly as it may have looked, he squatted and sat straddling the toilet from the front, facing the wall.

"Well, Jackson, you're on your own," he said with a sigh of relief as his bladder began to empty while the blue box beeped away.

Jack had finished and was sort of bouncing on the toilet seat to shake himself off when Sheriff Young came into the room. He didn't see Jack in the bed but could hear the beeping sound coming from the bathroom and see the end of the IV pole sticking out of the doorway.

"Mr. Jackson?" he called questioningly.

Jack grunted from the bathroom, and the sheriff stuck his head in the doorway about the same time Jack bounced for the last time.

"Son," the sheriff said in his Montana drawl, "What in the world are you doing in there?"

Jack sat with his forehead and both soccer-ball hands against the green tile wall. It looked like he was worshipping a ceramic Buddha.

"Fuck you! I'm trying to take a leak. What does it look like I'm doing?" Jack answered very hoarsely, kind of through his teeth. "Please, get the nurse!"

The sheriff took the wet call button from the bed, held it with two fingers and called for the nurse. Jack motioned with his head for the sheriff to come closer. The sheriff leaned into the bathroom, and Jack said in a whispering voice without looking at him, "Shoot me! Please, Sheriff, just shoot me!"

The sheriff fell back laughing. Still, he knew the situation wasn't funny. He knew Jack was hurting, hurting very badly.

A nurse came to the room almost as soon as the sheriff called. She called for a doctor and began tending to Jack's needs while Jack and Sheriff Young talked. The sheriff helped get him back into the bed, and stood alongside ready to help as the nurse changed his wet hospital gown; then, while she waited for the doctor to arrive, she began to remove the wet bandage from Jack's right hand.

Even the pain he felt couldn't hold back the humor as he recounted to the nurse, in detail, how his bandages got so wet in the first place. The lighthearted way he told the story had her laughing so hard she could hardly work.

Soon the conversation took on a more serious tone. Sheriff Young told Jack all he knew about what had happened. He told him Captain Bill Stanley had died of a heart attack without going into all the gory details. Jack remembered riding to his burning home with Bill, but had no memory of the Captain's heroism. He didn't know his friend had given his life to save him. He was sickened by the news but wouldn't allow himself to grieve. His mind was preoccupied with thoughts of Wendy.

The sheriff told Jack the fire had been arson and that it had destroyed everything on the hilltop except Jack's workshop. The tanker truck from the Thomasville Fire Department wasn't even supposed to have answered the alarm. Jack's home was outside the fire district of the fire station in Thomasville. They answered the alarm in response to the call from the dispatcher at the Justice Center.

The dispatcher was a friend of Wendy's named Linda. They had worked together when Wendy was a guard in the old jail. She knew it was Wendy's house. Jack's workshop and most of the pine thicket were saved from certain destruction by their response.

The scope and origin of the fire and the explosion were such that the local fire department advised the sheriff to call the FBI and the Alcohol Tobacco and Firearms (ATF) for assistance. Agents from both agencies had wasted little time getting to Thomasville.

They had arrived early Sunday morning. In a very short length of time they had learned that some type of oxidizer had been used to accelerate the flames after the fire started. They called the fire an "HTA", meaning that a High-Temperature Accelerant had been used, and believed it was toluene. Toulene is a clear liquid hydrocarbon, obtained from coal tar by distillation. Among its many uses is the production of explosives.

Very little evidence was left at the scene of the fire except for the remains of the propane tank and the C4 plastic explosive.

"That's kind of how one of them HTA fires works, as I understand it," the sheriff told Jack. "It usually leaves no trace of itself after the blaze, or, at least, it only leaves what the arsonist wants us to find."

Sheriff Young knew very little about fires; however, he wasn't afraid to show his ignorance. He had asked questions and scribbled down notes and kept asking until he got answers that he understood. The investigators explained HTA fires for an hour and a half before he understood.

"They tell me that them fires can burn at 5,000 or more degrees Fahrenheit. They burn so hot everything is destroyed, even traces of what started them. Now get this," he said pointing at Jack, "When the fireman try to use water to put them out, the water actually accelerates the flames. The fire is so hot it actually strips the water atom of its oxygen molecules and they too are consumed by the flames."

"I wrote down something they told me," the sheriff added, pulling a small spiral notepad from his pocket. "He said," the sheriff continued, reading his notes, "Some fellow out in California or somewhere out there said that 'Comparing HTA fires to all other arson fires is like comparing a jet plane to a bicycle.'"[1]

Putting the notebook back into his pocket, the sheriff continued, "The investigators from the ATF said the same arsonist who had started the fire at your house probably started the other fires that occurred during the football game. Witnesses of the other fires said that they saw the same kind of whitish flames that we saw at your house. The ATF boys are very much interested in the fires because there had been several fires recently up in Atlanta where the arsonist used a cellular phone and a road flare just like they done here."

"Jack," Sheriff Young said as he placed both hands on the foot of Jack's bed. "We're doing everything that we can to find out what happened, who caused the fire, and most especially,

---
[1] Tallahassee Democrat, October 25, 1993

where Wendy is. We believe the fires and the auto accidents during the football game are all part of the mystery of her disappearance, but we don't know yet how they connect. We'll question everyone at the stadium if we have to, but it's gonna take some time."

"What has happened here in Thomasville will be on the television tonight on Channel 6, WCTV, on the 11 o'clock news. Nurse, will you make sure someone has his television on then?" the sheriff asked.

The nurse nodded her head, and the sheriff continued, "An announcement will also be on the local cable television network on the Public Access Channel for persons who might have seen something out of the ordinary at the game. They'll carry the announcement every hour on the hour beginning Monday morning."

It was a surprise for Jack to learn it was Sunday. Saturday had passed without any recollection.

The sheriff asked Jack if there was anything he needed or he could do for him, and Jack called upon the spark of humor inside that always seemed to get him through tough times.

He laughed, and replied, "I want my wife, my chair and my dog. In that order."

Sheriff Young answered, "Don't worry about Wendy. We'll find her. Your chair, I'm afraid it's vaporized. But as for your dog, Earnhardt's at my house destroying my back yard, trying to dig escape tunnels.

"Damn! I loved that old chair. It fit my old ass just right. All them farts in the cushion probably caused it to burn. Hell! It could have been my chair that exploded," replied Jack, laughing.

Jack's comment about his chair would have made one think he thought more of the chair than the fact that Wendy was missing, but the sheriff was beginning to understand Jack and his safety valve of humor.

As the nurse tended her duties, Jack told the sheriff he would be out of the hospital by the next morning, but Sheriff Young doubted the pledge. He knew Jack was hurt badly but didn't belabor the point.

The nurse didn't need the sheriff's help with Jack. She would have topped the scales at an easy 230 pounds. She tossed and turned Jack's body on the bed like he weighed 25 pounds.

A doctor came into the room shortly afterwards, and the first thing he did was tell Sheriff Young he would have to leave the room. The sheriff asked Jack again if there was anything he needed or wanted him to do, and Jack asked him to call his brother in Texas.

"Try to explain to him what has happened," Jack said.

"Do you want me to tell him to come to Thomasville?" Sheriff Young asked.

Jack replied, "You won't have to tell him that." He told the sheriff that his brother's phone number should be in Wendy's phone index.

"It will take me half the night to find her index in her office. I wouldn't let anyone straighten up in there. I don't want her raising hell at me when she..." the sheriff's words trailed off into silence. Jack saw the outline of the sheriff's Adam's apple move up and down in his throat as he swallowed a few times and cleared his throat.

"I don't, ah, ah," he said, clearing his throat and trying to continue. He turned his face away from Jack, looked toward the window, and began again with a slight tremble to his voice. "Ah... I don't have your way of laughing when I should feel hurt. Wendy means a hell of a lot to the department and me. She was there when I took this job. Wendy and Bill Stanley stood behind me when I didn't know my ass from a hole in the ground. There were many times during the first months when I wanted to tell some of these uppity Thomasville rednecks to kiss my Montana ass, but she wouldn't let me quit."

"It wasn't anything she said in particular, it was more the way she worked. She put her heart, mind and soul into her job while earning just about nothing. Every time I thought about giving up, I'd go talk to her."

"She told me a lot about the way she was raised. That woman's got guts to keep on going day after day after what she has been through. I owe a lot to her and Bill Stanley. Bill Stanley took me under his wing when I entered the Marines and force-fed me what I needed to know to survive."

"Wendy Jackson didn't tell me anything, she showed me what it takes to survive. I don't know where she's at, Jack, but I can tell you one thing, she's a survivor. I'll find her, and not just for you. I'll find her for me, Matthew Young."

By the time his statement was completed, Sheriff Young stood at the window of Jack's hospital room. The trembling in his voice was gone and had been replaced by a tone of steadfast anger. Without looking toward anyone in the room, Sheriff Young turned, lifted his hat from a chair, and walked toward the door.

"Nurse, I'll be at my office for a while in case you need to find me for any reason. Don't forget about the news at 11 o'clock, okay?" He silently left the room.

Jack heard a sniffle and looked to see the nurse blotting at her eyes with a tissue. "You old softy," he said, fighting back his own tears.

"Shut up," the nurse whispered in reply.

The doctor examined Jack. At first, he said he was going to have Jack taken back to ICU, but some persuasion from Jack and the nurse swayed the doctor otherwise. The nurse insisted that she could look after him there in the ward, so he was moved into an isolation room closer to the nurse's station. There, Jack would be near the ones who could help him when he needed them and the isolation would be another precaution against infection. A small table with yellow rubber gloves, yellow masks, yellow hair covers, yellow booties, and yellow paper gowns was placed in the hallway outside the room. Whenever anyone came into the room, the yellow garb had to cover them head to toe. A "NO VIS-ITORS" sign was hung on the door.

The doctor didn't have Jack's right hand wrapped again as it had been before. It wasn't burned as badly as the left. His left hand had areas where the meat had been burned from the bone.

Jack wanted the hood removed from his head, but the doctor said that it was necessary, at least for the night, to prevent him from rubbing his blistered face on the bed linen. Jack protested, but the hood remained. The gauze hood was very uncomfortable, but the other option the doctor gave Jack was less desirable. It was either allow the hood to remain over his head or be strapped to the bed to prevent his turning over and submit to a catheter for his bladder.

The doctor left Jack as soon as he was settled in the isolation room. The nurse soon followed after she straightened Jack's bed for the tenth time.

"The television is already tuned to Channel 6. If you need anything, just push the button," the nurse said as she switched off the overhead light. A different style button was in the new room. "You shouldn't have anymore trouble with it since your hand isn't wrapped."

"It's a good thing I'm right handed," he replied.

"I suppose," she answered. "Is there anything that you want, Mr. Jackson, before I leave?"

"There's a whole lot that I want, like my wife to tuck me in," he said. His voice was so hoarse it was difficult to understand what he was saying.

An injection had made Jack sleepy, but he wasn't asleep when the nurse came back into his room. He was remembering, remembering when he was in Vietnam.

Jack had gotten sloppy, crying, puking drunk one night with some of his boat crew and a college-age girl who was a student at the University of Hue', following the successful completion of an operation on the Perfume River just above Hue' in what was once South Vietnam. Jack's amphibious boat was the YFU-60 and the girl had acted as a pilot to help him navigate up the unfamiliar river.

During the evening of merriment and drinking in a tent in the US Marines' compound to release the tension of the battle, Jack's longing for the nearness of his wife seemed to draw him closer to the girl, who had reciprocated the affections for whatever reason.

The evening culminated with Jack and the girl leaving the tent together.

The next morning, while suffering from a tremendous hangover, Jack tried to remember everything that had happened the night before but couldn't. He believed he had been too drunk to have done anything of a sexual nature but he wasn't sure.

The following day, he asked one of his drinking buddies, the skipper of another YFU, if he had done anything. His friend replied, "I seriously doubt it! You left the tent with that sweet young thing on your arm, but you couldn't have put that thing of yours in with a forked stick."

Up to that moment, Jack had never been unfaithful to Wendy. For weeks afterward, he lay awake many nights wondering whether he and the girl had made love that night or not. And, when he finally slept, he had a nightmare.

In the nightmare, he awoke one morning and was alone. Everyone he had ever known was gone—no note, no nothing, just gone. His wife, or at least the person he thought was his wife, had vanished without a trace. She had left nothing behind that told that she had ever been on earth. He tried to call out her name, but he didn't know whose name to speak. Nothing remained of her except a memory that told him he shouldn't be alone. When someone awoke him from the dream, he was crying and screaming words that weren't words. He was screaming and calling the name of someone who had no name.

He racked his mind for several days, trying to figure out why he wasn't screaming Wendy's name when he was dreaming. It bothered him so badly that he saw a chaplain, who gave him a very straight answer.

"It's simple, son," he said. "If everything was gone, everything that told you that your wife existed, she wouldn't have ever been and wouldn't have had a name. She would never have happened in the first place. How could you have called a name of a person who never existed?"

Jack wondered that night while he was in the hospital if he was having another dream, if Wendy's disappearance had been another nightmare. He began to pray. It was something he hadn't done very much of over the past twenty years or so, but he made a feeble attempt as he begged God to look after Wendy and bring her safely back home. He didn't ask anything for himself, but then again, Wendy was a part of Jack Jackson. The hurt inside needed to be eased more than the hurt outside.

He fought back sleepiness, trying to stay awake until he could watch the news on the television above his bed. He wanted to see the report of Wendy's disappearance but kept nodding off. He was awakened every fifteen minutes or so by someone who looked like a very large redheaded canary when the nurse entered the room to take his vital signs and to ask if he needed anything. Jack quarreled and argued with her each time and threatened to kill her if she woke him again, but fifteen minutes later, she was back again, fluffing his pillow, making him drink water, and fussing like an old mother hen or canary would have done.

Soon Jack was resigned to the fact that he wasn't to be left alone, so he tried to put the pieces together of what had happened. He always enjoyed solving a good mystery movie or a book before it ended. To hold his interest at all, the mystery had to make him think a little in order to figure out the plot. If he was able to figure things out after watching half an hour of a movie, he left the theater, changed the channel or ejected the tape from the VCR.

What was happening wasn't a movie or a book and Jack knew it. He knew he couldn't simply stop what was happening by closing the book, ejecting the tape or leaving the theater. As unreal as it all seemed, he knew it was real, very real.

Nevertheless, Jack looked at his predicament as a mystery movie of sorts, and mentally began trying to figure out the plot by running every recent event through his mind. Things that had happened to him or Wendy were first; then the things she told him about the cases the Sheriff's Department was working, things in the news, anything, anything that might yield a clue, any clue. However, after an hour had passed, his mind seemed not to work, and before long, he was asleep. Not a restful sleep, but sleep just the same.

***

It took Sheriff Young nearly an hour after he arrived at the Justice Center to dig through the boxes in Wendy's office and find her phone index. It was around 8:00 p.m. when he telephoned Jack's brother in Texas. He attempted to explain things to him, but the sheriff didn't know a great deal. Carl Jackson asked many questions some that had no answers. The sheriff detected a lot of anger in his voice and couldn't really blame him for venting it toward him. The sheriff was mad as hell, too, but there was no one he could direct his rage at because he was the one in charge.

Carl told Sheriff Young, "It'll take me at least thirteen or fourteen hours to make the drive if I don't stop to rest. It might take longer because of the Labor Day holiday traffic, but I ought to be in Thomasville around noon tomorrow."

The Sheriff wrote reports of the little he knew and left the office around 11:30 p.m.

***

Just after midnight Monday, a camouflage-painted GMC Jimmy came to a stop in the quiet and nearly empty parking lot outside the emergency room of Archbold Memorial Hospital. No emergency vehicles were backed to the ramp at the double entrance doors.

A hand inside the Jimmy with long bony fingers reached and lifted a black western hat from where it had rested atop the cellular telephone in the floorboard. A long lanky leg and foot swung out of the opened driver's door, and the heel of a black western boot made a "tap!" sound as it fell upon the black asphalt pavement. A gritting sound followed as the heel turned counterclockwise and the driver's other leg swung out of the open door and made another "tap!" as the heel of the right boot fell beside the left.

The black western hat made a wide sweeping movement and came to rest atop a head that rose a few inches above the cab of the raised four-wheel-drive vehicle. Its silver band seemed to glide along the top of the Jimmy with a "Tap! Tap! Tap!" sound as if it walked alone.

The tall spindly frame of a man came into view around the rear tailgate of the Jimmy, wearing camouflage coveralls and carrying a small green canvas bag, what was known as an AWOL bag in the military. An insignia on the side of the green canvas bag read "United States Army".

The man walked toward the emergency entrance with his head held downward, looking at his feet. The toes of his black western boots were tipped with silver. The two halogen lights above the emergency room ramp reflected from the toes of his boots and cast lines of light on the weeping mortar facade of the building.

Jack's isolation room was on the fifth floor, about eight good steps north from the west exit door of the visitor's elevator. The elevator had two doors. They opened to either east or west, depending on the selection made by the passenger. The elevator and nurse's station were on a sort of island with the elevator being at the extreme south end and the nurse's station at the north end. Two patient wings ran east and west or right and left from the nurse's station like the cross of a "T."

When the west elevator door opened, the only person visible in the hallways, or anywhere else outside the patient's rooms, was a nurse's aide at the desk inside the nurse's station. She was busy charting patient vital signs taken throughout her shift that had ended at midnight. The remainder of the oncoming and outgoing nursing staff was in the nurse's lounge in "report".

The man, clad in camouflage and looking to be about forty or forty-five years old, stuck a small wedge-shaped piece of wood into the narrow upright gap between the elevator door and the outside door frame. He looked to his right and up the hallway, exited the elevator and walked on the balls of his feet to the table outside the door of Jack's room. He picked up two complete sets of yellow clothing and crept back down the hallway to an equipment room to the left of the elevator.

Less than a minute later, he came out of the equipment room rolling a wheelchair, dressed in the yellow outfit and wearing surgical gloves. The first few steps he took on the tiled concrete floor of the hallway, a dull "Tap!" was heard. He immediately shifted his weight to the balls of his feet again and crept up the hallway to Jack's room.

Jack was asleep when the man rolled the wheelchair into the room and closed the door afterwards. The room was very dimly lit. He stood at the foot of the electrically controlled bed, depressed the petal and the bed began to lower. He wiggled Jack's foot until his eyes opened.

"What in the hell do y'all want now? I could get more sleep laying in the middle of Jackson Street!" Jack exclaimed with a weak but disgusted tone to his voice.

"X-ray, Mr. Jackson. Gonna take some nice pictures of your chest," the man's voice drawled.

"X-rays?" Jack asked, puzzled. "How are you going to take me down to x-ray when I'm suppose to be quarantined or something?"

The man laughed a fake-sounding sort of laugh and replied, "We have to put this yellow suit on you, sir."

Jack asked, "Don't they have one of those portable things on wheels they could just roll up here?"

The bed reached as low as it would go. The man came from the foot of the bed with a metal chart in his hand and picked up the yellow things from the chair. He then dropped the chart on the seat of the wheelchair and replied, "Mr. Jackson, I'm just doing what I was told. If you don't want to put on this stuff; then call the nurse. It don't really matter to me one way or the other. I'd rather go back down to transportation and watch David Letterman, anyway."

Jack just shook his head, and said, "No, that won't be necessary. I'll go peacefully." Then, he rose to a sitting position very, very slowly and eased his feet over the side of the bed. "Let's get this over with so I can get some sleep."

Jack managed to put the yellow outfit on with the man's clumsy help. It stuck to the greasy ointment smeared on his arms and chest.

"Before they try to take this yellow shit off, order me a double shot of morphine," Jack said when the dressing was finished.

The man laughed the same fake-sounding laugh again, and Jack added, "Can I take this greasy hood off my head?"

The man picked up the metal chart, opened it, closed it, and replied, "It don't say you can, so you can't."

"Figures," Jack answered as he rose from the bed with the man's help and was seated in the wheelchair.

The man laid the metal chart in Jack's lap, opened the door, looked toward the nurse's station, and pushed Jack hurriedly out of the room, down the short hallway and into the elevator. He reached up and pulled the wedge of wood out of the crack and the door closed.

Jack glanced over his shoulder, and asked, "I thought they gave y'all a key for that?"

The scent of the air inside the elevator suddenly changed. Jack was about to ask what the smell was when a wad of cotton was clamped over his nose and mouth, and a bony arm surrounded his body and held him firmly against the back of the wheelchair. Jack fought, but only a little, for he was very weak. In seconds, he was unconscious.

The elevator door soon opened and the man pushed the wheelchair out into a vacant hallway on the first floor. Across the hallway from the elevator was a waiting room used for the families of patients in surgery. The wheelchair was pushed into the room and the door closed.

The man pulled another pair of camouflage coveralls, a pair of boots, and a baseball cap from the AWOL bag he had left there before taking the elevator to Jack's room. He removed the yellow attire from himself and Jack, and then dressed Jack in the coveralls and boots.

He adjusted the plastic band of the baseball cap to its maximum size and tried to place in over the gauge hood but the bandages were too large. So, taking a large hawk-blade knife from his pocket, he removed the plastic adjustable band from the cap, and then put the cap on Jack's head.

He folded the knife and threw the plastic strap, the metal chart and the yellow clothing into a waste paper basket before he wheeled Jack into the hallway and to the emergency room exit. The "Tap! Tap! Tap!" from the heels of his boots was the only sound that echoed down the deserted corridor.

When Jack was wheeled out of the emergency room doorway, two men dressed in white clothing stood just outside, smoking cigarettes. The wheelchair chauffeur nodded his head at the two men as he passed them and kept his head lowered and cocked to one side with the brim of the black hat concealing his eyes and most of his face.

One of the smokers nodded his head in return and asked, "Hunting accident?"

Without looking up, the man with the black hat replied, "Yeah," as he began to push the wheelchair down the ramp.

"What's with the surgical gloves? HIV?" the smoker asked.

The man replied, "Yeah." Then he rolled the chair to the Jimmy, put Jack in the passenger side and walked back to the ramp with the empty wheelchair and his head down. The lights reflected from his silver tipped boots into the smokers' eyes.

One of the smokers started down the ramp and said, "I'll take that wheelchair for you. Nice boots."

The man pushed the chair toward the smoker and said, "Thanks." He wheeled around on his heels and walked back to the Jimmy. Soon he drove from the parking lot and was gone.

***

Sheriff Young had just gone to sleep when the call came from the hospital. When he was told Jack Jackson was missing from his room, he first thought Jack had made good on his pledge to be out of the hospital by Monday morning. However, after he thought about it for a moment, he discarded the idea. He knew Jack wasn't in any kind of condition to leave the hospital on his own.

The sheriff arrived at the hospital around 2:00 a.m. The Thomasville City Police had already conducted a search of the hospital and grounds. The sheriff checked and rechecked the room and talked to the personnel on duty in the ward. The hospital administrator, as well as the off-going shift for the fifth floor ward, were telephoned and requested to come to the hospital. The administrator arrived in fifteen minutes but another hour passed before all the off-going staff arrived.

In the meantime, while waiting for the staff, Sheriff Young began questioning every staff member he could find at the hospital. During the questioning, one of the two orderlies who had been smoking outside the emergency room entrance was found and questioned. He hadn't told hospital security or the Thomasville City Police about the tall skinny man with the black western hat and silver tipped boots because the orderly knew he wasn't supposed to have been where he was when he saw them. It wasn't a designated smoking area.

The sheriff got a description of the vehicle and called dispatch. An alert was broadcast of the Jimmy and its passengers. Also, the sheriff's departments in the surrounding counties and the Georgia State Patrol were alerted. Since Wendy's disappearance was being handled as a kidnapping, the Georgia Bureau of Investigation and the FBI were already in the area. They were notified and given the information concerning Jack Jackson's abduction from the hospital.

***

The noise of a vehicle outside the cabin woke Wendy. She didn't know what day it was or the time of day. Her days consisted of the periods of time between consciousness and the shots of the drug. She only knew it was dark. She heard the wooden door creak and slam, and the "Tap! Tap! Tap!" of footsteps. She saw a dim light through the hood and caught a smell that again woke memories of long ago.

She smelled the odor of a kerosene lamp burning, and instantly she thought of Lester, the shack where they were forced to live, and the second time he came to her in the night. Her head jerked involuntarily toward the light. She didn't want to move, but she couldn't help herself. Fear made her body respond.

"Give her another shot," the muffled voice of a man commanded. Wendy knew it was the same harsh voice that had spoken from behind her before her home began to burn.

"Please don't," Wendy begged.

"By god," the man said, "she can talk." Then, he added in a very angry tone, "Why in the hell ain't she got tape over her mouth?"

"There's nobody here but me. I took it off to give her some water and forgot to put it back. I'll put it back," the muffled voice of the woman answered. Her voice sounded anxious or nervous. Her hand was shaking as she untied the hood, reached under, and gently put the tape across Wendy's mouth again.

"Please don't! Please..." Wendy begged as the tape cut off her words, but begging was of little use. It hadn't helped before, she thought. Her mind began to remember the times in her life when she had been forced to beg, and she bit her tongue to keep from begging again. She tried with all her might to keep her mind from slipping back to her old memories, but she couldn't help herself. The drugs left her with little will of her own.

A moment passed, and the woman said, "Why are you giving her this stuff? She can't go nowhere. What are you going to do with her? She'll be a ..."

Wendy heard the voice trail off; then heard a slap and the sound of glass breaking. Wendy didn't know what glass object had broken, but she knew the sound of a slap. That sound had been branded on her memory.

"Don't you question me!" the man's muffled voice jeered.

The woman was forced back some, and as she rubbed her jaw, he continued, "And the next time I tell you to do something, you better damn well get it done! The next time it might not be just a slap you get!" the man's voice said in a very harsh tone.

Wendy didn't hear the woman answer. She heard the woman's soft steps approach and heard her sniffling as she knelt at her side. Her hand was trembling as she rubbed Wendy's upper left arm and whispered, "This arm's all banged up. I'll put it in the other."

Wendy felt the motion of the air change as the woman stepped over her outstretched legs as she moved to her right side.

"What are you doing in there?" the man yelled.

"That arm's black and blue," the woman answered.

Wendy could hear the fear in the woman's words. She knew what words spoken in fear sounded like, too. The woman's hand shook as she rubbed the muscle of her arm and pushed the needle into the flesh.

Wendy felt her consciousness begin to slip away almost before the needle was withdrawn. She heard the "Tap!" of the man's footsteps as he walked in the other room. It sounded like he was walking inside a wooden barrel. She heard the door creak, then only silence around her, again fighting the oncoming unconsciousness.

The woman followed the man outside the cabin to the Jimmy. He opened the right side door and the woman saw Jack Jackson inside and slumped to his left side. "What's he..." she began to ask but stopped. She was about to ask what Jack was doing there but thought again about questioning the man and the slap that still stung her cheek.

Wendy could hear voices from outside the cabin but she couldn't make out the words being spoken.

The man removed the yellow mouthpiece from his mouth and answered the incomplete question as he grabbed Jack's ankles and started pulling his feet and legs outside the cab of the truck, "It was on the news that he was in the hospital. It wasn't very difficult to figure out which hospital since there's only one in Thomasville. Finding which room he was in was as simple as stopping at the front desk and asking when I was in town this morning. I called again before I parked the truck in the parking lot and knew he was in one of the isolation rooms on the fifth floor."

"What's that on his face?" the woman asked with the mouthpiece still in her mouth.

"That's how our Mr. Jackson was when I got to his room," the man answered. "Almost like the poor bastard was gift-wrapped and ready for transport. You can remove that mouth piece."

The woman removed it, and asked, "Aren't we going to use these things?"

"No. We don't need them any longer," the man answered as he grabbed Jack, pulling him outside the cab of the Jimmy and tied his ankles together with a long tie-wrap.

"Why?" she asked not thinking until the question was already out of her mouth.

He looked at her with an evil look, and answered, "I've about had it with your questions. You're gonna keep right on until I have to hurt you, aren't you?"

"I'm sorry," the woman replied as she moved backward in a cowardly sort of way. She kept moving until she was out of the man's immediate reach; then added, "I just need to know what's going on."

The man took Jack by the ankles and told the woman, "I'll tell you what you need to know when you need to know it. Here, grab his feet and pull him out of the truck. I'll grab his head."

The woman asked, "Is he gonna wake up before we get him inside?"

"Not hardly," he answered. "I gave him a shot of that stuff on the way here. He'll be out for hours. Besides, he's in pretty bad shape as it is. I would have got him from there yesterday if he hadn't have been in ICU."

"He looks like he's got one foot in the grave," the woman answered. "If he dies on us, we'll be charged with murder. You know that, don't you?"

"He ain't gonna die unless I want him to die," the man snapped. "Now, grab his feet!"

The woman dutifully did as she was told, took Jack's ankles and pulled him from the front seat of the Jimmy. As his head and shoulders were nearly clear of the edge of the seat, the man tried to grab hold but the gauze hood was too slick. Jack's upper body fell to the ground and his head hitting the running board.

"Ouch!" the woman said with a cringing sound to her voice. "That's gotta hurt!"

"He ain't felt a thing," the man replied. "Drag his ass in the cabin."

"How'd you know he was in ICU?" the woman asked about the time Jack's head crossed the threshold of the cabin door.

The man reached down, grabbed Jack by the shoulders of the camouflaged coveralls and lifted him.

"That radio of hers has come in handy. Glad I didn't throw it away," he replied. "Where's Mex and Cage?"

The woman answered, "They're not here," as Jack was dropped on the floor close to Wendy.

They tied him to another set of beds like Wendy was tied. A black hood was placed over his already hooded head. The man attempted to put a piece of duct tape across Jack's mouth, but the tape wouldn't stick. He cursed and hit Jack hard on the side of his head in frustration. Jack never felt a thing.

Wendy wasn't unconscious yet, but she faked it by leaning her hooded head to one side as much as she could without the tie-wrap cutting into her neck. She heard the blow to Jack's head and the un-muffled voices of the man and the woman talking, but nothing made any sense to her.

"Where did you say Mex and Cage got off to?" the man asked as he walked into the kitchen area following the woman.

Hearing his un-muffled voice again surprised Wendy. She tried to listen but the drug finally took effect and she drifted into unconsciousness before she heard the woman answer, "I didn't."

The woman placed the lamp on the small table in the kitchen and walked to the potbellied stove in the corner. The man pulled a chair from the table, sat, and asked, "Well? Are you going to tell me where they are or not?"

"I don't know," she answered. "They left here yesterday afternoon. They were drunk and fell in that stinking mud hole out there. I told them to get the hell out of here and go wash it off. I haven't seen them since. You sure picked a pair when you picked those two—a drunk wet back and a drunk coon ass!"

"Damn it!" yelled the man, causing the woman to cringe as she reached for a coffeepot on the potbelly stove. "Did they go to Thomasville? I told them two not to leave this cabin!" He seemed to hear only what suited him.

He had an expression on his face that wasn't quite a smile. It was more like a smirk as he watched the woman's reactions. She seemed to shrink before his words. He liked the feeling of dominance.

The woman lifted the large coffeepot from the stove and answered with a slight hesitancy in her voice, "They both were drunk as skunks. I'm glad they left. They probably went to the closest place they could find more whiskey. That's across the state line in Florida."

She filled a cup on the table using both hands to handle the big coffeepot. "Coffee's not too old and it's hot. Want a cup?" she asked without looking into the eyes of the man. He stared at her from across the table with a cold look.

When the man didn't answer, the woman put the coffeepot on the table and sat. She sipped the hot coffee and waited for the man to speak. He seemed to be looking straight at her; yet, his blank stare seemed to be looking at something off in the distance, far away.

"No," the man said suddenly replied and caused the woman to jump just a little. His eyes focused on her, and he added, "But I'll take a drink."

The woman laughed a mock sort of laugh, and said, "Well, you'll have to drink water or coffee. What whiskey those two brought with them when they arrived, they drank."

She placed her coffee cup on the table; then added with her voice showing concern, "I'm afraid for her in there when Mex and Cage get back here. Mex was in there with her and he put his hands all over her. He was standing over her and jerking off when I found him in there. Cage came in there when I was giving her a shot. He stomped hard right down on her thigh. Then, the bastard jerked the syringe from me, and drove it deep into her leg. He jammed that long needle all the way to the bone. I told you that needle was too long. That's why I gave her the shot just now in the other arm. I've been real gentle with the shots I've given her but still the muscle of her arm is black and blue."

"I told you!" the man yelled as he jumped up from his chair. The chair fell backwards to the floor. The woman's forearms immediately rose to a defensive posture before her face.

"I told you," he repeated, putting the palms of his hands in the center of the table, leaned toward the woman and yelling into her face, "I told you to keep them two assholes away from her!"

She turned her face away from him, ready for a slap that she believed would soon follow.

"Damn!" the man shouted and slammed his fist down on the table. Most of the coffee in the woman's cup splashed onto the tabletop. The lantern flickered as the man's words echoed in the small room.

He left the table and walked to the door, opened it and stood in the doorway with his hands braced against the upper frame, staring outside into the darkness. Deafening silence came over the cabin for about a minute. The woman sat at the table and tried to drink her coffee. Her hand trembled so she had to put the cup down.

The man spun around on the sharp heel of his boots and looked at the woman with an icy stare. She thought he was about to charge across the room to her. She defiantly lifted the coffeepot and looked at him as if to say, "Come on."

He grinned at her, thinking her demeanor was only a bluff, but if he had charged the table, he would have found out differently.

The man took a few slow cautious steps toward the table, and lifted the overturned chair with the toe of a silver-tipped boot. He saw something in the woman's eyes he hadn't seen before. He wasn't accustomed to that sort of look. She was older than he was by about fifteen years or so. Still, he looked at her in a way that said he was the boss, the master. He knew a confrontation would happen between them, but in his own time.

He sat slowly and pushed a coffee cup toward the woman.

"I think I will have some of that coffee. Any sugar?" he asked. His voice was calm, sounding almost courteous.

She filled his cup and hers and sat the pot slowly on the table, answering, "No, you'll have to drink it black."

She looked at the man with a look of bewilderment. She hadn't expected the sudden mood swing. She took advantage of the moment and asked, "How was I suppose to stop them? You need to be the one who does that."

He lifted the cup from the table and blew slowly into it. He took a sip, and replied, "No, you'll have to take care of it yourself, and I don't care how you do it. I've seen you shoot a gun before. Shoot the bastards for all I care."

He paused for a moment, sipped the coffee, and continued with soft-spoken words, "Just don't let them mess with her. Them Jacksons in there deserve everything I'm going to do to them, but it'll be me who does it. I earned that right. If they touch her again, they can kiss their asses goodbye. Let me rephrase that, sugar. All of you can kiss your asses goodbye."

"I'll keep them away from her," the woman replied, reacting to the threat on her life. "I don't know if I can kill somebody, but they won't touch her again. But I need to know what you are going to do with those two in the other room."

She knew she shouldn't have said it before she finished speaking, but she felt she had to find out what was going on.

The man slammed his fist on the top of the table again, and replied, "I didn't ask you to kill the bastards. Shoot them in the foot, in the leg, in the ass. Just stop whoever tries to touch her."

His answer wasn't what she wanted to know. She wanted to ask him the direct question again but decided to leave it for the time being.

The man removed his hat, and withdrew a large red bandanna from a rear pocket of his camouflaged coveralls. He wiped his forehead; then the inside band of his hat, and said softly, "I told you when I called you to come down here that I had something special planned for her. If they get to her and screw up my plans, I'll deal with those two; then I'll deal with you. Is that clear? Nobody touches her except me. She's mine, all mine. I own those two now and my hand alone will determine what happens to them."

He took a sip of the coffee, and added, "Besides, you'll probably only have to shoot at them to do the trick." He sat the cup back on the table, and continued, "Another thing: keep our guests doped up and gagged. I don't want them talking to each other. How long has she been out after a shot?"

The woman asked, "You mean out cold or just out of this world?"

"What in the hell is that supposed to mean?" he asked.

She replied, "Right after I give her one of them shots, I can lead her around like a puppy. I usually take her to the toilet before it knocks her ass out."

The man looked at her, shook his head, and replied, "Okay, how long is she like that?"

The woman answered, "Sometimes ten or fifteen minutes, then she's out cold. Why?"

The man's face turned red slowly when he heard the why. He polished the silver hat band with the handkerchief, and answered, "Just make sure they're awake around eight o'clock tonight. In the meantime, while she's kind of groggy, like when you're taking her to the toilet, ask her some questions. That doctor I got that stuff from said it could be used like a truth drug."

"Truth drug, my ass. I've been asking her question after question and she hasn't answered one yet, not one. She's not going to tell us anything. I don't think she knows anything. She was only ten years old then," she said.

A few moments passed; then the man said, "What do you mean, lead her around like a puppy? If that puppy you're leading around gets loose, it's your ass. Anyway, it don't matter whether she talks now or not. It would be nice if I knew for sure, but it don't matter. Don't screw around with her until she cracks you over the head. She might be tougher than you think. I've got some business to take care of in town before daylight. In the meantime, keep that tape on her mouth, and keep those two assholes out of that room!"

"I'll be back here just about dark," he added as he left the cabin.

The woman wanted to ask him again what he planned to do, but she held her tongue. She wasn't exactly sure what she was going to do if things turned out for the worse, but she made up her mind not to cause physical harm to the two people in the other room.

11
"THE UNHEEDED CLUE"

Carl Jackson hadn't been off his feet in nearly thirty-six hours. He was a tired man, a very tired man. He had been looking forward to the weekend to relax and catch up on some needed rest. He hadn't had a weekend off in three months.

When he left the refinery late Friday afternoon, he stopped at the first package store and purchased two quarts of his favorite sour mash whiskey. His plan was to get some rest even if he had to drink himself into oblivion, and that's exactly what he did that evening. By 2:00 a.m., one quart was empty and he was passed out on the couch.

Then, at 6:15 Saturday morning, he received an emergency call-in from the boss of the skeleton weekend crew. There was a fire at the refinery near Houston. The call went out for all fire fighters, as well as every off duty man who could be contacted by phone.

Carl was still about half drunk when he reported and took charge of a fire team. It consisted mostly of roughnecks and laborers who had been working at the site. Most of them had started their long weekend like Carl had, and a few were in about the same shape. However, after a few hours in front of a gas and oil fire, most of the alcohol had been sweated from their bodies.

Carl was exhausted and could barely put one foot in front of the other. He was supposed to be a supervisor, but he couldn't make himself hold back and let others do the work. This held true during his regular shifts as well as during the fire. His way of taking charge of the fire party was to be the nozzle-man on the hose.

His body was out of shape and somewhat overweight, but he carried his 215 pounds well. His days of drinking all night and working all day were slowly becoming times of the past.

The blaze raged until sunset Sunday afternoon before the fire was controlled enough to allow some of the tired men to leave. Carl ordered his men home, and his boss ordered him home. As he clocked out, he was reminded his regular shift was only a few hours away.

"Don't fail me now," he said as he threw his hard hat into the back seat and turned the key in the ignition of his old gray Cadillac. The huge engine started with a roar and belched a cloud of black smoke. He put on an old floppy felt hat that lay on the front seat, rubbed the dashboard, which had more gray duct tape on it than original covering, and said, "That's my girl. Now, take daddy home, please."

The stainless steel skin of his Air Stream trailer had long since lost its shine. After his last divorce, the car, the felt hat, and the small trailer were all he had salvaged from the marriage. The house and everything else went to Mrs. Carl Jackson number three, or was it number four?

Since the divorce, he lived alone with a cat. It was a very strange pairing, to say the least, since Carl hated cats. If it had been up to him, he wouldn't have had a cat; however, it wasn't left to him. The big yellow tomcat decided the shiny object was his new home. Besides, he figured the cat had squatter's rights. He was already living in the trailer park when he parked the Air Stream. As it worked out, both seemed perfectly happy with the arrangement, except since the past Wednesday. Carl hadn't gotten much sleep because of the tomcat's noise as he courted the female cat next door.

The fire at the refinery had taken a lot out of Carl. His body was greasy, black, and filthy dirty when he swung a stiff-jointed leg out the car in front of his trailer and slowly rose to his feet. It had been a very long and hard day. His back felt as if it had been welded in the sitting position.

When both feet were planted firmly on the ground beside the car, he moved both hands toward his back. The handle of his coffee thermos was in one hand and the handle of his lunch box was in the other. He pushed both fists into the small of his back, closed his eyes as pain shot from his neck to his heels and began a very painful maneuver to the upright position.

When he unlocked and opened the door of the trailer, the telephone was ringing off the hook. He dreaded answering a phone, especially that evening. He figured it was a call to go back and fight more fires. He answered each ring as he walked toward the kitchen with a stream of phrases showing his indignation:

RING! — "Up yours!" — RING! — "Yo momma!" — RING! — "The shit's deep!" — RING! — "I'm on the throne!" — RING! — "Fuck you!" — RING! — "The bastard's dead!"

He said only "Hello?" as he lifted the receiver of the phone. It was Sheriff Young. Carl Jackson was on the road headed to Thomasville by 9:00 p.m. Texas time, 10:00 in Thomasville.

Adrenaline kicked in and gave him the necessary strength and alertness to drive the first hundred miles or so, but by the time he was halfway across Louisiana, he could hardly keep his eyes open. He finally stopped at an exit on the interstate and bought a soft drink and some fishing snacks, as he and Jack called them: a can of vienna sausage, a can of potted meat, some cheese, and a package of saltines.

He returned to the car, ate, and reached to open the glove compartment. His soot-darkened fingers caressed an old friend, the pint bottle of whiskey.

"I've never taken a drink that I thought I had to have," he said aloud as he removed the cap from the bottle. He turned the bottle to his mouth and took three swallows; then drank some of his soft drink as a chaser. As he replaced the cap, he added, "But I needed that one," and put the bottle back into the glove box.

Carl was soon on the road again and headed east. His eyes soon became so heavy he could barely keep them open. He fought to remain awake until he could get to the next rest area. His head bobbed downward several times and snapped back up before he finally saw a sign indicating a rest area was just ahead. He pulled in and stopped, knowing he couldn't drive another mile until he rested some. He made sure the doors were locked, tilted the power seat back, leaned his head back on the headrest, pulled his hat down over his face and closed his eyes. In seconds he was asleep but only his body, for his mind constantly thought of Wendy and Jack as he dreamed.

Jack was more than a brother and Wendy, more than a sister-in-law. They were his anchoring points in the real world. No matter what he did or where he went, the same two people awaited his return with open arms never asking what, where or how. Once inside their home, he could shut out the world and just be himself.

***

Another person received the news about the Jacksons that Sunday evening, someone not as far away from Thomasville as Texas. It was Tom Wenslow, in Conway.

Usually he would have been in bed and asleep by 11:00 p.m. Sunday evening. Having to be at work by 4:00 a.m. each workday morning put a damper on his nightlife. Being the general manager of the concrete plant meant only that he had to be at work earlier than nearly everyone else to make sure the concrete was ready to load into trucks by 6:30 a.m. each business day. However, since Monday was Labor Day and a holiday, Tom had allowed himself the luxury of staying up late to catch the late news.

The first report he heard was the story about the Jacksons from Thomasville, Georgia. The report included the fact that Wendy had once lived in Conway. Tom was shocked almost to tears; then anger took over. Seven and a half hours later, at 6:30 a.m. Monday morning, he entered the city limits of the South

Georgia town with Emily asleep in the back seat and Bill asleep on the other side of the front.

They stopped at a drive-in restaurant for coffee and a breakfast biscuit; then Tom leaned his head back and closed his eyes for a moment to rest. At almost the same time his eyes were closing, Carl Jackson's were opening at a rest area in Louisiana.

***

By 8:00 a.m. on Labor Day, the investigation was moving forward through the bureaucratic system. The holiday had things in a stagnant condition. The fire investigators had determined that the fire at the Jackson's home and the other fires around town the night of the game were related. The nature and evidence in the debris were the same.

At about 9:30 a.m., the siren of a law enforcement vehicle awakened the Wenslow troop. As Tom rubbed his eyes to clear away the sleep, he saw at least four police cars zoom past the restaurant. He had never been to Thomasville nor had his brother or sister and they had no idea where the sheriff's office was, but Tom said, "I'll bet we'll find it if we follow those sirens."

Tom had never seen as many law enforcement officers in one place as there were when he entered the Justice Center that morning with Emily and Bill in tow. He tried to get them to wait in the car but talking to them was like talking to a stone wall.

It took them nearly an hour to get into Sheriff Young's office to talk with him. The sheriff was polite and cordial as he relayed everything he knew of Wendy's abduction and Jack's disappearance from the hospital. Tom was angered by the scarceness of facts and didn't believe that the sheriff was telling him everything he knew.

"You mean to tell me that this is all you know about all of this?" he exclaimed, leaning forward in his chair.

"I know how you feel, Mr. Wenslow, but at this point, that's all there is," replied the sheriff.

Emily was crying. "Is my sister still alive?" she asked.

Bill put his arm across her shoulder, pulled her to him, and added, "Is there anything in what you've uncovered that suggests that she's okay—a ransom note, a phone call, anything?"

The sheriff shook his head and answered, "I've told y'all everything that we know at this point. Why don't y'all find a motel room and get some rest? There's nothing y'all can do at this point, anyway."

It was about 11:30 a.m. when they left the sheriff's office carrying a map he had drawn showing how to get to the Holiday Inn and to the Jackson's burned home.

***

At noon, a hero's funeral began for Captain William H. Stanley (Master Gunnery Sergeant, United States Marine Corps, Retired). The military funeral included marines from the Marine Logistics Base in Albany acting as honor guards. It seemed every marine from Albany and every police officer in southwest Georgia was present in Thomasville.

"God help the person or persons who caused the death of a Marine and a brother police officer," said Sheriff Young to himself.

***

"Where's the sheriff's office?" Carl's hoarse voice asked the receptionist at the hospital.

His throat was sore from breathing the smoke of the Texas fire and from smoking three packs of cigarettes on the drive to Georgia. He was tired, hungry and didn't want to hear any more from the woman who sat at the information desk. Her endless ranting had been going on for the last five minutes. He looked so much like Jack that she had been caught off-guard and frightened. She knew Jack Jackson was missing from the hospital and that he had been burned badly. Her mind rejected the fact that another soot-faced Jackson was standing in front of her.

Carl couldn't take anymore. "Madam, would you please tell me where the sheriff's office is?" he asked again.

The woman's voice lost all of the anxiousness and apprehension it once had as she answered in an angry tone, "It's out on Smith Avenue, but it won't do you any good to go there, young man!" Then, she stopped talking and turned her face from Carl. She was angry at being interrupted and not allowed to finish what she had been saying.

Carl was somewhat familiar with Thomasville. He knew that Smith Avenue was one of the main arteries. "Where on Smith Avenue?" he politely asked.

"It won't do you any good to go there, young man. Everyone will be at the church for the funeral at noon, in about twenty minutes. You know they had more flowers for that funeral than I ever saw. Why, they had to haul them to the..." the lady replied.

"Thanks," Carl said, stepping on her words. She was primed again. She talked faster than Carl could understand, faster than anyone could understand.

He didn't know where the funeral services were being held, but he remembered that the large First Baptist church was downtown across the street from the old courthouse. When he drew near to it and saw all the cars parked nearby, he knew he had the right place.

His face looked almost ghostly as he walked into the church. He hadn't taken the time necessary to thoroughly scrub the oily black smut from his face before his hurried departure from Texas. The greasy blackness that remained in his eye sockets gave his already haggard appearance a skeletal resemblance.

Carl always felt uncomfortable at funerals, and the funeral for Captain Stanley was no exception. He sat on a pew in the rear and watched a continuous stream of uniformed law enforcement officers enter. He waited until the congregation stood to sing the first song and then left. He could hardly keep his eyes open. He knew he had to keep moving or he would fall asleep.

He didn't know where he should start looking for Jack and Wendy, but he knew he had to start somewhere. He drove out of town headed toward Wendy and Jack's home. He had been there many times in the past few years. He had been with Jack the day construction started on the house. From time to time over the past few years, he returned to help him with little projects like planting grass, pouring cement for the carport, stringing the wire grid for the ivy-covered walk, building an arbor for the grape vine, and dynamiting stumps from where Wendy wanted to plant a kitchen garden.

When he turned his old Cadillac from Summerhill Road onto the lane leading to the house, he had to suddenly stop. A strip of yellow tape was strung across the drive.

The words, "DO NOT ENTER—CRIME SCENE," were stenciled in black along the tape. The word "CRIME" made his temper boil. He couldn't understand why someone, anyone, would want to hurt either Wendy or Jack.

Wendy had always been just like a sister to him. He envied Jack for having a wife like her. He loved her almost as much as he loved his brother. Jack and Carl had always been inseparable. If Carl itched, you could scratch Jack. If Jack got drunk, Carl threw up. If one hurt, both hurt.

Carl got out of his car and approached the tape barricade. A loop was in one end of the tape and had been dropped over the mailbox post. He could have lifted the tape for entry, but he was angry. He drew a buck knife from the leather sheath on his belt, flipped the razor-sharp hawk-bill blade open, and hacked at the tape as if it were the bowels of the person responsible for hurting a member of his family.

He drove slowly up the lane, not expecting the sight that greeted him. The once beautiful home was a scattered pile of black nothingness. He was about halfway up the lane and around the curve when he began to see pieces of charred wood and roofing shingles. The center of the lane had been cleared of the debris, and he followed the cleared path as it turned left; then right, ending about ten yards behind the burned hull of Wendy's car. Another car that Carl had never seen before was parked near the workshop. It was Tom Wenslow's car.

The black, partially burned rubble seemed to be mostly in the front of the house. The sub-flooring was almost completely cleared. It looked as if it had disintegrated in the area of the kitchen. Part of the bathroom plumbing fixtures remained, but other than that, it looked as if someone had swept it with a broom.

Tom stood near the area where the front porch should have been and was looking at Carl. Emily had been emotionally drained and tired, so Tom had taken her by the motel and Bill stayed with her.

At first Tom thought it was Jack, but he knew it couldn't be because the sheriff had told him how badly Jack had been burned.

Whiffs of smoke still rose here and there from the debris in the front yard, and the smell of the fire lingered. Carl knew fire, and what fire could do. What he saw before him was proof enough. However, the fire had burned more than just a house. It had burned dreams and futures. More than a building once rose from that hilltop in South Georgia. Two people's lives once stood there.

Memories began to flood his consciousness but he tried to push them aside. He heard a vehicle approaching up the lane, and saw that it was a Thomas County Sheriff's Department patrol car. It stopped behind Carl's car and a tall, skinny deputy got out.

Deputy Jamerson walked around the back of his car and opened the rear door. Earnhardt jumped out and nearly flattened him. The big red bloodhound's nose went immediately to the ground as if he had been ordered and he began to methodically search the debris all around the yard. He sniffed everything except the places where smoke rose. When he approached the spot in the front yard where Captain Stanley had fallen, he paused for a moment. Suddenly, he lifted his big red head with slobber streaming to the ground and howled the saddest sound Carl had ever heard.

The deputy approached Carl with his hand held out, and said, "That's where the Captain was when he died and where Mr. Jackson was when he was burned so bad. I'm Jamerson, and his name is Earnhardt."

"I know the dog's name!" snapped Carl. "But who's that man over there?" he asked, pointing to Tom.

Jamerson slowly let go of Carl's hand and took a step backward. Ice water couldn't have been any colder than the reception felt by the deputy, but Carl hadn't meant it to sound like that.

"You look ja...just like the other one," the deputy said, breaking the ice and stammering a little. "That's Tom Wen...Wenslow, Wendy's brother. I sa...saw him and his brother and sister at the sheriff's office a little while ago. The...they ja...just got here from South Carolina."

Carl didn't reply. He just stood there looking at Tom.

"Sheriff sent me out here to bring you the dog," Jamerson continued. "He...he's about to turn his ba...ba...back yard into a great big hole. He figured you...you'd be out here. Said you...you'd probably want to look around. When you...you've finished, Sheriff wants you to stop by his office. He says an arsonist did this. They used some kind of oxygen-a-riser or something like that to make the fire burn so hot." Jamerson talked with the same drawl as the sheriff but with a stammer.

"Do you mean an oxidizer, deputy?" asked Carl with a friendlier tone to his voice.

The deputy hesitated a moment and answered, "Yes sir, ah, that's it, oxidizer. An investigator called and said an oxidizer was used when they said it was a HTA fire, or something like that."

Carl knew a little about HTA fires from what he had read in recent journals, but his knowledge was limited at best.

Tom had climbed down from the sub-floor and now stood beside Carl. "I'm Tom Wenslow," he said, reaching out to shake Carl's hand.

"I'm Carl Jackson. Jack's brother," Carl answered. "The deputy just told me that you and your sister and brother just got here from South Carolina?"

"Yes," Tom answered. "Conway. Drove most of the night after I saw what had happen on the late news."

"I'm just in from Texas myself. Drove most of the night, too," Carl replied, then tuned toward Jamerson, and snapped,

"Where's my brother, deputy? Where's Wendy?" All of the pleasantness seemed to leave his face as he looked at the deputy.

The deputy turned his eyes from Carl's piercing stare, looked at Tom, and replied, "We...we don't know." He paused for a moment, took a deep breath, and continued. His speech stammered less when he added, "We think we...we know how they got him out of the hospital, but we...we don't know why either of them were kid...dd...napped. We know how this fire sta...sta...started, but we don't know very much more than that. The Sheriff will expla...ain everything to you when you see him. He's already talked with Mr. Wenslow."

Tom replied, "If he doesn't tell you any more than he told us, you sure won't know very much."

"What's going on around here, deputy?" Carl asked, the tone in his voice changing again to reflect his disdain. "Why would anyone want to harm either of them? Jack is the kindest man I ever knew, and Wendy! Why in god's name would anybody want to hurt her?" He didn't really expect a reply from the deputy.

"We don't know yet," replied Jamerson. "But you can bet we're going to find out. Our Captain was killed here, and somebody will pay for that!" His tone showed his anger, and he didn't stammer.

"Down at the office," Jamerson continued, "there are about fifty or sixty more law enforcement officers, and a mass of reporters. Even the FBI and ATF are in town. We've got enough cops and marines around, the Sheriff says, to start a war. He says if them people who did all of this so much as fart, we can tell you what they ate for lunch." Jamerson still spoke without stammering.

"Deputy," Carl said with the cold stare again in his eyes. "It's been two days now. It seems to me more should have been done than has been done!" The sound of his voice rose several decibels toward the end of his statement reflecting his concern.

Jamerson kicked about in the ashes with the toe of his shoe, and replied with a returned stammer, "To...to...today's a holiday, ma...ma...Mr. Jackson."

"Holiday!" Carl lashed out. "Holiday, my fucking ass. When I was in the navy, we painted all the time. Hell, the whole goddamn world was haze gray. If it moved, we saluted. If it didn't, we painted it. If a spot was missed on a bulkhead, it was called a holiday. I believe you people have missed a spot somewhere." Tom nodded his head in agreement.

The deputy took Carl's outburst as his cue to make his exit. He walked to his car and was soon gone. He couldn't really argue the point. He believed Carl Jackson was correct, for every time they had attempted to follow up on a lead on Saturday afternoon and Sunday, trying to find out more information on this or that, the person with whom they needed to talk to was out of town for Labor Day.

Carl and Tom didn't talk much after Jamerson departed. Both seemed to be in deep thought. Finally Tom said, "I'd better get back to the motel. My sister was tore up pretty bad when I left her there. If I know her, Bill's got his hands full. I'll talk to you later. Maybe we can all have supper together, okay?"

"I won't promise you about supper. That's too far away, but I'll probably see y'all later," Carl answered.

***

Carl looked through the debris a little longer after Tom left, and Earnhardt seemed to sniff and lift his leg on everything that wasn't smoking. Carl had to let his temper cool some before he tried to talk with anyone else that afternoon. He was tired and angry and felt he had the right to be.

Jack's workshop was the only structure left on the hilltop. The windows were shattered and some of the tin was missing from the roof, but the building still stood. Carl found the keys, though burned and twisted, still in the lock of the open trunk of Wendy's burned car. He walked toward the workshop wondering if there was a key on the key ring that would fit the lock on the door of the shop. Carl wasn't looking for anything in particular, just looking.

He found the workshop door unlocked. In fact, the door was barely on its hinges. "Looks like some energetic fireman put his ax through this," he mumbled to Earnhardt. "The goddamned door was probably unlocked all the time!"

Carl pushed the door open. The inside of the shop looked like someone had put everything into a blender, wet. He was sure the sheriff would have searched the shop for clues, but he decided to look around for himself.

After about ten minutes of looking at the wet, burned remains of what was left of Jack's private place of solitude, Carl decided he was just too tired and sickened by the mess to go much farther for one day. He could hardly keep his eyes open. He decided he would come back later after he had time to rest and had talked with the sheriff. He wasn't sure what he could do on the burned hilltop, but he figured his time would be better spent cleaning up the mess than waiting in a motel room to find out what had happened to Wendy and Jack.

As Carl was leaving the workshop, he saw a four-cell flashlight, and said, "Better take this along. Won't be any lights out here tonight when I come back."

He clicked the flashlight on, then off, stuck it in his back pocket, and left the workshop. As he stepped out of the door, he glanced to the left and looked at the spot where he and Jack worked so hard to clear a place for Wendy's kitchen garden.

"We sure worked our asses off," he said smiling to himself, and added, "and what did she plant? Herbs! No butter beans, no tomatoes, just fucking herbs."

His tired steps staggered some as he walked toward his car repeating over and over, "Herbs, fucking herbs." His body told him his day was about over whether he liked it or not. He planned to check into the Holiday Inn where Sheriff Young told him he would make reservations, take a long hot shower, and find something to eat before he met with the sheriff.

He reached his car, looked around but didn't see Earnhardt, and grumbled, "He was just behind me! EARNHARDT! EARNHARDT!" he yelled but he still didn't see the dog.

Then he turned and looked toward the workshop and saw the dog sitting near the doorway.

Carl shook his head, and called again, "Come here, boy. Come here." But, Earnhardt just sat there. Not knowing what else to do and not wanting to leave the dog behind, Carl backtracked to the workshop to bring the dog to the car.

As he approached, he noticed something in Earnhardt's mouth. He thought at first that it was a piece of wood or something. When he was directly in front of the dog, Earnhardt dropped the object to the ground and Carl saw it was a small piece of gray duct tape.

Puzzled for a moment, Carl looked at the piece of tape and at his old Cadillac. The gray duct tape was the same type he had used to repair the padded dash.

"Now, I know you haven't been eating my dashboard, have you?" he asked the dog. Earnhardt's head tilted to one side as his fiery red eyes stared at Carl.

Carl gave Earnhardt a good scratch behind his long red ears, gently took him by the collar, and led him back to the car. He thought little more about the piece of tape.

"Just in case," Carl said as he reached the car, "you better ride in the back. Can't have you eating parts of my car."

12
"THE NOSE KNOWS"

Within the relatively short distance between Wendy and Jack's burned home off Summerhill Road and the motel in Thomasville—about six miles—Carl was detained at three roadblocks, delaying his shower and hot meal. His stomach growled as he waited his turn to pass. The fishing snacks he had purchased in Louisiana were long since gone. However, he was encouraged to see an active effort being made to find Wendy and Jack and didn't really mind the delay.

Seeing Jamerson at the last roadblock made Carl remember how he had talked to him. He knew his attitude was uncalled for; in short, he knew he had been an ass and made a mental note to apologize the next time he saw Jamerson.

When Carl arrived at the motel at about 2:00 p.m., he could hardly find a place to park. Two large tractor-trailer rigs with satellite dishes on the tops sat in the center of the parking lot. The check-in counter in the lobby looked the way a bar in a saloon must have looked the night before prohibition. Women and men in business clothes stood three deep. Carl didn't know what was going on and didn't ask. He had reservations and all he wanted was the key, a drink, a shower, and food, in that order.

He waited patiently in line for his turn at the counter while the three-piece suits flashed their gold cards and begged for accommodations. Finally, Carl had had enough. He elbowed his way forward above prissy moans of displeasure and soon had his key in hand. He turned toward a group of grumbling three-piece suits, who were staring his way and jeering their displeasure very loudly, jingled the room key over his head, and said, "Up yours," punctuating his comment with an upheld middle finger as he departed the lobby.

The clerk was too busy to ask about a pet and Carl didn't volunteer the information. He drove around the motel and parked in front of his room, took the bottle of whiskey from the glove box, Earnhardt from the back seat, and walked very slowly to his room. His energy was gone. All he could think of was a drink of whiskey. He had been thinking about how good it would taste for the last hour, and his mouth literally watered with anticipation. All he needed to fulfill his desire was two or three ice cubes.

He unlocked the door to his room, let Earnhardt inside, threw his old AWOL bag on the bed, took the ice bucket from the dresser top, and walked with a new spring in his step toward the ice machine. He passed several three-piece suits on the way to the ice machine; each carried a large ice chest.

He thought to himself, "Must be one hell of a beer party," and was smiling when he reached the ice machine, thinking of the keg parties that he and Jack once had when they were in the navy.

He reached to raise the lid of the ice machine, and someone yelled, "Hey, asshole!"

Carl turned and saw the trio of three-piece suits standing where he had passed them. One of them shot Carl the bird, and yelled, "Up yours!" with the same punctuation he had used earlier.

Carl smiled, surprised a little at the nerve of the young man. However, when he lifted the lid of the ice machine and found it empty, the smile turned to a frown. Not one ice cube remained in the well of the machine, not even a sliver or a chip. Carl returned to his room cursing each step and drank the warm whiskey straight from the bottle without a chaser.

While Carl showered and shaved, Earnhardt lounged on one of the beds and napped. Carl dressed and decided to lie on the other bed for a few minutes.

"Five minutes, just five minutes," he said as he closed his tired eyes. In less than a minute, he was snoring as loudly as Earnhardt.

***

Jack was just regaining consciousness when he heard the sound of laughter. He remembered the hospital, the elevator, and the man dressed in yellow, but he had no idea where he was.

His face hurt and burned like it was on fire. He would have called for help but his tongue was thick and felt like it was glued to the roof of his mouth. Every time his rib cage expanded, pain tore through his body. He tried to move his tongue to make the saliva flow but it was swollen and his mouth was dry. It was as if he were licking a board.

He tried to move his hands and feet but soon discovered they were tied to something that wouldn't move. His hands felt numb. He believed they were still wrapped in the giant ball of gauze, but he wasn't sure. He knew his body was in the sitting position with his legs extended outward. Something was drawn over his head. Something other than the gauze hood, but he didn't know what. He could see tiny windows of light through a black web of hood.

He listened and waited to hear the laughter again. The resonant rumbling in his chest and the pain was more painful than the worst chest cold he had ever had. He stopped his breathing so he could listen more intently.

He heard a slight movement not far away from him. He wasn't sure what it was. At first, he thought it was a rat and a chill ran up his spine. He detested the sight of the furry little rodents. He held his breath and listened for the sound again until his lungs hurt, but all he heard was silence.

Slowly he eased the air from his lungs and took another breath of fresh air. The expansion of his rib cage sent a wave of sharp pains through his chest again. An involuntary moan escaped from his throat. He didn't want to make the sound, but he couldn't help it. He wanted to keep quiet. The pain, however, betrayed him.

He sat absolutely still for a moment and listened. The pain in his chest felt like hot oil boiling inside of him. He gritted his teeth to keep from crying out again and beads of sweat soaked into the gauze at his forehead and the salt stung like a thousand angry bees. The burning pain was almost unbearable. He felt like that he was drifting away on an ocean as another quiet moan escaped.

Suddenly, he heard a soft-sounding moan answer his own. At first, he thought it was an echo, but then he heard the moan again. He knew the moan hadn't come from him. It had come from the area where he thought he had heard the rat. It came from somewhere to his left. Seconds passed. In the silence he stopped breathing again, listening.

Slowly he turned his head in the direction of the soft sound and strained to listen. All at once, the front door of the cabin opened and slammed against the wall. Jack jumped in fright. The pain that shot through his body was so severe, he passed out.

Wendy teetered between consciousness and unconsciousness. She had begun to feel someone's presence in the room near her, and she knew whose it was. She could literally smell her husband. Not the kind of detestable odor emitted by the likes of Mex or Lester, but the sweet scent that greeted her senses when she opened her eyes in the mornings with her head on Jack's shoulder.

Over the years, Jack had been very patient with her. At first, she would almost cringe away when he would touch her. But he was gentle, and little by little, he drew her out of her shell. Their lovemaking was always something special to her, almost like the first time. No bells, no whistles, no cannon exploding, only gentleness that seemed almost orchestrated.

Wendy thought at first it was only her imagination or the longing within her for her husband, but then she heard a moan. She moved each foot; then each hand to see if maybe she could touch him, but the reward for her movement was pain as the tie-wraps sawed into her skin. She heard another moan and tried to call to Jack, but the tape over her mouth only allowed a very quiet sound to escape from her mouth. She could hear each labored breath that Jack took and struggled to get to him. She forgot her own pain and twisted her arm around and around, struggling to get her hand free. That was when she heard the cabin door slam open.

She was sure it had been Jack she had heard. It had to have been. She believed her prayers had been answered, and he was there to rescue her. Her heart pounded in her chest like the first time he told her that he loved her. She wanted to call out his name. She wanted to reach out and touch her knight in shining armor, but she couldn't. She knew he needed her. She could feel his need, but she couldn't reach him. The tears that others couldn't force her to shed now ran freely from her eyes.

"I love you," Wendy finally said for the first time, but the words behind the tape only sounded like another moan.

***

Cage and Mex returned, very drunk, to the cabin. They stumbled through the door and almost tore it from its hinges. They were even drunker than they had been. Their words were slurred and unmasked by the yellow mouthpieces but most were unintelligible, anyway.

"You can kiss my ass. That's what you can do. You can just kiss my ass. Drink I will when I want and y'all can kiss my ass, bitch!" Wendy heard Cage yell.

He turned and pointed his finger at his behind. Mex attempted the same pointing maneuver, but fell off-balance toward the center of the room. Like a cat, he turned in midair so that his hands were out in front of him. They floundered in the air, trying to grab the edge of the table that was approaching his face at a very high rate of speed. The very ends of his fingers met the edge of the tabletop and pushed the table across the worn wooden floor. His fat chin came down hard on the edge of the table with every ounce of his heavy body behind his fall.

His head snapped backward as if he had been hit by an uppercut from a sledgehammer. His bloodshot eyes rolled back in his fat head and his knees buckled forward, causing his body to pause momentarily in a praying posture. Slowly, the upper part of his body fell to the floor, landing face-first. His head never moved to the right or to the left. It looked nearly as if his face had been permanently flattened.

The woman was sitting at the small table when the two entered the cabin. She jumped up when Mex began to fall and moved backward against the rear wall of the cabin. She tried to maintain a stern, "I'm in charge here!" face, but couldn't help but laugh at the antics of Mex. She was glad he had fallen and was out cold on the floor. She disliked both of the men.

Cage looked down at his fallen comrade with a dazed and unbelieving stare and angrily looked up at the woman. He stepped over the fat mound in the middle of the floor and moved in her direction. When his foot touched the floor on the other side of Mex, she thumb-cocked the 44 magnum. Cage looked directly down the barrel and stopped dead in his tracks.

"I'll blow your drunk ass away if you take another fucking step!" the woman said with a very stern voice. Her eyes left little doubt of her sincerity.

"But baby," Cage said, slurring his words in mock earnest. "I was just going out the back door there to take a leak," he added as his body slowly leaned toward her.

"Yeah, I'll bet!" the woman replied with a doubtful sound to her voice.

Cage's body leaned forward, and she lowered the pistol's aim until it pointed at Cage's groin.

"I mean it, Cage. You take another fucking step and you won't have to worry about peeing ever again." She stepped toward him, and added, "You'll be peeing through a plastic tube into a fucking Zip Lock bag!"

She was as tall as Cage but about twenty pounds heavier. She pushed into the middle of his chest with the barrel of the pistol, and added, "Or, I can put this pistol down and stomp a mud hole in your fucking ass." Her words were very slow and deliberate.

Cage looked dazed, as if he had already forgotten what the confrontation was about. He staggered backward a step and his heel hit Mex in the head. Cage almost fell backward, but Mex didn't feel the blow. His body hadn't moved a muscle since it hit the floor.

"Now, grab that fat tub a shit and drag his fucking ass out of here! If either of you comes back in here or tries to touch that woman in the other room again, I'll kill you, Cage! I swear I'll kill you," the woman said, using the barrel of the pistol to point in the direction of the door.

Cage staggered against the wall between the kitchen area and the room where Wendy and Jack were held. He saluted the woman, grabbed Mex by the ankles and began to pull him out of the cabin.

"Whatever you say," he said. "Your servant I is," he added, bobbing his head up and down like a coolie.

"And you can drop the phony fucking Justin Wilson Cajun shit, too," she said. "I've already heard you talk like white people."

Cage didn't say another word, but the woman could see that what she had said had made him angry. She could see the muscles in his jaw tighten as he gritted his teeth.

***

Wendy heard the ruckus in the other room and kept struggling to reach Jack. She knew he was close. She tried to ignore the pain as she twisted her right wrist, but soon it was almost more than she could stand. She knew it was probably hopeless to pull and twist her wrist, but she had to try. She knew she had to do something no matter how badly it hurt. She knew she had to find a way to get free and get to Jack. She strained to hear his movement or a moan again, but all she could hear was his hoarse breathing.

She heard the sound of Cage dragging Mex's body from the cabin and heard the door slam shut. She waited for a moment, listening but couldn't hear any sounds coming from the other room. She knew it was risky, but she had to take the gamble. She moaned as loud as she could beneath the duct tape, listened for a response, and moaned again. Still she didn't hear an answer from where she knew Jack had to be. Panic gripped her and she jerked her right arm until she could feel the tie-wrap cut deeply into her flesh.

Jack began to regain consciousness very slowly. He could hear sounds around him but they sounded far, far away. He tried to speak, but his voice was so hoarse and raspy he barely heard himself speak. But his voice was loud enough for Wendy to hear.

"Wendy," his voice said, and only Wendy could have understood. She answered with the only sound she could make, a moan. Tears flowed again from her eyes, but they were tears of joy.

It nearly broke Jack's heart when he heard Wendy's moan, for now he was sure she was there in the room with him. His chest hurt from trying to breathe but not the way his heart ached. He could hear her so near and could do nothing. He felt more helpless than he had ever felt in his entire life.

"Are you okay?" he strained to whisper. He had to swallow to fight the urge to cry. The words weren't out of his mouth before he thought how stupid they were. He tried to see something funny in his stupid question, but his old friend "humor" wouldn't be summoned.

Wendy cried out with another moan and Jack answered, "I'm sorry, baby."

They were the only words he could think to say. He paused to try and wet his tongue and to swallow the lump in his throat, his head slumped forward, and he was unconscious again.

***

It was after 6:00 p.m. when the sound of Earnhardt lapping water from the toilet woke Carl from his nap. He washed the sleep from his eyes and telephoned the sheriff's office. The sheriff wasn't in, but he was told that he was expected back very soon. He left a message to tell the sheriff that he had fallen asleep and to apologize. He added that he would grab a burger and that he would be at his office shortly.

Later, when Carl left a nearby drive-in restaurant and headed up Jackson Street, which was also US-319, or the Tallahassee highway when south of town, Earnhardt lay prone on the back seat. He didn't smell like a housedog by any stretch of the imagination nor was he very particular about when he expelled gas. A green cloud could almost be seen engulfing the inside of the car. Carl hit the power window button for the rear windows and lowered them about halfway. The odor must have been difficult even for Earnhardt to tolerate because he stuck his big red head out of the window like he was the one who needed the air.

Carl was impatient to hear what the sheriff could tell him about what had happened. As it usually is when someone is in a hurry to get anywhere, he seemed to catch every red traffic signal. He grumbled but sat, tapping his finger on the steering wheel, waiting.

A Thomasville Cement Company truck pulled alongside the Cadillac on Carl's side with its windows down and loud music blaring from its radio. He smiled as he looked at the truck because he knew all about construction work. Holiday or not, if the sun was shining, you poured cement. He had worked his share of construction jobs after he got out of the navy and had worked many holidays.

Suddenly, Earnhardt seemed to go completely berserk. The only thing that kept him from jumping from the car was the fact that the window wasn't down far enough. Carl was afraid he would break the glass. First, he tried to raise it, but it only resulted in Earnhardt being choked. He also yelled at him but Earnhardt wouldn't pull his head back into the car.

Carl turned around in the seat and caught Earnhardt by the collar, and said, "You crazy bastard! You just ate two hamburgers. What do you want? A cement truck for desert?"

The traffic signal changed and the cement truck began to move through the intersection. Carl was still facing the back seat, holding Earnhardt's collar. His car didn't move forward when the truck moved. Earnhardt jumped over the back of the front seat on top of Carl. Carl was half turned in the seat, and the back of his head hit the frame around the windshield. His felt hat was knocked off, and it fell to the rear floorboard.

Carl only had time to yell, "You son of a bitch!" before mayhem erupted inside the car.

Earnhardt crashed into the dash and windshield as if he planned to jump through and run after the truck.

"You crazy bastard!" Carl yelled.

Suddenly, Earnhardt was over the top of him on the left side of the front seat. His long body was across the steering wheel. Carl held to a roll of loose skin on his back, trying to pull him back. Earnhardt's rear end was directly in Carl's face. The dog's big red tail was about the diameter of a giant kosher dill.

It moved back and forth in Carl's face like a hairy red windshield wiper while Carl kept repeating over and over, "What in the hell? What in the hell? What in the hell?" Thankfully, for Carl's sake, it was Labor Day afternoon and Jackson Street was nearly deserted. Very few people saw the fiasco.

Earnhardt finally moved to the other side of the front seat and stuck his big red head out of the right front window. Carl had very little to do with his decision to move. He had probably gotten tired of the gearshift lever poking him in the ribs.

Earnhardt knew exactly what he was doing but Carl didn't have a clue.

The dog acted just as crazy on the right side of the front seat. He seemed possessed with a determination to eat the tandem rear wheels from the cement truck. As long as he could see the truck ahead, he tried to paw or eat a hole through the dash and windshield of the car.

As the cement truck approached the intersection a half block south of the football stadium where Wendy had been kidnapped, Carl saw the traffic signal change to yellow. It was the intersection where Carl intended to make a left turn to go to the Justice Center for his meeting with Sheriff Young. A left turn at that intersection was also the truck route through town, but the truck didn't take the truck route. It went through the intersection under a yellow light and headed straight for downtown Thomasville.

Carl went through the intersection under a red light. His curiosity told him to follow the cement truck to see what Earnhardt was so worked up about.

Carl thought the truck would stop soon at a construction site somewhere downtown, however, it continued straight through the downtown area with its gears grinding each time the driver shifted. Carl tried to follow the truck closely, but as long as Earnhardt could see it, he threatened to eat the right side of the dashboard. Carl had to back off from the cement truck by about four blocks. At that distance, Earnhardt settled down some but still tried to bark—a deep, lonely-sounding bark that was more like a sad wail.

A police roadblock was set up at the city limits on the Tallahassee highway. Carl waited in line to pass through. His car was separated from the cement truck by two cars and a semi. The semi blocked the view ahead, and Earnhardt had become somewhat quieter.

Carl had time to retrieve his hat, and he sat waiting. Soon he became impatient and wanted to find out why the sight of the cement truck had set Earnhardt off. He was trying to keep his cool and watched Earnhardt as he moved to the left, then to the right of the seat.

Carl soon figured out Earnhardt was a very smart old hound. He would dart to the left side of the seat, pushing on Carl and trying to look around the back of the trailer. Then, he would dart to the right side of the front seat and stick his head out of the half-open front window, trying to look around the other side of the trailer.

Carl saw Jamerson at the roadblock and wanted to talk with him to tell the deputy about Earnhardt and the cement truck ahead, but the deputy was checking vehicles in the lane coming into Thomasville. By the time Carl cleared the roadblock, he was so engrossed in hurrying to follow the truck, he forgot about talking with the deputy.

The highway between Thomasville and the Florida state line was in the final stages of being converted into a four-lane divided highway. Labor Day weekend or not, big road graders, bulldozers and other heavy equipment worked on parts of the highway. Carl thought the cement truck could be headed somewhere along the construction route but that still didn't answer the question as to why Earnhardt was acting the way he was. He accelerated his old car, trying to catch the truck. Blue smoke bellowed from the exhaust as if it came from a diesel engine.

Carl caught up with the semi truck about the time he was at the Pebble Hill Plantation entrance, about five miles south of town. The dual-lane was complete along that section of road. Carl pulled into the left lane and passed the semi and a few cars. But a mile further up the road, the dual-lane ended and a single road began again. The road was very curvy with very few clear stretches to pass. He took the opportunity to pass other vehicles when he had the chance.

He expected to come upon the cars that where behind the cement truck soon, but curve after curve showed short stretches of empty road ahead. All of the construction was taking place on the new road to the left that ran parallel to the old road. He kept looking for the cement truck in the lanes under construction, but mile after mile went by without seeing it.

After five more miles, Carl rounded a curve on top of a hill. Ahead on the top of the next hill, he finally saw the cement truck as it was just going out of sight down the other hill. There was a car near the bottom of the hill in front of him. He pressed the accelerated of his car to the floor. With the added down hill force, the old car seemed to launch itself down the hill. The speedometer bounced on 115 miles per hour and the heavy car seemed to float in the valley of the two hills. The car ahead was about halfway up the upcoming grade.

Carl had hoped to reach the car and pass on the upgrade. The old Cadillac started up the hill at 120. Its four-barreled carburetor sucked all the air it could into its breather vent. It sounded almost like an airboat. He eased the steering wheel gently to the left to make the pass and was almost alongside the other car when a Georgia State Patrol car topped the hill in front of him.

Carl figured if the trooper wanted to stop him, it wouldn't make any difference whether he completed the pass or not. The accelerator of Carl's car was already on the floor. Earnhardt's head was out of the right window and his ears streamed straight back, looking like a red Snoopy. The flabby skin on his face was forced backwards and parted his lips, exposing his teeth. He looked like he was grinning as Carl's car cleared the other car and darted to the right just as the oncoming GSP car passed close enough to take the shine off the paint on the left side of Carl's car, if there had been any.

The GSP car was moving fast and was followed by at least ten cars. Some were marked sheriffs' department vehicles and some were unmarked. When Carl finally topped the hill and started down the other side, he passed another group of five or six cars, all headed toward Thomasville, all traveling at the same fast speed.

The cement truck was nowhere in sight. A crossroads was at the bottom of the hill where Metcalf Road intersects US-319. Carl breezed past a sign that read "Beachton." He slowed his car and continued for about a quarter of a mile. He always drove the route when he came to Thomasville and knew the highway well. He knew there wasn't a town at Beachton, only a country store and gas station.

He turned the car around at the store and headed back toward Thomasville. He was curious about all the police cars he had met and was anxious to get back to town and find out what was happening. He knew the sheriff was waiting on him. Besides, he knew a cement truck couldn't be running faster than he had been traveling. He believed the truck had to have turned somewhere.

However, Carl couldn't stop thinking of how Earnhardt had acted. When he backtracked to the crossroads, he stopped and looked at the dog.

"Alright, son. I'm gonna give you a little while longer," Carl said. It was approaching twilight and would soon be dark.

The road to the left at the crossroads was paved and the road to the right was red clay. Thinking the heavy truck would have remained on the paved surface, Carl turned to the left. However, after he had gone a couple of miles without seeing it, he stopped and headed back to the intersection.

He crossed 319 at the Beachton crossroads and headed east on the red clay surface of Metcalf Road. "Well, dog," he said as he lowered all four windows, "We are about to find out how good that bloodhound nose of yours is."

Carl eased the car along at about five miles per hour, hoping Earnhardt would be able to detect the scent or whatever it was that set his alarms off in the first place. It was a long shot, and he knew it. He could see the giant red ball of the setting sun in the rearview mirror. Almost instinctively, his naval memories returned, and he said to Earnhardt, "Red sky in the morning, sailors take warning. Red sky at night, sailor's delight."

Earnhardt looked straight at Carl as if he understood what he had said.

"You heard Jack say that before, haven't you boy?" he said. His bottom lip trembled and his eyes watered some. "I wish me and him were back on the old Gilmore again. Lord, what's going on?" he said as he scratched Earnhardt's neck.

The protective fortress of humor that Carl maintained around his emotions suddenly crumbled. Tears streamed down his cheeks. He wiped the tears with his upraised shoulders, and said, "Damn!" He swallowed hard a few times, regaining his composure and continued the slow drive along the dirt road.

He had driven about two miles on the hard red clay surface and it was almost like driving on red asphalt. It was impossible for him to distinguish the tire tracks of a truck or any other vehicle.

Finally he said, "This is stupid! It's like looking up a goat's ass to find a silk worm." He turned into an old road to turn the car around and switched the headlights on at the same time. The light from the headlights revealed an iron gate across the entrance of the old road.

"You probably saw a nice big tire back at that intersection you wanted to piss on, didn't you?" Carl mumbled as he put the shift into reverse.

He reached across the seat to scratch Earnhardt behind the ear just as the dog turned his head toward him. Carl's fingers went into his slobbering mouth.

"Ain't you got no manners?" he exclaimed, jerking his hand back. "Slobbering all over the hand that's gonna have to feed you for a while."

Earnhardt barked a sort of half-bark. "That better be an apology," Carl said, paused for a moment, and added, "Carl, if you're talking to a dog and he's just answered you, you better take another drink."

As soon as the car began to move backwards, Earnhardt jumped across Carl's lap and straight out of the window, taking Carl's hat with him.

"Fuck!" Carl yelled as he crammed the shift lever into park while the car was rolling backward.

CLANK! the universal joints clanged, and the car choked down, leaving the headlights shining.

"Dog?" Carl called as he flung the door open. Earnhardt hadn't gone far. The car door nearly hit him in the head. Carl reached out of the door and grabbed his collar and said, "Get back in here!"

He reached with the other hand for his hat that lay on the ground about three feet from the open door. Earnhardt turned his big head to the side and jerked Carl out of the car and he landed on top of his hat.

Earnhardt moved toward the iron gate with Carl hanging to his collar. Then, getting partially to his knees, Carl made a feeble, crab-like crawl.

When Earnhardt reached the gate and jumped up, he put his front paws on the six-foot high top-rail, pulling Carl to a half-standing position alongside. Carl struggled to stand and found himself looking eyeball to eyeball with Earnhardt. The headlights of the car made the two figures at the gate cast long shadows beyond.

"You red bastard!" Carl exclaimed, trying to catch his breath. "You trying to kill me or something?"

Carl squatted beside the gate and pulled Earnhardt down with him. He petted, scratched and rubbed him, trying to calm him down some as he looked through the gate pickets at the road on the other side and saw deep impressions in the soft dirt.

"I'll be," he said. "That truck went right in here, didn't it, boy? You could've just pointed. You didn't have to drag me in the dirt." Carl had to strain to hold Earnhardt down.

"That truck's got to have something to do with Wendy and Jack!" Carl mumbled to himself, then to Earnhardt, continued, "I'm quick, ain't I boy? Hell, you knew that an hour ago. If you're that smart, next time just tell me. Point like a bird dog and don't eat my Cadillac, okay?"

Earnhardt's head seemed to freeze along a line of sight beyond the iron gate and down the old road. He acted as if he knew exactly what Carl had said. He lowered his nose to the ground, inhaling and exhaling, causing the red dust to blow from the ground under his nose.

13
"THE SCENT IN THE WIND"

It was about 7 o'clock Labor Day evening in Thomas County and many things were beginning to happen. Some of the events were new for the quiet little city of Thomasville, nestled in the southwest corner of Georgia.

The wire services picked up on the news reported by a Tallahassee television station of Wendy Jackson's disappearance and it had made the national news. Reporters from all the major networks flocked to Thomasville and the motels were booked to capacity before noon Sunday.

When the string of automobiles led by a GSP car sped through the roadblock at the Thomasville city limits, Jamerson left his assignment and followed them back to the Justice Center. The center literally buzzed with activity and there were so many cars in the parking lot, he had to park his patrol car in parking lot across the street.

Most of the reporters and some uniformed marines stood outside the main entrance. The lobby and hallways were packed with law enforcement officers as Jamerson worked his way through the building, finding the hallway outside the sheriff's office nearly as crowded as the lobby. When he got to the open doorway, he couldn't even see the sheriff for all the people inside. So, he decided he would get a hot cup of coffee from the machine down the hallway and try to talk with him later.

The sheriff's persistent military-like investigating style had overcome the bureaucratic system and was beginning to yield some results. An FBI agent from Albany had arrived in town and had assumed command of the investigation "officially." It was being handled as a kidnapping, although, as Sheriff Young had told the Wenslows, no ransom demands had been made nor had there been any attempted communications.

The Thomas County Sheriff's Department more or less headed the investigative team. More agents from ATF were scheduled to arrive at the Tallahassee airport just after midnight. The GBI agent assigned to Thomasville was already working closely with the sheriff. Sheriff Young coordinated the different segments and generally ran the investigation.

The information in the statements obtained from the questioning of the two hospital orderlies was, in the sheriff's mind, the end of the thread that slowly began to unravel and expose what had happened. The speed at which the pieces of the puzzle suddenly began to fall into place could have overwhelmed a lesser person. However, his slow, methodical, and systematic investigation progressed at a deliberate pace.

Believing the tall man described by the orderlies was a hunter, the owners and employees of the gun and pawnshops in Thomasville and nearby towns had to be found and questioned. The shops were closed on Monday for the holiday so most were located at their homes.

The sheriff had plenty of personnel to carry out the investigation. He had an almost unlimited pool of manpower—if anything he had too much. Many law enforcement officers from Southwest Georgia were still in Thomasville for Captain Stanley's funeral. To add to his troubles, he had to deal with twenty or twenty-five hotheaded marines. He could speak their language but was thankful they weren't armed.

None of the people questioned from the gun and pawnshops gave any usable information. Some thought they had seen a man who wore a black western hat and some thought they remembered seeing the Jimmy but nothing was tangible.

Then the first real lead presented itself, and as it turned out, the lead was unsolicited. A young man who worked at a service station near the shopping center on US-19 in Thomasville walked into the Justice Center and gave a statement that exposed another thread.

He remembered seeing a Jimmy on Friday afternoon at the station about a half-hour before the football game. The young man remembered the time well because the man in the Jimmy caused him to be late closing the station and getting to the game.

The Jimmy with two passengers had pulled into the "self-service" island. The driver was a man wearing a black silver-banded western hat, and the other passenger was a large, big-boned woman. The driver demanded that his windshield be cleaned of the love bugs. The young man argued with the driver, explaining that he must pull to the other pumps and buy a full tank of gasoline before he could clean his windshield. He explained that it was the owner's rule.

However, the driver of the Jimmy wouldn't accept an excuse. He reached from the window of the Jimmy and seized the young man by the shirt and jerked him part of the way into the window of the Jimmy. Then the driver laid his hand on a pistol on the console between the seats, and said, "Clean the damned window, boy! Clean it now!"

The young man cleaned the windshield of the Jimmy, went to the game and had waited until Monday afternoon before coming to the sheriff's office to make out a complaint.

The young man didn't even know the sheriff was looking for a camouflage-painted Jimmy. He couldn't remember much beyond the description of the Jimmy, the black hat, the size of the woman passenger and a very shiny, very large pistol.

"Do you mean to tell me," asked the sheriff, "that this man threatened your life and you didn't even get his license plate number?"

"No, sir!" answered the man. "As soon as I could, I got the hell out of there!"

Just before the man left the sheriff's office, he added, "Oh, yeah! Almost forgot! Me and the old lady was at Wal-Mart this afternoon, and I could swear I saw the same Jimmy parked in the parking lot."

Sheriff Young knew there couldn't be many vehicles around Thomasville that would answer the description of a camouflaged GMC Jimmy, so he dispatched a patrol car to the Walmart. Also, he had an officer contact a representative of the local GMC dealership.

By the time the officer had recorded the VIN number from the Jimmy at Walmart and had called it into Sheriff Young, Lou Miller, the manager of Spence Oldsmobile and GMC, who happened to be in his office at the dealership on US-19 doing some paperwork, was on the phone with the sheriff telling him that he had sold the Jimmy to a plantation near Thomasville.

At least twenty-five law enforcement officers in nearly as many cars headed south from Thomasville on the Tallahassee highway about 5:00 p.m., and, although not invited, nearly as many reporters followed the convoy. The vehicles closed in on the plantation at about 5:30 that afternoon.

After the caretaker, his family and a few employees were nearly frightened to death, it was discovered that the Jimmy was missing from the plantation. The last anyone remembered seeing it was Friday afternoon when the caretaker allowed all of the employees to take the afternoon off to go to the football game. The Jimmy had been parked under the shed at the blacksmith's shop.

The raid on the plantation turned out to be a fiasco with people literally bumping into each other. Sheriff Young was about as mad as anyone had ever seen him as he hurried everyone out of the plantation's gate and ordered everyone back to Thomasville.

Most of the employees of the plantation were off for the holiday weekend. The caretaker gave the sheriff a list of all of them. However, in his haste to leave and end the disastrous raid, some questions that should have been asked weren't.

The raid was the reason behind the roadblock on the Tallahassee highway as well as the many police vehicles Carl Jackson passed while following the cement truck. The main entrance to the plantation was about three miles north of the crossroads at Beachton. The cabin Wendy and Jack were being held captive was on the plantation of the aborted raid. The cabin was only two miles from the caretaker's house. The caretaker's wife had heard a rifle shot that afternoon in the direction of the cabin but didn't tell this to Sheriff Young.

Before the sheriff could get out of the mess at the plantation and back to Thomasville, a deputy at another roadblock north of Thomasville at the Ochlocknee River Bridge on US-19, radioed and reported stopping a white van. The deputy was excited and started talking on the radio without waiting to find out if anyone was receiving his transmission. However, that question was answered as soon as he released the key of his radio, when almost every officer in the convoy tried to talk at once. For a time, Sheriff Young couldn't determine who was saying what to whom. However, as soon as he could crowd into the conversation, he called for total radio silence.

"I better not hear so much as a squawk from any of your radios! I mean not one more squawk!" he yelled into the hand microphone.

A few moments passed and he told the deputy at the bridge, "There are two cars at the roadblock. I want you to leave one car there, go to the nearest telephone, call my office, and wait on the phone until I get back to Thomasville. Do you understand?"

"Yes, sir! Out!" he replied.

Sheriff Young's call for radio silence was an attempt to prevent what had just happened at the plantation south of town. He knew some of the reporters had radio scanners. He also knew that the radio Wendy had been carrying at the game had not been found, and he didn't want to give her kidnappers the advantage of hearing a transmission that might aid them.

Other incidents in Thomas County were important to the sheriff, but the abductions of Wendy and Jack and the death of his best friend, Captain Stanley, overshadowed almost everything else. He had turned over the normal operation of his office to his newly appointed Chief Deputy.

Sheriff Young rode in the GSP vehicle and told the trooper to lead the pack of vehicles directly to the Justice Center as fast as he could. Carl passed the convoy on the Tallahassee highway about a minute later. The trooper's Ford Mustang was running 125 miles per hour and still accelerating when it passed his Cadillac.

As soon as Sheriff Young entered the Justice Center, he was summoned to the telephone. The deputy from the roadblock was on the other end. The deputy filled him in on what had happened. He told him that when the van was stopped, two men jumped from the van and ran underneath the bridge and into the woods alongside the river.

When the sheriff hung up the phone, he telephoned the county road maintenance facility outside of town where the tracking hounds were boarded.

Almost as quickly as the second hand on the wall clock in Sheriff Young's office could sweep from 6 to 12, the direction on the search for Wendy and Jack swung from south of town to north of town. Nearly every patrol unit was ordered to direct their search in that area.

"Hurry and take the tracking hounds to the Ochlocknee Bridge," he ordered, knowing that if the dogs couldn't pick up the scent of the fleeing occupants of the van and track them down before sunset, their chances were slim-to-none of apprehending the two men.

"YOU WHAT?" Sheriff Young yelled into the phone while jumping to his feet behind his desk. Everyone inside his office and in the hallway stopped talking.

"WHO IN THE SAM HELL AUTHORIZED THAT?" he said, and then he was silent for a moment. "Oh, okay," he said, his voice changing to a much soft-spoken tone. "No, no, you did what you were told. I'm sorry I lost my temper... Yeah, we're going to miss him around here," he added and slumped into the chair behind his desk after he hung up the telephone.

Captain Stanley had authorized the tracking dogs to be lent to Brooks County to help train their dogs. Sheriff Young sat in silence for a moment, looking with a blank stare as he saw something no one else could see. He saw his company sergeant jerk him down behind a rock as a Cuban bullet ricocheted off the top of his helmet when he was on the island of Grenada and heard the trumpet still playing taps over his friend's grave.

Only a moment passed before the sheriff snapped back to reality. He telephoned Brooks County but they didn't have anyone to bring the dogs back to Thomasville. It seemed every off-duty deputy, as well as the Brooks County Sheriff, was in Thomasville already.

Then Sheriff Young remembered Jack Jackson's bloodhound, Earnhardt. He yelled for Jamerson about the same time that Jamerson took the first sip of the hot coffee. The word, "Jamerson!" wasn't out of his mouth before he remembered sending the deputy to take the dog to Carl Jackson.

"Jamerson!" he yelled again.

The FBI agent was standing closest to the sheriff's closed office door. He opened the door and called, "Jamerson!" and Jamerson's name could be heard being repeated down the hallway like echoes in a canyon.

Jamerson came running from the area where the coffee machine was and ran straight into a 270-pound deputy sheriff from Grady County. The paper coffee cup Jamerson carried was smashed between their two stomachs. The hot coffee erupted from the cup and spewed upward, scalding the fat jowls of the Grady County officer. He looked at Jamerson in disbelief, and without even flinching from the hot coffee, grabbed the cup from Jamerson's hand.

"Sorry," Jamerson's voice quivered, sounding like he was twelve years old. He shyly lifted the end of the deputy's black clip-on polyester tie and blotted the coffee from his cheeks.

"Jamerson!" the sheriff yelled again.

Jamerson grinned sheepishly at the deputy, and said, "Keep the cup," sidestepped the deputy and wormed his way through the many people in the hallway.

"Yeah, ma...Matt," Jamerson said as he opened the sheriff's office door. Sheriff Young stood up behind his desk, lifted his arm in the air so it could be seen from the door and waved Jamerson toward him.

There were many people in the office, including the sheriffs from Grady and Brooks Counties, the Thomasville Police Chief, the FBI agent, the sheriff's Chief Deputy and Chief Investigator, a GBI agent, and an arson investigator from Atlanta.

Jamerson entered the office, closed the door behind him, and walked to the sheriff's desk.

"I'm sorry, Matt," he said as he stood in front of the desk. He thought the sheriff had called him across the room because he had said "Matt" instead of "Sheriff."

"Jamerson," the sheriff said, without looking up, seeming not to hear what Jamerson had said. He was preoccupied, writing something on a note pad. He folded a piece of paper, rose from the chair, reached across the desk and handed it to Jamerson. The note read: "Holiday Inn, Room 107."

Jamerson read the note and looked at Sheriff Young with a puzzled look. The sheriff reached across the desk, grabbed Jamerson's forearm, and loudly said, "Just go there, get him, and bring him and the dog back here to me."

"I don't th...think he's th...there," Jamerson replied.

"What do you mean, you don't THINK he's there? I just talked to the lady at the desk and she says he's in room 107. Don't THINK, Jamerson, just GO!" Sheriff Young answered harshly.

"I'll ga...go, Matt, ba...but he ain't there. I saw him headed toward Tallahassee around si...six or si...six...th... thirty," Jamerson answered as he twisted his hands in front of him.

"TALLAHASSEE!" Sheriff Young yelled as he slapped the desk top again without thinking. His brother was already so flustered he couldn't talk without tripping over his words.

Sheriff Young knew better than to yell at his brother and shook his head and fidgeted with the pencil between his fingers.

Everyone in the room sort of stared at the sheriff, and the FBI agent said, "Why don't I buy all of you gentlemen a cup of coffee?" Everyone then looked at the agent, some looking slightly puzzled. The agent nodded his head toward the door and everyone filed out of the office in single-file. The agent was the last to leave and nodded at the sheriff as he closed the door behind him.

"Now," Sheriff Young said as he came from behind his desk, sat on one of the corners, put his arm around his brother's shoulders, and added in a very soft tone, "Now Jammy, tell me about Carl Jackson."

"Wa...when," Jamerson began, but the sheriff stopped him by saying, "Easy now Jammy. I'm not mad at you. Settle down and talk slower, okay?"

Sheriff Young tightened his arm around his brother's shoulders. Jamerson, smiling from ear to ear, continued, hardly stammering, "I was at the roadblock, and I saw him headed toward ta...Tallahassee."

"Tallahassee," the sheriff repeated, stood, paced in front of his desk rubbing his chin, and added, "Now, why in the sam hell has he gone to Tallahassee?" He circled behind his desk, sat, and asked, "Why?" rhetorically.

Moving the papers around on his desk, he added, "All I need is another missing citizen, another missing Jackson gone off God knows where!"

A knock sounded at the door and a deputy stuck her head through the opening, and said, "Sheriff, there's two men outside who say they have to talk to you."

"Ms. Clark, I'm a mite busy round here," the sheriff replied making his voice drawl more than usual. It was a little game he enjoyed playing with people who didn't know him very well; then added, "Get Captain Stan... I mean, get somebody else to take care of them."

"But...Sheriff!" Ms. Clark forcefully replied, stepping just inside the office door.

Deputy Susan Clark was about the same age as Jamerson. She knew Wendy and Jack Jackson through her father, Cecil Clark. Her father was one of Jack's friends. They had met each other in Vietnam.

Susan was a graduate of the University of Georgia and had just completed a school for law enforcement officers in Tifton, Georgia. She wasn't scheduled to report for duty until the Tuesday following the holiday, but she had reported a day early just to help out. The sheriff knew that she was young and green but she showed spunk. She would wear lieutenant's bars when she put on her uniform.

"Don't 'but' me, Lieutenant! Do what I said!" the sheriff said sternly and banged on his desktop again. Clark retreated toward the doorway.

"Wait," the sheriff added.

"Sir?" Clark answered, turning toward him.

The sheriff took a folded piece of paper from his shirt pocket, motioned for her to come to him, and said, "Look over these names. Have you ever heard the Jacksons mention any of these people?"

Susan took the piece of paper from the sheriff, looked at the names and shook her head.

"Well," replied the sheriff, "run them in the computer and let's see what turns up. We might just get lucky. You are checked out on how to do that, aren't you, Lieutenant?"

"Yes, sir," she confidently answered, turned on her heels and marched out of the office. The sheriff watched her leave and just smiled. He was thinking that she would have made a good marine.

The piece of paper the sheriff gave Clark was the list of employees at the plantation the caretaker had given him.

***

Wendy and Jack both heard the roar of the cement truck's diesel engine as it plowed through the mud hole and strained to carry its heavy load up the hill to the thicket of oaks. The driver of the truck had made a fast run down the hill and hit the mud hole with enough speed to make it across without bogging down. Most of the water and some of the mud splashed out of the hole but most of it oozed back as soon as the truck reached the other side.

They listened as the sound of the truck passed the side of the cabin and heard the air escape from its brakes as it came to a stop behind the cabin. Its engine continued to run with a low rumble.

The woman hadn't carried out her orders, for she hadn't given either Wendy or Jack the shots of the drug. She had lost the desire she had felt at the beginning when she was met at the airport in Tallahassee and was told: "We're only gonna frighten them."

She had been willing to go along with that plan; however, that plan had changed drastically. She didn't like the direction everything had turned and didn't want to be a party to what was happening but doubted she would have a choice. She was afraid of the man who wore the silver tipped boots, for his moods could change as quickly as he could remove the hat from his head.

Cage and Mex attempted to enter the cabin several times during the afternoon, but she kept them outside at gunpoint. Keeping them away from Wendy was one command she had obeyed. They hadn't entered the cabin since Cage dragged Mex outside.

Cage attempted to force his way inside about a half-hour before the cement truck came up the hill, but the woman fired two shots with the 44 magnum into the doorframe over the door. The bullets tore large holes the size of softballs in the wooden facing and splinters showered down on Cage's head as he ducked and backed away.

Wendy was working to get her hand free when she heard the very loud explosion of the gunshots in the other room. It caused her to jump and she jerked her left hand almost free. The pain was nearly too much for her to withstand, but she had gritted her teeth and kept pulling. However, the instantaneous and severity of pain she felt when she jumped caused her to become faint headed and dizzy. He stomach churned and the taste of bitter bile filled her mouth.

Not long after the cement truck stopped, the rear door opened and Wendy and Jack heard voices in the other room. None of the voices were muffled. Wendy could clearly hear the man who had been talking to the woman when Jack was brought to the cabin. She knew it had to be the same man who ordered her house to be burned. She thought the man's voice sounded familiar but didn't know why.

"Where's the Jimmy?" the woman asked.

The man snapped, "Why do you need to know about that?"

The woman replied, "I was just asking." Her voice sounded nervous and apologetic.

"Don't worry about it. I've got everything taken care of," the man said, confidently.

He had abandoned the Jimmy in the parking lot at the Wal-Mart and walked the short distance to the Waffle House. It wasn't the first time he had been there. Earlier in the day, when he rode past the restaurant, he saw a Thomasville Cement Company truck parked between the restaurant and the bowling alley. He circled the restaurant once and noticed that the truck's engine was running and the large cylinder on the back was rotating. He parked the Jimmy behind a trash dumpster that sat in the rear of the building and went inside.

When he walked through the door, he saw the logo of the concrete company on the back of a man's shirt that was seated at the counter. The man was drinking coffee and flirting with a waitress.

The waitress said, "Hold that thought, stud. Let me see what the man in the cowboy hat wants."

"I'll hold on to something, but it won't be a thought. It's something just for you, baby doll. I'll be back around three o'clock or so and we can play circus. You can sit on my face and I'll try to guess your weight," the driver said, laughing as he stood and went out of the door.

The waitress laughed, and said in a mumbling voice, "Yeah, right! Like that's the first time I've heard that. I'm glad my shift ends at two-thirty. The fat bastard ought to go home and take a damned bath."

At 3:00 p.m., the man in black was hidden in the scrubs beside the bowling alley and watched as the cement truck parked and the driver went into the Waffle House. Three minutes later, the truck was stopped at the traffic light when Carl pulled alongside and Earnhardt went berserk.

Mex and Cage entered the rear of the cabin and the man turned toward them and shook his head in disgust. Turning to the woman, he asked, "Is he conscious?" and began to move toward the doorway to the room where Wendy and Jack were.

"I think they both are," the woman answered.

Wendy heard someone coming toward her. She could hear the "Tap! Tap! Tap!" of each footstep. In the darkness the sound made her insides tighten in fear—fear for herself and for Jack. She became sick to her stomach and started to gag. Her body moved as she swallowed hard to keep from vomiting.

The man wheeled around, squinting his eyes as he looked at the woman in disgust, pointing at Wendy. The woman looked into his eyes and quickly looked down at the floor to avoid his icy stare. He saw her cowardly reaction and enjoyed the weakness he could bring out in her from only a look.

He smiled, and said, "Cage, come in here!"

The woman stepped backwards out of the doorway to let Cage enter the room.

"Bring our guest outside," he said to Cage, pointing toward Jack.

Cage stepped toward Jack, withdrawing a hunting knife from a sheath at his waist. The man stepped to the side so Cage could pass and stood near the doorway between the two rooms. Cage bent forward and cut the tie-wrap at Jack's right ankle.

Wendy listened intently; trying to judge the distance to the person she could hear near her feet. Then, without considering the consequences, she jerked her right hand out from under the tie-wrap and swung it across her body in the direction she thought the man should have been. She missed the back of his leg by an inch, hitting only his trousers.

Cage stepped to one side a little, drew his fist into the air and smashed it downward onto the top of Wendy's head. She was knocked unconscious and her head slumped forward.

He drew back his fist to hit her again, and the man yelled, "Don't hit her again!"

Jack heard the commotion around him, but his body was so wracked with pain, he didn't know what was happening.

Cage turned toward the man and said in a very distasteful-sounding tone without any of the phony-sounding Cajun dialect, "You don't order me to do nothing. I do what the hell I feel like doing, and I feel like cutting her throat for trying to hit me."

"Don't touch her again!" the man ordered. "If you do, I'll kill you, Cage!"

Cage laughed, turned toward Jack and jerked the black hood from his head. The gauze hood was also partially removed, and he reached down and pulled it the rest of the way off. He looked directly at the man, took the tip of the knife blade and pricked the skin of Jack's neck. Then, looked at the man again, grinned as the blood ran onto the end of the blade. Jack tried to focus his eyes on Cage but couldn't. He tried to speak but couldn't do that, either.

Cage drew back his fist and hit Jack hard across the side of his head. Jack wasn't far from being unconscious and was out cold in an instant.

Cage lifted the point of the knife to his extended tongue, wiped Jack's blood off, took a half-step toward the man, and jeered, "Then, after I'm finished, I might do a little carving on your ass."

The man retreated slowly until he was standing in the doorway between the two rooms. The woman was behind him in the kitchen, lighting the lantern when she heard Cage's threat. She raised the lantern above her head and eased across the room, watching Mex, who was standing at the rear door.

She tapped the man's right elbow with the barrel of her pistol. Mex kept his position, leaning against the door facing. He seemed oblivious to everything happening in the cabin. His nose still bled a little and both eye sockets were beginning to blacken. His fat head looked even larger.

The man glanced quickly down at his elbow and shifted his body to one side of the doorway. The dim light of the lantern reflected off of the nickel-plated pistol and Cage's eyes opened wide.

He remembered his earlier confrontation with the woman and immediately raised both arms and retreated backwards, saying, "You got the bitch, boss man, and she got the gun."

The backward step brought him back in front of where Jack lay. He leaned over sideways to his right side and cut through the tie-wrap that tied Jack's right wrist to the post of the bunk bed. Jack's hand fell lifelessly to the floor.

Cage slowly straightened his back until he stood, put the knife back into the sheath, and said with a grin, "When you got the gun, you be the boss man."

The man stepped backwards into the kitchen, took the lantern from the woman, and said, "You better remember that. Next time, I'll kill you. Now, bring him out to the backyard."

He raised the lantern over his head, turned and saw Mex standing at the door.

"Mex, get your fat ass in there and give him a hand!" the man ordered, stepping backwards so Mex could enter the room. He had hardly moved since he came into the cabin or spoke. He was still so drunk he could hardly stand.

When Cage pulled Jack's feet through the doorway of the bunkroom, Mex grabbed an ankle and helped drag him out of the cabin. Wendy was beginning to regain consciousness. She overheard part of the confrontation. She wanted one of them to kill the other. She wanted all of them to die.

***

Carl decided he would walk down the road a short distance to see if he could find the cement truck. He was curious, very curious. But first he decided he would move his old Cadillac. If it proved to be a wild goose chase, he didn't want his car blocking the entrance to the road. He thought it could be the driveway to someone's country home. It would have been strange to be pouring cement at that time of day but stranger things have happened, he surmised.

After he picked his crumpled old felt hat from the ground, he put Earnhardt in the back seat of the car, and attempted to start the engine. It turned over very grudgingly about one and a half times, painfully slow. The headlights were still on and they dimmed to only a glow.

"You big dumb ass. You've managed to get way out here in the middle of nowhere with a dead battery," Carl said laughing at himself. He got out of the car and kicked the left quarter panel. Clots of dried Texas mud fell from under the car.

He opened the rear door and took Earnhardt's collar in hand. He led him out of the car and pulled upwards on the collar until Earnhardt's eyes were looking at him, and said, "You better hope that truck's down that road."

He laughed for a moment at what he had just said. It felt good, he thought, but he saw little humor in what was happening.

Carl knew he had little choice but to take Earnhardt along on the walk down the road. He knew he couldn't leave him alone at the car because he figured Earnhardt would start barking and put an end to a stealthy search.

He opened the trunk of his Cadillac to see if he had anything that he could use as a leash. He felt around in the trunk until he found the flashlight he had taken from Jack's shop. And, with the flashlight, he soon found a nylon-towing strap. He cut eight or ten feet from the strap and made a makeshift leash.

Soon the twosome was on its way, Earnhardt leading with Carl in tow. Carl used the flashlight to guide his way up and over the iron gate while Earnhardt crawled between the strands of barbed wire next to it. Carl shut the flashlight off and put it in his back pocket once on the road on the other side of the gate. It wasn't a full moon, but there was enough light to see.

He followed Earnhardt down the road. Earnhardt worked one side of the road then the other. The two hadn't walked very far before Earnhardt stopped and raised his head into the air. He began to move his head slowly from side to side, sniffing the light northeast breeze that blew through the pines. Carl was impatient to move down the road but he waited on Earnhardt, wondering what he was doing.

Finally, Earnhardt began to move, but not down the road. He moved to the left into a shallow ditch and put a strain on the nylon strap, trying to go into the woods.

Carl tried to pull him back saying, "That truck ain't in the woods."

However, Earnhardt turned his big head to the left and plowed forward, dragging Carl over the ditch. Carl stumbled and nearly fell coming up the bank on the other side.

"What in the world are you after, a deer? Bring your sorry red ass back here," Carl said, straining with both hands on the strap, trying to hold Earnhardt back.

"What's wrong with the road?" he asked through his teeth as his feet were beginning to slide on the loose pine straw. Earnhardt barked and dragged Carl headlong for about twenty-five feet as if he were water skiing. The bark didn't sound like a bark. It sounded like the starter on Carl's car when it died of voltage starvation.

Soon, Carl got his footing and began to run behind Earnhardt, taking giant steps. He had very little to say about the adventure he embarked upon, for he was like a trailer behind a semi. Running wasn't his strongest suit, but he sprinted for a short distance, trying to keep up with Earnhardt. He couldn't have stopped running if he wanted because he had made a loop in the end of the strap and the loop had drawn tightly around his wrist.

Earnhardt only barked the one bark. He didn't bark again as he ran through the woods like he was two years old. But soon, his speed slowed to a trot. Carl had time to look ahead to try and figure out where they were headed. He seemed to be making a large half-moon to the right.

When Carl finally figured out what was going on, his only comment was, "I'll be. You're smart, ain't you?"

The wind was out of the northeast, and Earnhardt was following the scent of the cement truck or its driver by smelling the air. His head remained high in the air as they went through the woods. Carl was amazed. He had heard how bloodhounds could track and had seen it in movies, but hadn't actually seen one in action, doing what he was bred to do.

Soon, Earnhardt's half-circle began to head back in the direction of the road, with his pace slowing considerably. He was old, had heartworms and was too fat. Jack gave him medicine daily, but the veterinarian kept the dosage low. He told Jack that Earnhardt was too old for a strong dosage.

Carl was about in as bad of shape as Earnhardt. He didn't have heartworms nor was he that old, but he was fat and out of shape. It would have been even money on who would have to stop and rest first—him or Earnhardt. As it turned out, it was Earnhardt. His pace slowed to a slow walk just as the two started down a hill.

The trail Earnhardt's nose took them on led them through a wet boggy area with tall cattails. It intersected the road again about twenty yards from the mud hole Cage and Mex had fallen into. Once on the hard surface of the road, Earnhardt fell back from the lead and walked behind Carl, and he could hear Earnhardt's labored breaths.

Soon, Carl could make out the outline of something large and white ahead of him and to his left. His heart thumped hard in his chest as he stepped into a ditch on the left of the road. The runoff of water down the hill had gouged a three-foot-deep gully in the red clay.

Carl waited for a moment, hyperventilating with shallow quick breaths. His wits soon returned and he crept down the gully, approaching the white object ahead. After he had gone fifteen feet or so, he could see that the object was a pickup truck. He stopped again and listened. He could hear a distant noise but no sound was coming from the pickup. Carl raised his head so that he could see above the edge of the gully and saw that Earnhardt was behind him with the leash pulled tightly.

Carl heard more sounds that were louder than before. It sounded like someone laughing and an engine running. The sounds came from the top of the next hill. He waited for a few more moments, listening. Then, standing bent at the waist, he tugged slightly on the strap and Earnhardt followed until they were at the rear of the pickup. When he stopped, Earnhardt had reached his end. Carl rubbed his head and untied the nylon strap from his collar.

Carl slowly eased along the side of the pickup, listening. The pickup was now between him and the sounds he had heard. He stopped when he reached the left rear tire and squatted while he listened more intensely, but he heard nothing close to him except Earnhardt's hoarse-sounding breathing.

He removed his hat and began to rise slowly until his eyes cleared the top of the truck's bed. He looked through the rear window of the cab but couldn't see anyone inside the truck. Holding the flashlight like a club, he moved slowly forward until he could look through the window of the driver's door. No one was inside the cab.

Carl took a deep breath of relief and moved back toward the rear of the truck and, more or less, collapsed on the ground alongside Earnhardt. He rested a moment, trying to regain his strength as well as his courage. Then, he peered over the top of the bed and looked toward the top of the hill. He could still hear voices and a diesel engine running. He could see lights and heard a squeaking sound.

Earnhardt's breathing sounded worse than it had earlier. Carl whispered the dog's name but couldn't hear him stir. He knelt beside him and tried to see his face, but it was too dark. He didn't want to use the flashlight, but he believed he had no choice. He moved so that his back would be toward the top of the hill and switched the flashlight on.

Earnhardt's head lay on the ground, resting on his lower jaw. The excess skin that hung from his bottom jaw lay spread on the ground on either side of his head like two halves of a pancake. Bright red blood tricked from his nostrils and each time he exhaled, tiny red bubbles formed and burst.

Carl turned the flashlight out and rubbed Earnhardt's head. "You crazy old dog. Why did you go and do a fool thing like running through the woods like you were a young stud or something? Why did you do that, huh? You stupid dog," Carl said, swallowing hard a few times.

"Damn dog," he said as he turned his face away. "You lay here and rest awhile. You've done your job. I'll do the rest. That truck's up there, and I'm gonna find out what's going on. I'll be back soon. Watch my hat."

Carl placed his felt hat next to him and stood. He believed Earnhardt would die soon. He had seen deer hunting dogs in South Carolina, fat from staying in a pen all summer, run deer on the first day of deer season in August in 95 degree heat and 90 percent humidity. Some ran until their hearts burst, and they always bled at the nose, like Earnhardt. They almost always died. Carl didn't want to see Earnhardt die, for he had earned a spot of respect in his heart.

***

The sounds Carl heard at the top of the hill were the voices of Mex, Cage and the other man. They were near the well at the rear of the cabin. The engine of the truck was idling so the drum on the back of the truck could continue rotating. The light he saw was the truck light. The men behind the cabin were using them to see as they drew a rope through the rusty pulley above the well. One end of the rope was tied to Jack's ankles, and he had been lowered into the well, headfirst, like a plumb bob.

***

Carl moved from behind the pickup truck and approached the mud hole but paused before he crossed. He knew he couldn't just charge up the hill. He had no idea what awaited him but believed Wendy and Jack were up there somewhere.

He moved back behind the pickup truck, hoping to find something he could use as a weapon—a tire iron, a chain, anything. He looked in the bed of the pickup and couldn't see anything but empty beer cans. He looked in the window of the cab and started to open the driver door but stopped. He remembered the light inside the cab and reached through the open window, fumbling around on the ceiling, searching for the dome light. When he found it, the cover was missing and so was the bulb from its socket, so, he opened the door slowly, listening as the hinges creaked. He searched under and behind the seat but found nothing except but more empty beer cans.

He reached across the seat and opened the glove compartment. He found a pint vodka bottle with one swallow remaining and a medium-sized screwdriver. On the floor he found two empty quart whiskey bottles. He eased back out of the truck cab and closed the door so that it rested on the jamb.

"Well," Carl whispered toward Earnhardt. "I guess I could throw empty whiskey bottles at them and stab them with this screwdriver if I get to dance with one of them." Some of the humor was returning in the tone of his voice. He screwed the top from the pint bottle and sniffed its contents.

"Never did like to drink this clear shit. It reminds me of water," he said as he turned the bottle up, draining what remained.

Carl drew his arm back to throw the bottle into the back of the pickup but stopped in midair with a strange look on his face.

"A stupid move like that could get your John Wayne ass killed. Why don't you just blow the horn, Carl? If I only had a brain! If you only had a brain," he said. Then, an idea suddenly came to him. Not a good idea, but an idea just the same.

He crawled underneath the pickup with the screwdriver in his hand. He felt around until he found the gas tank and tried to punch a hole in its bottom with the screwdriver, but his efforts were useless. The metal of the tank was too thick. He hit the handle of the screwdriver with the heel of his hand and the blow made a loud noise. Carl bit his lip and waited to see if the sound had been heard.

After a few moments, he felt around the side of the tank until he found the outlet for the tubing that ran toward the engine. The metal tubing was connected to the tank with a short piece of rubber tubing. With his knife, he cut the rubber tubing and filled the bottles. When they were full, he was afraid to leave the gas draining from the tank because Earnhardt wasn't far away. He had begun to crawl underneath the truck toward Carl with the felt hat in his mouth.

Carl fumbled around on the ground beneath the truck for something he could stick into the end of the rubber tubing, and when he couldn't find anything, he used the screwdriver.

He crawled from beneath the truck and stuffed his handkerchief and part of his torn shirttail into the neck of the bottles to be used as wicks. He had never thrown a Molotov cocktail before, but he knew what gasoline could do when it was subjected to fire. It had only been what seemed like hours since he had been fighting a gas fire in Texas.

He checked his pocket to make sure he had his cigarette lighter as he walked toward the mud hole, paused for a moment at the edge, took a deep breath and waded into and across the knee-deep puddle. He stopped for a few seconds when he reached the other side to stomp some of the mud from his feet, then walked up the hill toward the cabin.

14
"COME-UP'NS"

Sheriff Young's patrol car and another car stopped behind Carl's Cadillac at the iron gate on Metcalf Road at about the same time Carl started up the hill from the mud hole. Deputy Jamerson and two other men were with the sheriff as he climbed over the gate and began a slow cautious walk down the old road. The only thing that could account for the sheriff finding Carl's car as quickly as he had was luck or a gut feeling.

When Jamerson told him about Carl Jackson heading toward Tallahassee, the sheriff left the Justice Center with Jamerson through a side door and saw two men standing near the edge of the parking lot. The sheriff remembered the men Clark had told him were waiting to see him, wondered if those were the same men and looked to see if he knew them; however, their backs were turned.

When the sheriff and Jamerson crossed the small parking area to a side street that led out to Smith Avenue to get Jamerson's car that was parked across the street, the two men followed.

Sheriff Young hoped they were police officers and not reporters or marines. He didn't want anyone following just in case Carl Jackson knew something he didn't. He believed if Carl had the tenacity of his brother, he wouldn't stop until he found them or got himself killed along with Wendy and Jack, so he told the FBI agent some of what he had planed and left to find Carl Jackson.

Sheriff Young and Jamerson were bent over at the waist so they could pass between the cars parked in front of the Justice Center without anyone at the front of the building seeing them. But, when the sheriff glanced back about halfway across the lot, he saw the two men following. They were bent over and moving through the cars the same as he and Jamerson. He wanted to stop and find out who they were but was afraid he would be seen, so he and Jamerson kept moving. When they reached Smith Avenue and were about to cross, the two men doubled back through the parking lot and disappeared between the cars.

Jamerson turned his car left out of the parking lot and headed west on Smith Avenue. Before he reached the first traffic signal, a car with two passengers followed them.

"Do you want me to turn around or try to lose them, Matt?" Jamerson asked.

"No. Just head out the Tallahassee highway," the sheriff replied.

Jamerson drove toward Tallahassee as ordered without a word being spoken until they approached the first road south of the plantation they had raided earlier in the day.

"Turn left here!" Sheriff Young suddenly ordered. Jamerson slammed on the brakes and turned left at the crossroads at Beachton with the car carrying the two men still following them.

***

Wendy's hands hung at her sides as she stood just outside the rear door of the cabin. The woman stood behind her with her arms encircling the upper part of Wendy's body, pinning her arms to her sides. The black hood was still in place over her head and the duct tape still covered her mouth. Mex and Cage stood one on either side of the well, each holding a whiskey bottle and leaning against an upright. The man was near the cement truck.

Mex let the upright go as soon as he saw Wendy and started walking toward her. He staggered and almost fell, but continued. His blackened eyes were only thin slits and looked like two over-ripe purple plums. The woman didn't see his approach; however, Wendy knew someone was coming toward her. She could hear the acorns crunching under his feet; then, as he came closer, she could smell him. She could smell Lester. She could smell his whiskey breath and his urine.

As Mex's hands reached toward Wendy, he stumbled on his own feet and fell into her with his right hand grabbing her shirt at the first button. Wendy was forced backward by his falling weight but the woman held her upright. Mex's hand ripped down the front of Wendy's shirt and tore off the buttons down to her belt, ripping her bra in half between her breasts. His fingernails sliced long bloody lines in her flesh from between her breasts down to her waist.

The woman saw what was happening and released her hold on Wendy. Wendy's hands shot forward as quickly as the blade of a switchblade. Guided by Lester's scent, they clamped the sides of Mex's head at his ears, holding his head like a vise. Her thumbnails dug into his eye sockets like nails shot from two nail guns. They were rough and jagged from her struggle to get free and tore at his eyeballs like dull knives cutting ripe tomatoes.

Mex let out a howl, jerked his head up, and grabbed Wendy by the throat with his hands. He gritted his teeth and choked her so hard that the veins bulged on the backs of his hands. But Wendy wouldn't let go. She wouldn't be denied the chance to gouge out the eyes of the man who had made her feel dirty when he looked at her. She had been too little then to keep him from looking at her but now she wasn't.

She rose to the tips of her toes and drove her thumbs deeper into his eyes while screaming, "I'll never love you, you bastard!"

Mex broke his hold on Wendy's throat and grabbed her thumbs, trying to pull them out of his eyes, but the hold, fueled by adrenaline, would not be broken. He cursed as he started moving backward, trying to pull himself free but she stepped forward with him and held on.

The woman could see what was happening but held her position behind Wendy and didn't try to stop her.

"Now the fat bastard's gonna get his come-up'ns!" she mumbled.

Mex heel stumbled on a small limb in his backward movement and his knees bent forward. He began to sink to the ground but Wendy's fingers gripped his ears like handles. Her thumbs dug into his eyes as if they were rooted there. His knees touched the ground and she pushed down as hard as she could, causing her thumbs to be driven deeply into his skull the same way Lester's finger had been pushed inside of her.

Blood gushed from around her thumbs and sprayed all over her chest and dripped from the nipples of her exposed breasts. She felt the warm blood and thought of the blood she had found in her panties the morning after her stepfather had come to her room.

Finally, the man wearing the black hat yelled, "STOP HER! STOP HER!"

The woman hesitated; then started pulling Wendy away from Mex. She had to tear Wendy's hands loose. Mex grabbed at his eyes and fell face down on the ground. His head hit Wendy above the ankles and she drew her foot back and kicked him before the woman could push her away.

Mex clambered to his feet and blindly ran toward Cage. Cage pushed him aside, and he ran into the shadows on the east side of the yard, screaming with one hand over his eyes and the other flailing in front of him, reaching for something in the darkness.

The woman stood in front of Wendy and held her by the shoulders. Wendy could have lashed out at her but didn't. She could have removed the black hood but didn't. She hadn't thought to do either. Her anger and revenge had been directed toward Lester. It may have been Mex to everyone else, but to a ten-year-old girl named Wendy Wenslow, it was Lester Flanders, her stepfather.

Carl heard the screams from Mex. He couldn't see the cabin clearly, but he could see one of the headlights of the cement truck and began to run, half-stooped, up the hill. He saw the cabin as soon as he was in the clearing on the west side of the hilltop. He ducked behind a tree and now could clearly hear the voices coming from behind the cabin.

Sheriff Young and those with him heard Mex, as well, and began to run down the road. They hadn't reached the mud hole yet.

Carl strained his eyes, trying to see more of what was happening behind the cabin, but the bright headlights of the truck prevented him from seeing clearly. The right headlight cast a diagonal shaft of light across the clearing to the west of the cabin. He shielded his eyes from the light with his raised hand and was able to see the well behind the cabin. The cement truck's unloading chute was extended and resting on the wooden railing around a well. The huge cylinder on the back of the truck was rotating.

Carl thought of Earnhardt, and whispered, "That old red bastard should get a medal."

Carl decided he would move to his right toward the cabin until he was out of the direct beam of the headlight; then he would creep along in the shadows until he reached the cabin. He felt he had to find out what was going on and, to do that, he had to get closer.

"Well, here goes nothing," he mumbled as he moved from behind the tree and quickly ran into the shadows near the cabin. He stepped on a small limb, stumbled and nearly fell. The dried limb made a loud noise when it broke in half but he doubted the sound could be heard over the roar of the diesel engine. Nevertheless, he ducked behind a tree two-thirds of the way to the cabin and waited for a moment, listening.

The man wearing the black hat circled and grabbed Wendy from behind the same way he had in the parking lot at the football game. Wendy fought to get free but he lifted her feet from the ground and held her firm.

Cage still stood at the well. He leaned against the railing with a grin on his face and looked like he had enjoyed the fight with Mex. It had lasted less than half a minute but Wendy had done enough damage for a lifetime.

"Son of a bitch!" the man holding Wendy yelled at the woman. "You mean to tell me that you couldn't hold her back. You could..." his words were broken as he struggled to hold Wendy.

Her heels were kicking hard, backward, and he kept his knees together, trying to block the kicks as the woman tried to catch Wendy's feet and hold them. The man's hat was tipped from his head and it sailed like a black felt Frisbee a short distance.

"Grab her!" the man yelled at the woman, "If she kicks me in the balls again, I'll kick your ass." The woman attempted to grab Wendy's feet but, each time she tried and missed, Wendy kicked backward with the heel of her shoe.

"Ouch! Shit!" the man yelled each time that a heel hit his shinbone. "Here, grab her arm. Hurry! She's gonna break my leg," he yelled as he began to dance from one foot to the other, trying to avoid Wendy's backward mule-like kicks.

The woman grabbed Wendy by the upper right arm, and the man spun out of his hold and grabbed the other arm. They held Wendy's feet almost clear of the ground and forced her to the well with Wendy fighting every step of the way and continued to fight as they tied her wrists to the two uprights. The blood on her thumbs and hands was smeared on the hands of the man and woman as they tied her hard and fast.

***

Carl started to run for the cabin when he saw Mex running with staggering steps through the trees on the east side of the clearing. He was saying words Carl couldn't understand while holding one hand over his eyes and the other in front of him.

Carl hid behind the tree and waited a little longer. He had devised a simple plan. He would run to the cabin, ease around the west side to the northwest corner and try to see what was going on around the cement truck. If he saw Wendy or Jack, he planned to return to the front of the cabin, light the wick of a bottle and throw it against a tree on the east side of the front yard where he had seen the man running. He hoped the explosion and fire would draw everyone from the rear and around the east side of the cabin long enough for him to get to Wendy and Jack. If he didn't see them behind the cabin, he planned to search for them inside.

He took a deep breath, mustered his courage, and ran for the cabin.

***

After Wendy had been tied to the well, the man quickly turned and walked to where his hat had landed. As soon as his back was turned, Cage sprang toward Wendy and grabbed at her breasts. He began to laugh wildly and started rubbing his hands all over her. The blood from Mex covered her chest and Cage looked like he was trying to transfer it to his hands. Wendy wiggled her body to get away and kicked her freed feet in all directions.

The woman fired the pistol into the air to get Cage's attention, trying to stop him. He looked at the woman and started walking toward her holding the palms of his hands open so she could see the blood on them.

"I want your blood now, bitch!" he said in a hissing almost evil-sounding tone.

The man in black was about twenty-five feet from Cage.

"Stop! Cage!" the woman ordered.

The man in black turned and started walking back toward Cage, and yelled "CAGE!" but Cage didn't stop.

"You had better stop," the woman said with a calm-sounding voice. "I meant every damned word I said, Cage," she added as she drew the pistol's hammer back with both thumbs.

Cage kept coming at her, grinning and rubbing his hands together. He was about ten feet away.

The woman lowered the barrel of the pistol until it pointed at Cage's belt buckle and squeezed the trigger. The round hit him just where she was aiming and exited through his backbone, leaving a large hole.

His body was propelled backward onto the ground, and he wormed around in a small circle as his blood spurted from his mouth, making gurgling sounds while looking at the woman through disbelieving eyes.

The woman pulled the hammer back again and aimed the pistol at Cage's head. The muscles in her hand had begun to tighten, when the man yelled, "Stop, Kaye!"

Wendy heard the name called but it didn't register in her mind. Everything happening seemed to be a blur or a dream.

The man walked to Cage, and said, "I tried to tell you to stop, didn't I?" Then he drew back his foot and kicked Cage in the left temple with the sharp toe of his black boot.

The toe was like a silver-tipped spear burying itself in Cage's skull. He withdrew the boot and blood spurted from the hole. Cage's body jerked a few times, rolled onto its back, and lay motionless in a growing puddle of blood.

***

Carl had reached the front of the cabin when he heard the gun shot. He flattened himself along the wall and began to ease himself along to the east corner, moving faster now. His hand trembled and caused the bottles of gasoline to clank together; he pressed them against his thigh to silence them.

Then, from the bottom of the hill where the white pickup was parked, he heard voices. He thought it was the man he had seen running away from the cabin, but it was Sheriff Young and the others.

Carl rounded the corner, stopped, and listened again for the voices down the hill, but he only heard the rumbling of the cement truck's engine. Then, he heard Wendy's name called by someone behind the cabin.

***

The man walked from where Cage lay and stood behind Wendy.

"Wendy," he said.

Wendy heard her name but didn't move.

"WENDY!" the man shouted.

Wendy's head jerked upward, and he added, "Now that I know you can hear me, listen. In a few seconds, the hood will be taken from your head. I want you to look down in front of you and tell me what you see."

Wendy heard the instructions but they didn't make any sense to her.

The man stepped back from Wendy and motioned for Kaye to come to him. He put his arm across her shoulders, and said, "When I get over to the truck and reverse that big drum, pull that hood off of her head; then shine this flashlight into the well. Make her look down. If she turns and sees you, it won't make no difference. She already knows your name, but it don't matter. She'll never be able to tell anyone."

Kaye looked at the man in disbelief. She knew what it was coming to and knew she had to try to stop what was going to happen. She remembered how Wendy had run to get help when she was doubled over with pain on the front porch of her parent's home long ago. She opened her mouth to speak, to plead for Wendy's protection, but the man placed the tip of his right index finger on her lips.

"Just listen, Aunt Kaye, and do what I tell you for once. Don't make me hurt you. Just take the hood off of her head and the tape off of her mouth. Can you do that?" he asked.

Kaye's legs were trembling. She knew what he could do when he was mad. She didn't speak. She only nodded her head.

The man started to walk away, and Kaye grabbed his arm, and pleaded, "But, but, wait a minute. You can't do this! Please don't..." Her words were stopped by a slap across her mouth.

She stumbled backward, attempting to draw the pistol from her waistband. The man grabbed her wrist and dislodged it from her hand and it fell to the ground between her feet. He held onto her wrist and seized her by the throat with the other hand. She grabbed at his hand and tried to pull it loose, but he tightened his grip until she began to fight for air.

His knuckles were almost white when he hissed into her face, "Bitch! You'll learn one day. The next time, I'll kill you and throw your body into that well on top of them. If you want to stay alive, don't question me again."

Then, he slung her toward the well, and added, "Get your ass over there and do what I told you to do!"

Kaye wiped the blood from her mouth and nose with the back of her hand and stood trembling behind Wendy. The man picked up the pistol and walked to the truck.

***

The sound of engine became louder by the time Carl had reached the rear corner of the cabin. He saw the man standing at the open door of the truck with a pistol in his hand. The large cylinder on the back of the truck stopped rotating momentarily; then started turning in the opposite direction. Carl could see the end of the unloading chute resting on the railing of the well. He saw the pulley and rope hanging down into the well. The rope was moving gently back and forth. He knew Jack must be down there. He could see the person tied at the well was wearing a uniform. He knew it was a woman and that it had to be Wendy.

***

"Now!" the man yelled but Kaye didn't move.

"DO IT NOW, KAYE!" he yelled.

Kaye shook her, and defiantly replied, "No, D.L.! I've had enough of this."

Wendy heard another name, but like the other, it didn't register.

D.L. stood looking at Kaye with a look of bewilderment as Kaye began to untie Wendy's right hand from the well upright.

"I'm sorry, Wendy," she begged, crying. "I'm so sorry. Forgive me. Please forgive me."

"Damn it, Kaye! Stop!" yelled D.L.

Kaye continued to untie Wendy's wrist as if she didn't hear him. Carl wanted to run to Wendy's side and help Kaye, but D.L. started walking toward them, pointing the pistol at Kaye. Carl judged that there was too much distance between him and the well. Time seemed to drag by, but everything was happening so rapidly. From the time Carl ran up the hill and stood at the corner of the cabin, less than five minutes had passed.

Wendy's head was still covered with the hood. Her mind raced, trying to figure out what was happening. She thought of the two names again, Kaye and D.L., but her mind wouldn't or couldn't make the connection. She could feel someone's hands and fingers at her right wrist. She heard a woman crying.

Wendy tried to pull her hand free, but her struggle only hampered Kaye's efforts.

D.L. walked up behind Kaye, grabbed a handful of her hair, and yanked her back.

"Kaye! What in the hell are you doing?" he exclaimed.

Kaye fell to the ground. D.L. cocked the hammer of the pistol and reached for the hood over Wendy's head, and said, "Damn it! I want her dead!"

Kaye jumped up and yelled, "NO D.L! NO!"

Carl had seen enough. He ran for the front of the cabin, reaching in his pocket for his cigarette lighter.

Kaye tried to grab the pistol from D.L's hand. He quickly whipped it around and the barrel slashed saber-like across her face, laying her cheek open from her nose to her ear. Blood poured down her neck as she stumbled backward, staring wildly at D.L.

D.L. knew he had hit her hard enough to have knocked her down, but her man-sized body still stood. He shook his head in disbelief as Kaye began to come at him again.

"Aunt Kaye!" he yelled. "When are you going to learn? Now, come over here and do as I say!"

Kaye wiped the blood from her month, and said, "Fuck you, D.L.!"

D.L. shook his head and said, "I told you a long time ago not to say that word, didn't I?" then, pointing the pistol point blank at her face, he pulled the trigger.

Kaye took the full impact of the bullet, and the entire left side of her head exploded as she was propelled backward ten feet to the ground.

Carl ran around the front of the cabin, trying to light the wick as he ran. He was crying, fighting mad.

D.L. turned away from Kaye and what he had just done without the slightest hint of remorse on his face. In fact, he was grinning the same way his father had grinned when he was drunk, for D.L. was D.L. Flanders, Junior—Wendy's half-brother.

D.L. jerked the hood from Wendy's head, and yelled into her ear, "What happened to my daddy, Wendy Wenslow?"

He pulled the hammer back on the pistol, put the barrel behind her head and pushed her head forward and down. "What happened to my daddy?" he jeered again through gritted teeth.

Wendy heard what D.L. had said. She couldn't help but hear him, but she didn't know what he was talking about. Her mind still didn't make the connection with what was happening to her now and what had happened long ago in Horry County, South Carolina. She could only shake her head. She could see the well in front of her and could smell the musky scent it emitted but still her mind was a total blank.

D.L. moved the gun from behind Wendy's head, and pointed the barrel down into the well. Wendy could see the pistol in his hand, and she saw the slightest movement of the rope hanging down into the well. She knew someone was at the end of that rope, and it could only be Jack. She could see D.L's finger as it tightened on the trigger of the pistol, and she bumped into him just as the gun fired. The shot exploded into the one of the railing boards.

D.L. cursed and shifted the pistol to his left hand. He tried to push Wendy away with his right, but she resisted. His hand pushed against her shoulder, and as she wiggled her upper body, it slipped from her shoulder to push against the side of her face, and she bit down hard on his fingers.

D.L. yelled and hit her on the head with the barrel of the pistol twice before she would let go of his fingers.

"You bitch!" he yelled, shaking his hand.

His fingers were bloody. He pointed the pistol down into the well and fired.

"JACK!" Wendy yelled as the shot exploded and echoed inside the well. The shot nicked Jack's right shoulder but didn't cause any serious harm. Jack didn't feel the bullet. He was somewhere between consciousness and a dream. He could hear voices and the pistol shot, but he only heard jumbled up sounds.

His whole world was the dizziness inside his head. He tried to call for help but nothing came out. He was lost inside the darkness of his memories. The blood had drained down to his brain and nothing made any sense.

"Wendy," he cried, then the darkness changed to a bright red, and he was unconscious again.

No one could have heard Jack except for Wendy. She heard him more with her heart than her ears. He sounded like a little child who thought it was lost, a little baby crying for its mother. She had seen tears in his eyes, but she had never heard him cry. She kept calling his name and struggling to get to him, to hold him, to hush his cries.

The faint sound told Wendy that her husband was still alive, and she said, "Jack! Oh God! Jack! Please God! You've taken everything I've ever loved! Please God, please don't take Jack, too!"

D.L. kept repeating the question, "What happened to my Daddy?" But Wendy didn't hear him as her ears strained for the slightest sound of Jack's cries.

***

Carl heard the first gun shot as he fumbled with the lighter, trying to make it light. Finally, the flame flickered enough to light the wick of one of the bottles and lit another bottle from the wick of the first. He had his arm raised to throw the first bottle when he heard the second shot, and Wendy scream Jack's name.

"Oh God," Carl cried. He just knew the man called D.L. had murdered his brother. His hand trembled for an instant over his head as he threw the bottle of gasoline as far as he could in the direction of the mud hole.

Sheriff Young had crossed the mud when he heard the two gunshots. Jamerson was halfway across when Carl threw the first bottle of gasoline. The bottle hit a big oak directly to the sheriff's right. He flattened himself marine-like in the road, and Jamerson dove down into the mud. The others in the sheriff's party hadn't started across yet.

In an instant, Sheriff Young jumped to his feet and ran up the road to the top of the hill with his pistol drawn. He could see someone at the front of a small building, holding what he knew was another bottle of gasoline.

***

Wendy listened intently. She couldn't hear Jack inside the well, but Jack was alive, though barely. But if he wasn't pulled from the well soon, he would die. Not just from the injuries caused by the fire and hanging down in the well for so long; Jack would soon be drowned and buried in wet cement. The well was filling and it was only a foot from his head.

Wendy began to say Jack's name over and over, trying to push forward toward the well. She could smell the scent of the spent gunpowder.

"He's dead, Wendy. Your dear sweet Jack is dead, just like my daddy!" D.L. sneered into her ear. Wendy tried to move her hips to push D.L. away, but he grabbed her by the hair and pulled her head down hard; then he put the barrel of the pistol to the back of her head. "I said look, damn it!" he yelled into her ear as he pushed her head forward.

"WHERE IS MY DADDY?" he said even louder than before.

Wendy's right hand slipped from under the rope that Kaye had loosened. She reached for D.L. and grabbed a handful of his hair at the same time Carl threw the second bottle against an oak on the east side of the cabin. When the gasoline exploded, the entire hilltop was illuminated.

A piercing scream came from the area where the bottle exploded, and Mex ran from behind the tree, looking like a human torch. He stumbled toward Carl, screaming, but fell after only a few steps, rolling over and over on the ground. The heavy layer of leaves and acorns began to burn.

"Die, you bastard! DIE!" Carl yelled.

D.L. was able to break free from Wendy but not before she lifted part of his scalp as clean as one of her Cherokee ancestors could have accomplished.

"They'll never get to you in time!" D.L. said. "Cause you're going to die right now," he added as he stepped back from her and rubbed the bloody spot on his head.

Carl ran around the corner into the light from the cement truck headed for the rear of the cabin.

"That's Carl Jackson!" Jamerson yelled. Sheriff Young had almost reached the cabin.

"Tell me what happened to my Daddy, bitch, before you die! Tell me what happened to Lester Flanders!" D.L. snarled.

Wendy instantly recognized the name, Lester Flanders, and anger, pure as love, gripped her. She looked D.L. directly in the eyes, and said, "Fuck you, you bastard!"

D.L. looked at the blood on the tips of his fingers, aimed the pistol at Wendy's head, and said, "You shouldn't have said that word!" and pulled the trigger, but it didn't fire. He looked at the pistol in disbelief and threw it into the well, pulling a stiletto out of his pocket. The blade sprang open as he grabbed Wendy by the hair and put the blade under her chin, grinning.

The grin and the pulling of her hair reminded at Wendy of Lester when he was drunk, the way he had pulled her hair when he pulled her from underneath the house and whipped her like a dog.

Again, she starred into the eyes, laughed, and said, "Fuck you! You go to hell, you worthless piece of shit!" Then she turned her face toward the well, grabbed the rope with her freed hand, and started pulling it through the pulley as if D.L. wasn't even there.

Carl ran behind the cabin with the wick in the pint bottle of gasoline blazing. D.L. turned, saw Carl and jumped to the other side of Wendy; then ran into the shadows toward the outhouse. Carl threw the bottle at him and it exploded on the front of the outhouse and to the right of D.L. The liquid flame spewed outward and caused the legs of D.L's trousers to catch fire. He screamed as he ducked around the outhouse.

Sheriff Young ran around the cement truck, saw D.L. running into the woods, and fired a single shot in that direction. Jamerson came around the corner of the house and down the other side of the cement truck. He stopped just short of the well with his gun drawn and leveled toward the trail of fire that D.L. had left.

"Hold it! Hold your fire!" Sheriff Young yelled. Jamerson's body stiffened as if frozen in time and didn't move.

Carl yelled, "TURN THE TRUCK OFF! TURN THE IGNITION OFF! STOP THE CEMENT!"

Carl was already at the well. He had shone his flashlight down into the dark hole and had seen his brother. The cement was touching his forehead. Wendy was crying Jack's name over and over as she struggling with her one freed hand to pull the rope through the pulley. Carl grabbed the rope from her and the pulley began to squeak as the rope was slowly drawn along its rusty wheel.

"Shut the truck off!" Carl yelled again just as Jamerson reached the open door of the truck, reached inside, and pulled out the diesel's kill-switch.

Wendy was trying to untie her hand from the upright when Sheriff Young ran to the well to help her. As soon as the big drum on the back of the truck stopped turning, Jamerson ran back to the well to help Carl pull on the rope.

About that time, Tom and Bill Wenslow came running around the corner of the cabin. The sheriff yelled toward Jamerson while pointing toward the burning outhouse, "One of them ran into the woods with the legs of his trouser on fire! I got a shot off. Don't know if I hit anything. Get him!"

Jamerson ran toward the area the sheriff was pointing at, taking a flashlight from his pocket. He had little trouble finding D.L's trail because the burning outhouse lit up the night. There was also a path of little fires dotting through the underbrush where D.L. had run and Jamerson found a small stream of blood.

Tom and Bill ran to the well and helped free Wendy and get Jack pulled to safety. Tom removed his shirt and wrapped it around the shoulders of his sister.

When the commotion died down, D.L. Flanders, Junior had escaped. Kaye Flanders was dead. She had lost her life trying to stop D.L. Mex and Cage were dead and Jack was all but dead.

Wendy looked like she was in bad shape, too, and she was. However, her thoughts weren't for her own conditions. Her every action as soon as Jack was pulled from the well was directed toward him. She held his head as he was lifted to the seat of the cement truck. Her arms encircled him as they began the ride out to the iron gate on Metcalf Road.

Tom drove the cement truck, something he was very familiar with, while Sheriff Young, Bill and Jamerson climbed on the back and the running boards. Earnhardt was laid on the floorboard at Wendy and Jack's feet. The three that lived on a hilltop off Summerhill Road would live to see another day.

***

Wendy and Jack were taken to Archbold Hospital, and Tom and Bill Wenslow went to the motel to get Emily.

Two weeks later, while Sheriff Young searched for D.L. Flanders Jr. and continued the investigation, Jack regained consciousness. He was still in ICU. Wendy was doing much better and Emily wheeled her into Jack's room with Bill and Tom following.

Carl was at his brother's bedside. He had only left the hospital briefly since they came from the cabin.

The newspapers said that Wendy Jackson was a hero, but it was difficult for her to feel like a heroine when she felt like a victim. The wheelchair was pushed alongside Jack's bed, and she reached out and laid her hand on his forearm. Jack turned toward her with half-open eyes. His face was still covered with bandages.

Wendy rose from the wheelchair, stood beside the bed, leaned down so that her mouth was near Jack's ear, and whispered, "I love you."

When she stood again, Jack's eyes were closed.

15
"THE EPILOGUE"

The investigation into the background of D.L. Flanders Jr. and the Flanders family led to Conway, South Carolina, Wendy's birthplace. From members of her family and others, they pieced together what probably caused D.L. to behave as he had.

D.L. was more-or-less abandoned at the hospital after his mother, Grace Tanner Wenslow Flanders, died January 26, 1958. His father, Daniel Lester Flanders, simply disappeared after the funeral. Some said he moved back to Baltimore, Maryland, but no one seemed to know for sure. The last time anyone saw him was at the setting-up.

His grandparents, Eleanor and Daniel Flanders, reared D.L. until Eleanor's death when D.L. was two years old. His grandfather continued to rear him until his death when D.L. was twelve. Two daughters, Kaye and Alice, survived them.

Alice was the oldest when her father died and should have taken D.L. to rear, but she refused. Since no one on the Tanner side offered to look after him, Kaye reared him. None of the Tanners or Wenslows would acknowledge that there was a drop of their blood in the child.

Kaye didn't finish high school. She was a very unruly young woman and in and out of trouble constantly. After a year, D.L. was taken from her and sent to an orphanage in North Carolina. Thinking he was sure to be adopted, Kaye didn't attempt to contact him nor was he adopted. He remained there until he escaped at the age of sixteen. In the meantime, Kaye's way of life caught up with her and she was sent to prison for stealing and cashing social security and welfare checks.

D.L. eluded the law for two years, but at eighteen, he stole a car, was apprehended and given a choice of either going to prison or joining one of the armed services. He was induced into the US Army in 1975. He served three years, two of that in a Special Forces unit, the Green Berets, until he was forced to accept a general discharge. He was implicated in the death of his platoon sergeant during maneuvers at Fort Benning, Georgia.

D.L. was sent to prison in 1980 for robbing a convenience store near Conway. Kaye was still in prison. Her original sentence had been added to several times. Her youthful unruliness carried forth into her adulthood.

In 1991, D.L. had served his time, was paroled, and returned to Conway. Kaye likewise had been paroled and had returned to her hometown a year earlier. She was in her early fifties and D.L. in his early thirties. They lived together in the same house that the Flanders had lived in when Wendy spent her unforgettable summer.

D.L's girlfriend lived with them. Her name was Deborah Jenkins. D.L. and Kaye continued to have brushes with the local law because they still walked very close to the line between right and wrong.

The statement of Ms. Jenkins made up most of the information in the final report. She was only too willing to tell all she knew of D.L. Flanders Jr. She had her own axe to grind. However, some of what she had to say caught everyone off-guard, but shouldn't have, considering how things turned out.

Kaye had told Ms. Jenkins some things about her and D.L's early childhood. She told Ms. Jenkins that her father had molested both D.L. and Kaye and that Lester and Kaye had had an incestuous relationship before he married Grace.

Ms. Jenkins told them that D.L. loved to beat women, and he had beaten her and Kaye often. When they found Ms. Jenkins, she was still in the hospital from the last beating D.L. gave her. He had beaten her and thrown her out of a car that was running

50 miles per hour. Her back was broken and she was paralyzed from the neck down.

Soon after D. L's return to Conway from prison, people noticed that something about him wasn't quite right. Sometimes he acted as nice as could be, but he'd quickly change to an extremely cruel and vindictive person. He never did anything to anyone openly but waited until the darkness came and burned something of the person who may have offended him. He even burned their pets. However, he wouldn't burn anything if he couldn't watch the flames.

D. L. changed his way of dress to reflect the darkness and emptiness he felt inside. He wore mostly black clothing complete with a black silver-banded western hat and black silver-tipped western boots. He said that he wished he had been born when outlaws ruled the old west so he could have killed people the way they did.

He had gained a lot of knowledge while he was away from Conway, learning many skills while in the Green Berets and prison. Through the underground and insurance fraud loop, he was able to prove his greatest skill, explosives and arson. At first, he only did small jobs for local companies and helped them out of their financial worries while money began to fill his pockets. Soon, the word of his talents spread and he contracted arson jobs all over the southeast, some in the Atlanta area, some closer to home.

A few months before D.L. came to Thomas County to search for Wendy, he seemed to become obsessed with finding out what happened to his father. He became withdrawn and melancholy, but in the blink of an eye, he could became extremely violent; then just as quickly, he became as nice a person as anyone could meet or be around.

He was away from Conway a lot at first, and when he was home between jobs, he began to methodically question anyone who had ever known his father. He learned the most from Mary Tanner. She was in a nursing home in Myrtle Beach dying of AIDS and syphilis that had gone untreated for many years.

Most of the time her mind rambled, but sometimes she spoke of the times when she lived with Grace and Lester outside.

Mary never talked much about her sister's death. She would talk for hours as if Grace was sitting on the foot of her bed. D.L. spent many days gleaning enough out of what she said to put the pieces together of what became of his father, or, at least, what he thought had happened.

After he learned what he had from Mary, he told Kaye his version of what he had learned. He told her that he had pieced together different phrases from Mary's rambling.

He told her that she had said, "Lester Flanders killed my sister. He murdered her just as sure as the sun will rise tomorrow. So, I tied the son of a bitch up, Tom conked him over the head with a concrete block; then we dumped his sorry, drunk ass into a well and poured wet cement on the bastard."

Wendy and Tom were the only names Mary spoke, so D.L. began looking for them first. He learned from some folks that lived around Conway and Myrtle Beach that Wendy lived in Thomasville, Georgia. He told Kaye that he would find out where the others were when he found her. Tom still lived in Conway and still worked at the concrete block plant.

D.L. was away from Conway less and less. He turned down more contracts as he seemed to lose himself into finding out more about his father. He began to make plans to go to Thomasville. Kaye didn't like the idea, but he promised her and Ms. Jenkins that he wasn't going to cause any physical harm to Wendy or to the others when he found them, provided they told him what he wanted to know. If they didn't, he promised he was just going to frighten them.

Ms. Jenkins was ready to get away from D.L. and the beatings she was getting almost every day. And, when D.L. told them that he leaving for Thomasville, Ms. Jenkins told him she wasn't going.

"Damn D.L.! I told him," Ms. Jenkins told the investigators. "The woman was only ten years old. How in the hell could she have thrown your Daddy into a well, let alone remember anything about it? I told him, that's stupid! I also remembered using the f-word and that's when he threw my ass out of the car! I shouldn't have said that word. I knew he didn't like that word. Kaye told me that her Daddy use to make him talk dirty and say words like that when he was molesting him. His own Granddaddy! Jesus! There's some strange people in this world, ain't they?"

They had been riding in a car when the conversation took place. D.L. had reached across her lap, opened the door and pushed her out. When a motorist found her and she was taken to a hospital, she didn't tell anyone what had happened. She didn't know that D.L. left for Thomasville the following day. She was afraid if she told anyone what had happened to her, he would come to the hospital and kill her.

D.L. found a job at a plantation near Thomasville. He was hired as a blacksmith but he could do just about anything. D.L. had been eager to learn everything while he was in prison. He finished high school, as well as many of the college courses. His favorite subject was chemistry. The interaction of different chemicals fascinated him. Under the tutelage of his arsonist cellmate, he learned about fire and what chemical oxidizers could do to enhance the flame. He used the prison laboratory and a mail order electronics course to practice and sharpen his skills and learn about timers and remote control devices.

In time, he perfected a process for setting fires that water couldn't put out and, armed with this knowledge, he had little trouble selling his talent.

Within a week after arriving in Thomasville, D.L. knew where Wendy lived, worked, and who her husband was. He called Kaye and told her he was ready to begin his plan and wanted her to come to South Georgia to help him. He called the airport in Tallahassee the same day and made reservations for Kaye on a flight from Charleston.

Sheriff Young believed that D.L's plan was just as simple as it sounded in the beginning because he didn't attempt to conceal anything. He used the cellular phone in the Jimmy that was sure to have been discovered and had used his own name and social security number when he started work. He had even given Kaye's name when he made the reservation, as well as, his name and the phone number of the plantation. However, the sheriff didn't believe D.L. told Kaye that Wendy worked at the Thomas County Sheriff's Department.

Mex and Cage were working at the plantation when he started to work. Both men had criminal backgrounds and were probably easily enticed into helping with the plan.

D.L. figured everything out almost to the letter, but there were a few things he didn't figure on, namely: Jack and Carl Jackson; Emily, Bill, and Tom Wenslow; Sheriff Matthew Young; an old bloodhound named Earnhardt; but primarily, a tough bitch named Wilhelmina Grace Wenslow Jackson.

Earnhardt recovered and stayed at Sheriff Young's house for a while. He had plenty of time to finish excavating the sheriff's back yard. Wendy went to South Carolina for Kaye Flanders' funeral. Jack was still in the hospital and still in pretty bad shape.

Earnhardt had turned out to be sort of a hero. Not only had he been instrumental in finding the cabin where Wendy and Jack were held captive, he also had been instrumental in helping the arson investigators begin to unravel the possible cause of the fire at Wendy and Jack's home. His keen nose found the spot where the fire had begun. Traces of toluene were detected at the scene, however, the investigators determined that it was probably only used as the matrix for the arsonist's mixture. A type of plastic explosive, commonly know as C4, was also found, as were some of the parts of a cellular telephone.

Kaye Flanders' body was kept in Thomasville for three weeks after her death until Wendy could travel. She put her old memories of Kaye aside and remembered Kaye trying to help her when she was tied to the well. She remember what her mother told her that day when she was making biscuits, but she knew she could never love Kaye. The closest she could come was to give her a decent burial.

Sheriff Young sent Susan Clark and Jamerson Young to South Carolina with Wendy. Carl Jackson also accompanied her. The graveside funeral service for Kaye took place late in the afternoon in the last week of September. The Indian summer's sunset cast an orange array of shadows as a small group of people, surrounding the grave, walked away in single file. Alice Flanders was not one of them.

A lone figure stood at the tree line of a little thicket of pine saplings that was about a hundred yards behind the graveyard. One of the people at the graveside saw a wink of orange reflected light from the direction of the trees or said he thought he had.

Wendy, Carl, and Tom Wenslow remained inside the car at the graveyard during the funeral. Wendy felt sad for all that had happened and for what had happened to Kaye, but she didn't cry. On the way back into town, Wendy, Tom, Bill and Emily visited their parents' graves. They talked for a while, laughed for a while, and cried for a while.

Carl took Wendy to the motel, brought her supper to her room and left to meet Tom. The two men were going to talk and have a few beers.

The next morning, while Clark and Jamerson drove Wendy and Carl Jackson to Charleston for a flight to Tallahassee, someone who had been at Kaye's funeral told the Horry County Sheriff about the reflected light.

Having been given a description of D.L., he played a hunch and investigated the possible lead. He found a footprint on the edge of the pine thicket behind the little graveyard where Kaye Flanders had been buried. The heel of the footprint was deep and narrow, and the toe was sharply pointed.

Not long after the funeral, some coon hunters were gathered again before a night hunt at a little country store not far from Conway. The conversation ranged from old hunting stories to bullshit gossiping.

One of the old timers who was just along for the ride and the stories, commented, "Did any of y'all see that cement truck out this a ways late the other night?"

No one spoke, only the nodding of heads were their answers.

A period of silence passed with the same old timers asking, "Has anyone seen that Flanders boy? The one that was in prison?"

One of the other hunters scratched his whiskered chin, and answered, "Hadn't seen hide nor hair of D.L. since before they buried his Aunt Kaye."

Printed in the United States
1969